DENISE ROBERTSON

An
Unsuspecting
Heart

Published in the United Kingdom in 2012 by Little Books Ltd,
Notting Hill, London W11 3QW

10 9 8 7 6 5 4 3 2 1

Text copyright © 2012 by Denise Robertson
Design and layout copyright © by Little Books Ltd

A CIP catalogue record for this book is available from the British Library.

ISBN 978 1 906264 22 2

Every attempt has been made to trace any copyright holders. The author and
publisher will be grateful for any information that will assist them in keeping
future editions up to date. Although all reasonable care has been taken in the
preparation of this book, neither the publisher, editors nor the author can accept
any liability for any consequences arising from the use thereof, or the information
contained therein.

Printed and bound by CPI Group (UK) Ltd, Croydon, CR0 4YY

Prologue

13 August 1945

THE ANNOUNCEMENT CAME AT midnight: Mr Attlee, declaring the end of a world war in the same voice he might have used to say it would snow tomorrow.

Stella had been getting ready for bed . . . at least she had been thinking about it. Now, suddenly, she felt wide awake. Churchill should've been giving the news: it had been his war, but now the buggers had thrown him out. She closed her eyes to imagine that unmistakable voice, the way he would have sucked on the words till they came out round as pebbles. 'The last of our enemies' – there would have been a pause there – 'is laid low.' Attlee had said it as though world wars ended every day.

She went to the window. Surely there would be movement in the street as the news got round? Suddenly she heard a ship's siren from the river . . . and then another . . . and a train whistle coming from the sidings at the end of the street. London was waking up. She pictured the scene, excitement growing inside her. They would all crowd into Piccadilly like they had on VE night. God, that had been a night, and no mistake! Stella smiled, remembering the young GI and the down on his upper lip. He had cried because his President, Roosevelt, had not lived to see victory. She could have told him that losing a President in his own bed wasn't half as bad as losing a husband in a blazing building, but she hadn't. Instead she had taken him into a shop doorway and let him celebrate in style. Afterwards, he had promised to bring her nylons and God knows what else, but it had come to nothing. Most things came to nothing in the end.

There were people in the street now, stopping to chat and then hurrying on. It had said on the wireless that the next two days would be holidays, and people should stay home. No need to get up in the morning. Shepherd would still expect her at his bloody factory, but he could whistle. The war was over! She hesitated, wondering whether or not to wake up the girls and tell them. But then she would have to stay in . . . better leave them sleeping, and go out, just for an hour or two. Plenty of time to tell them in the morning.

She had to be careful, moving around the bedroom. Little Stella was asleep in her half of the bed – little Stella, her youngest and her last. Alf had doted on her. Doted! Stella felt a tear spring up, and brushed it away before it smudged the kohl line she had drawn around her eye. When she was ready she straightened the skirt of her best two-piece, checked her leg tan, switched off all the lamps, and padded from the room, her high-heeled courts in her hand.

She looked in on the other three girls, Maggie and Edith in the double, Cathy on the camp bed. All sleeping peacefully. She had been right not to wake them. She'd be back in good time to stop them rushing off to work, Mags to the munitions factory, little Edith to the hairdresser's on Coby Street . . . the salon, she kept calling it, but it was a hairdresser's, nothing else. And Cathy to the pub kitchen. All of them earning, and paying their share. Not that Edith wasn't a little liar about her tips . . . still, Alf would have been proud of them.

She closed the door of the flat, crept down the stairs, and tiptoed past Mrs Schiffman's door before putting on her shoes for the street. There was movement out there now, all right, with everyone scurrying towards the celebration. She passed the huge blocks of flats with their playgrounds and community hall. Everyone said they had heaps of mod. cons. What you did to get in there she wished she knew. Like everything else in life, it was a fix. Still, the buggers had lost their nice lawns when Dig for Victory came, that was some consolation.

She was past the flats and on to the main road when the van drew up. 'You going up town? Hop in.' He looked all right – like a worker on his way home.

'I'm making for Piccadilly,' she said.

He nodded. 'Same here.'

As the van threaded its way towards London's heart, they agreed on how wonderful the news was. 'Better times ahead,' he said, as they passed Drury Lane. They were going down Long Acre when a thought occurred to her: no more war meant no more Yanks. No more tinned fruit, nor the hope of nylon stockings.

She was lost in misery for a while, and then she noticed that they had turned into a side street. 'We're going the wrong way . . .' she said.

But by then it was too late.

BOOK 1
1945

Chapter One

Cathy

CATHY WAS THE FIRSt awake. Sun was streaming into the room, and for a moment she lay still, trying to decide whether or not to get up. On the one hand, she wasn't due at work until eleven o'clock. On the other hand, her mouth was dry, and she could kill for a cup of tea.

It was a few seconds before she realised that no one else in the room was stirring. Maggie was due at the factory at eight, and Stella at school for nine. Edie's hours were irregular, and, anyway, Cathy didn't care if Edie got wrong. In fact, she would positively enjoy it. Still, better make sure, for Maggie's sake.

She scrabbled for the clock on the shelf beside her bed. Ten past eight! She shot out of the covers and shook one of the inert figures in the bed alongside. 'Get up! It's late. Our Stel will get killed if she's late for school. Mam must've slept in.'

Edith groaned and turned on to her face, but Maggie had caught the anxiety in her sister's voice. 'Wake Mam. She can't afford to be late, either. You know what Shepherd's like. And put the bloody kettle on.'

They were putting on clothes and rubbing sleep from their eyes when Stella appeared in the doorway. 'Where's Mam?' she said.

'She'll be in the kitchen, dimwit.' Edith had sat up in bed to snap at her little sister. There was no love lost there, Cathy thought. Edie was too sharp-tongued.

'She's not in the kitchen, she's not anywhere. I've looked. And there's no one in the street going to work. Has something happened?' Stella's voice was a wobble.

'Nothing's happened,' Cathy said, comfortingly. 'We've all slept in, that's all.'

But when she went to the window, it was true that there was none of the usual bustle in the street outside. She turned back to Maggie. 'It's not Sunday, is it?'

Maggie was already struggling into her overalls. 'I wish it was. Is that kettle on?'

Cathy slipped her feet into her slippers and pulled on her dressing-gown. The kitchen was eerily silent without Mam. She filled the kettle at the tap and lit the gas under it, then went through to the living-room to stoke the fire, ready for making toast. It was almost out, so she riddled the bottom to get rid of the ash, and placed some sticks on top to catch light before she added coal from the scuttle.

'Are you all up?' she yelled as she went back to the kitchen. There was a rumble of answers, and then they trooped one by one into the kitchen. It was not until someone switched on the wireless that they heard the news: Japan had surrendered, and the war was over.

'That's it, then,' Mags said, relieved. 'Mam will've gone off to celebrate. She'll be home any moment. Are you sure we don't have to go to work?'

There was a knock on the door and Cathy opened it to reveal their neighbour, Mrs Schiffman from the flat downstairs. 'Great news!' she said, advancing into the room. For once her hair and clothes were not absolutely immaculate. 'Japan has surrendered. No more dead boys. No more war. Thank God!'

They looked at one another in disbelief which quickly changed to joy. 'Thank God,' Maggie echoed. 'Now we can get back to living like human beings.'

Mrs Schiffman confirmed the fact of the holiday. She was already washed and dressed, her black hair drawn back into its usual bun, but obviously done in haste. 'No work,' she said. 'Only celebration. They're dancing in the street already. Drunk, I think, but whether with wine or joy . . .' she threw up her hands '. . . who knows?'

'Cup of tea, Mrs S.?' Mags was waving the tea-pot as they clustered round the table. 'It'll have to be toast, the bread's like concrete. And there's hardly any marge, so it's shares, Edith, don't you forget it!'

'Where's Mam?' Stella said again. She sounded tearful, and Cathy put an arm around her.

'She'll be in directly, chicken. You know Mam, anywhere for a party. Come on, get a cup of tea and eat your toast, and then I'll do your hair. In bunches if you like, or plaits. And no school. We'll go up the city later and see what's going on. There'll likely be fireworks and all kinds.'

Stella was looking unconvinced. Cathy looked around the table for support. 'Tell her! Tell her what it was like on VE Day.'

'I can remember,' Stella said. 'It was only in May. But why isn't Mam here? She was here on VE Day.'

Mrs Schiffman had been drying the dishes on the draining-board. She folded the tea-towel neatly into two, then four, then eight. 'Your mama has gone to see what's going on. She'll tell you all about it when she gets home.'

They were all trying to comfort Stella, but somehow their reassurances felt unconvincing, even to their own ears. 'No one parties at nine in the morning,' Edith said in a low voice.

'Shh!' Mags's reproof was interrupted by a knock at the door.

'See,' Mrs Schiffman said, 'she's back.'

'She's got a key, dafty,' Stella said, and then coloured up in case she had been rude.

'Well, who's going?' That was Edith.

'Not you, Lady Muck,' Cathy said. 'Fat chance of you doing something useful.'

This might have brought a sharp retort, but Maggie had crossed to open the door. A policeman stood there, with another behind him, and the sight of the uniforms brought a hush upon the room.

'Does Estelle Jackson live . . .' He hesitated. 'Is this the Jackson residence?'

It was Cathy who answered. 'Yes, we're Jacksons. What is it?'

He had taken out his notebook and was turning the pages. 'A Mrs Estelle Jackson?'

'Yes, what *is* it?' Behind her Stella was whimpering. 'What do you want? You're frightening my sister.'

'Sorry. I'm . . . it's . . .'

The other policeman stepped forward. 'I'm really sorry, but it may be we're bringing bad news.' He hesitated and cleared his throat before ploughing on. 'The body of a woman was found this morning in an alleyway. From articles found on her person we believe the body to be that of a Mrs Estelle Jackson of this address. We can't be sure, though, until there's a formal identification. Sorry.'

Stella let out a cry that was almost a howl. Edie also started to sob, her body shaking. Maggie and Cathy looked at one another, unable to take in what had just been said. It was Mrs Schiffman who took charge, then, asking where the body lay and who would convey someone to view it.

'It must be next of kin,' the policeman said. 'Sorry.' The youth of the Jackson family had suddenly become apparent to him as they huddled together and wept.

'I'll come with you,' Mrs Schiffman said firmly. 'Two of you must go, for each other. Edith, you must care here for little Stella. Margaret, you are the eldest – you should go for your mama, and Catherine will come with you.' She was smiling at Cathy as she spoke, bending to whisper, 'You are the strong one, Catherine, and God will be with you.'

The young policeman stepped forward. 'Try to bear up. We'll make it as easy as we can. There's a car outside. I'll be with you.'

They went out on to the street, a street alive now with bunting and jubilant people, leaving behind them a crying child and another girl, normally full of herself, shocked into obedience by the horror of what had happened.

'You will have to be brave,' Mrs Schiffman said, as they went towards the waiting police car. 'Brave like your mama and papa. And God will help you.'

There is no God, Cathy thought. No kind God like they taught you in school. If there was a God, he was a cruel one. He had left them with no one . . . and not much else. For a moment she felt her eyes prick, and then she straightened her shoulders and shepherded her sister and neighbour into the car.

At the station, the young policeman led them through a maze of stone corridors and then they were in a small room, divided by a curtain. 'Are you ready?' he asked gently. Maggie turned away suddenly, her shoulders heaving, and it was Cath who had to step forward. 'Ready?' he asked again, and she nodded.

Behind the curtain her mother lay on a trolley, a grey blanket covering her up to her chin. She looked pale, but as though she were sleeping. Her face was unmarked, and, for a moment, Cathy had a sudden wild hope that she might just be asleep. Then she saw the red weal around her mother's neck.

She felt the policeman's hand on her elbow, steadying her, and realised she had been swaying. 'Is that your Mam?' he asked gently.

She nodded. 'Yes, that's my Mam. Estelle Jackson.'

Chapter Two

Maggie

T HE POLICE CAR HAD taken them home and the young
policeman, the one who had come at the beginning, was
taking off his helmet and looking round for a chair. 'I need to
take statements,' he said apologetically as he caught Maggie's
look of surprise. 'Besides, you need someone with you, for a
while, at least. So I asked the sarge if it could be me, seeing as
I know you . . . well, a bit.'

'I see,' Maggie said but she didn't see at all. She wanted
strangers out of the house. She wanted to bolt the door so that
they could all huddle together and howl. 'It isn't fair,' she said
aloud. 'It isn't fair. We lost our Dad in the Blitz, and now Mam.
Do you know what happened?'

'Not really. We think it was probably random, though . . .
not planned, and probably not anyone she knew. You can
imagine what London was like last night. Mayhem! It's possible
your mother wasn't the only one. We won't know till the
reports come in from all the stations. Nationally – well, who
knows?' He was unbuttoning his tunic and taking out a
notebook. 'I'm sorry about this, but it's got to be done. I'll
make it as easy as I can. I'll have to get statements from the
others as well. And the lady . . . is she a family member?'

'Family friend,' Maggie said. 'Neighbour, really. She lives
downstairs. There's four flats. Mrs Essex is on the ground floor,

then Mrs Schiffman, then us, and the man on the top floor's away a lot. He's a musician. I think he travels around.'

Cathy came back into the room then. 'I've persuaded Stella to go to bed for a while. Mrs S. is with her.'

'Where's Edie?'

'In the kitchen. She said she'd make some tea, so that'll be a first if it comes off.'

The young policeman stifled a smile. 'I was telling your sister I need to take statements. I'm Paul, by the way, Paul Steele. I don't need a lot. Just the last time you saw your mum, that kind of thing.'

'Let's get it over, then,' Maggie said. 'You go first, Cath. I'll hurry up that tea.'

'OK,' he said, pen poised. 'Tell me about yesterday.'

'I went to work in the pub round the corner. I start about eleven . . . I'm a kitchen hand. I'm finished about four, but yesterday it was later: five o'clock, I think. Mam came home at the same time. She works . . . she worked . . .' Her words faltered. Would she ever get used to talking about Mam in the past tense? 'She worked in a factory, Shepherd's.' He was nodding. 'She was just the same as usual. She was lively, my Mam. Funny. Full of beans.'

He was fishing out a hanky, white and folded. 'Here. I know it's hard. Would you like a policewoman here if I can get one?'

'No,' Cathy said, blowing her nose. 'I'll get this washed for you. No, I'd rather it was you. Anyway, she was like I said, happy. She made the tea . . . well, the evening meal. We had sausage and chips and bread pudding. After that we sat around for a bit. No one went out, except Stella. She went to Mrs Schiffman's downstairs to play cards. She often does that. The lady lives on her own, and she's fond of Stella. She was only away a while. Then we went off to bed, me and Mags, Stella had gone already. Maggie works on munitions, so she had an early start. Edie had washed her hair so she sat up a bit, tonging it. She was still with Mam when I went off. Mam wasn't intending to go out, I'm sure of that. She must have heard the news when they broadcast it, and gone out to see what was going on. I was already asleep.

'After that, it was morning. I knew something was wrong as soon as I woke up because Mam always got us up, and she hadn't. And then you came.'

He leaned forward. 'Did your Mam have any close friends?' He sat back again. 'Sorry to ask this, but was there a man in her life – you said your Dad died in the Blitz?'

'No,' she said, trying not to sound outraged. He had to ask. 'She did go out sometimes, on dates. Men she met at work. There was an American soldier once, but I think he left the country. Anyway, she hasn't mentioned him for a long time. Jerry, his name was. I don't know his other name. But she was a good mother. We always came first.'

Maggie came in, then, carrying a tin tray full of cups. Edie followed with the teapot, for once subdued.

They drank the tea gratefully, everyone silent until Cathy spoke. 'Do you want any more?' she asked.

The policeman was studying his notebook. 'I don't think so. Except, did any of you have any idea she'd gone out?'

Cathy shook her head. 'As I said, she was here, in this room, when I went to bed.' She turned to Edie. 'You were the last one up?'

Edie's eyes filled with tears. 'Perhaps, I can talk to you next, Edith?' the policeman said comfortingly. 'My name's Paul, by the way.'

Edie's statement was punctuated by sobs. 'She's making a meal of it,' Cathy said when she and Maggie adjourned to the kitchen with the used cups.

'She's only a kid,' Maggie said. 'Don't be hard on her, Cath. Not now. It's going to be hard enough if we all pull together. If we start fighting . . . well!'

'I know,' Cath said contritely.

When they went back into the living-room, Edie's tears had dried and the young policeman was telling her what a help she'd been. 'Well done,' Cathy said, trying hard not to sound grudging.

'Shall I get our Stella up?' Edie asked.

Both her other sisters spoke in unison. 'No.'

'It's all right,' the policeman said soothingly. 'It'll wait till she gets up. It's pretty clear that none of you know anything about what happened last night, and I don't suppose Stella will know any more. Is there anything you can think of . . . any incidents, anyone your mum might have known who could have held a grudge against her? Anything?'

'No,' Maggie said. 'There was nothing. She was an ordinary woman, the kind you see on every street. She went to work, she did her housework, she liked a drink occasionally. She went out with a few men, but she never brought them home . . . and there was nothing like that until well after Dad died.'

'You never think things like this happen to ordinary people,' Maggie said slowly. 'You think gangsters and gangster's molls get murdered, people like that.'

'It's usually ordinary people,' Paul said. 'The victims, I mean. Murderers are extraordinary . . .well, usually. My guess is your mum was just in the wrong place at the wrong time – wrong because everyone was taken up with something else last night. There were lots of people about, but they wouldn't have been taking much notice. And a lot of them would have been drinking.'

'Drunk,' Maggie amended. 'Mrs Essex downstairs says publicans have been hiding supplies for VJ night, and they brought them all out as soon as the announcement was made.'

'She could be right. Still, what are you going to do with the rest of the day? And what about a meal . . . are you up to cooking something this evening?'

A voice came from the doorway. Mrs Schiffman stood there with a finger to her lips. 'Don't wake the *liebling* now that she's gone off. I will see to a meal. I have something downstairs.'

She was moving to the door when Paul stood up. 'Mrs Schiffman, I need to take a statement from you, when you're ready.'

She smiled at him. 'I don't know anything. At least I don't think I do, but you detectives winkle things out of people, don't you?'

He was blushing. 'I'm not a detective. Yet. All I need is a few words. The girls . . . the young ladies will tell you it's just routine.'

He went off with the older woman, his helmet under his arm. 'He's nice,' Maggie said as the door closed.

'He's all right.' Cathy was straightening the cushions as she spoke.

Edie sighed. 'I thought it was an ordeal. They shouldn't grill you when you've just been bereaved.'

'You can cut the Bette Davis act, Edie. It's us, your sisters, you're talking to. And if you think that was an ordeal, God help you when you really get grilled.'

'What do you mean?' Edie sounded alarmed.

'She doesn't mean anything,' Maggie said firmly. 'She's winding you up. So, stop mucking about, both of you, and let's get this place cleaned up. It's the least we can do for Mam.'

For a while they worked in silence, and then at last Edie spoke. 'Do you think it was someone she knew? Someone she went out to meet? I mean, it might have been a neighbour, someone we know?'

'No,' Maggie said firmly. 'I don't think it was anyone she knew or we knew, so don't you go saying those things around our Stella.'

'People round here are rough, Edie, but they're not

murderers.' Cathy was trying to sound reasonable, but Maggie could still hear the edge in her voice. She didn't have much room for Edie, and that was a fact.

'I think we'll find out that it was a total stranger . . . she probably never even knew it was happening. There would be a lot of people out on the streets last night, Edie, all sorts. Mam was just unlucky. And if she was enjoying herself, celebrating the end of the war, she'd be off her guard. I'm just glad she knew the war was over.'

'But we don't know she did know. It might have happened before they announced it!'

Maggie saw Cathy's mouth open to give Edie a dressing-down and she stepped hastily in. 'That's enough about Mam for now. We can't change anything if we talk till midnight. So let's just get on with it, shall we, and then we can have a nice cup of tea.'

'If we've got any milk,' Edie said gloomily, but Maggie let it pass.

Chapter Three

Cathy

IT WAS QUIET IN the kitchen except for the buzz of conversation beyond the living-room door. The neighbours had descended upon the flat as soon as news of the death had spread. They had not come empty-handed: tea . . . precious tea . . . in a half-quarter packet, a bowl of sugar, half a loaf, and a few knife-fuls of marge on a saucer. Mags stood by the kettle, waiting for it to boil as Cathy tried to assemble enough unchipped cups. 'What are we going to do, Cath?' she said at last.

Cathy turned, her shoulders slumping as she spoke. 'I don't know.' And then, 'What do you mean? About a funeral?'

'About everything. It was Mam's widow's pension and her wage kept us going, Cath, you know that.'

'They'll still pay for Stella. She's only twelve.' Cathy tried and failed to sound certain.

'Yes, there's that, I suppose,' said Maggie.

But what if they didn't, Cathy thought? The wife of a dead fireman was one thing as far as the state was concerned; his children might be another. You didn't count for much when you were dead: she had seen that today in the mortuary. Her mother, hair nicely combed and dressed in white, lying on a narrow slab, eyes closed as though she were sleeping – and people just walking around as though she wasn't there. Only the young copper had seemed put out by it all.

She felt her eyes prick, but Mags was on her like tiger. 'Brace up, Cath. We've got to go in there in a minute and put a good face on it for the other two, specially for our Stella. I can't have you going to pieces. Not now.' She paused. 'We'll get by, Cath, because we have to. Like Mam did when Dad went. I can't think about it now, but I will . . . we will. Later on, when they've all gone. Now pass that tea-pot and get those cups in there. There's not enough milk to go round, so best say there is none.'

The conversation died as the girls brought in the tea, but only for a moment. The topic among their guests was how they would manage for food if shops took the two days' holiday offered. 'It's hard enough at the best of times, going from shop to shop and they've got nothing in, or it's all under the counter for their favourites. But I'll see my day when rationing's over. See if I set foot in their bloody shops, then. They'll be begging for customers.' That was Mrs Essex from downstairs, who never ever had a good word to say for anyone.

'The butcher's been good,' another woman said. 'Tried to be fair to everyone.'

Mrs Essex was not to be swayed. 'Fair? On the surface. Top show. Best bits under the counter for the favoured few, just like the rest.'

Mrs Schiffman was tut-tutting. 'I think they've all done their best. It's a miracle, really, that we didn't starve. When you think about it, this is an island. Before the war much food came in by ship, and then the Germans tried to sink the ships and stop the food. They succeeded, but we didn't starve. We had our ration books, and everyone got their share.'

Mrs Essex sniffed loudly. 'Well, the situation wasn't helped by all the foreigners coming in, eating us out of house and home.'

'Refugees!' Cathy said firmly. 'They didn't come here from choice . . . and a lot of them came here to fight. Fight for us.'

'And a lot of them didn't.'

Maggie was stepping in, aware that Mrs Schiffman had retired hurt. 'Yes, ration books are fair. Buff if you're healthy, green if you're pregnant or under five, and blue for the over-fives. Our Stella's is still blue.'

'Well, it can't be over soon enough for me,' someone said. 'Is there any more of that tea?'

Talk turned then to the wonder of the war's ending and the unexpected holidays. 'There's half of them set off for work this morning,' Bella Hays was saying. 'Didn't twig the trains were running a Sunday service, and had to turn back when they found out. Our Tim says they were flooding out of the Tube like rush hour. The buses are bursting. Our Eddie says the clippies are not taking fares or watching the numbers. If you can hang on you can get a ride.'

'Where are they all going, if there is no work?' That was Mrs Schiffman, eyes wide.

'Up West. They're going up the West End. Or to see the King and Queen. In an open carriage, they say, in spite of the drizzle. I'm surprised they're still opening Parliament on a day like this.'

The talk turned to the new Parliament, then, and the electorate's ingratitude to Churchill. 'Good old Winnie,' was the almost universal refrain, except from Mrs Essex in the corner, who held stoically to the belief he had been all right for war but no good for peace. 'He's not for the likes of us,' she said, to murmurs of disagreement. 'Our Sidney's put it in his letters for a bit. None of them overseas were going to vote for him: they thought he'd postpone their demobs, look for another war to fight. They've had enough of war, and who can blame them? Attlee's a quiet little man, but he won't stir things up. He'll just quietly get on with the job. Churchill should've been on the stage, I've thought that many a time.'

There was a chorus of disagreement, but no one felt

strongly enough for proper argument.

Cathy poured tea and passed cups, mixed emotions churning within her. One half of her didn't want mention of her mother or the manner of her death – not with Stella, dry-eyed now but wrung out, sitting in the corner of the sofa like a little lost soul. But the other part of her felt outraged that they could talk about anything except the catastrophe that had befallen them all. 'Strangled,' the inspector at the mortuary had said, and then coughed, and the young PC had gone beetroot red. 'Any more tea?' she said aloud, because she couldn't bear to think about that cough, and what probably lay behind it.

They began to drift away when the tea had all been drunk. 'Anything, anything we can do. You only have to ask. She was a good woman, your mother. Wouldn't hurt a fly. He'll likely hang, whoever he is, and serve him right.'

Cathy was nodding and smiling and saying 'Thank you' and 'I know' – again and again, until it became meaningless. Suddenly she heard a voice behind her. 'Do you think there'll be bananas in the shops?' It seemed, suddenly, wonderfully funny. Wickedly, wickedly funny. Someone was laughing and it wasn't until Mags's hand caught her square across the cheek that she realised it was her.

It was a relief when at last the room emptied, and she and Mrs Schiffman were left alone in the quiet. Mrs Schiffman touched her cheek. 'You need to get out for a bit, get away from it. Take the little one. See the fireworks, or whatever there is. Forget for a moment, if you can. Tomorrow will be soon enough for thinking.'

'I hope you didn't let Mrs Essex upset you?' Cathy asked.

Mrs S. was smiling. 'Not that one, Catherine. She has had many little swipes at me. I shrug them off. When you have experienced real resentment, it makes the little swipes unimportant. What's important now is that we do things right for your mama.'

'Do you think she suffered, Mrs Schiffman? Would she have known what was happening?'

The older woman was shaking her head sadly. 'We will never know that, Catherine. But it's best to think that she never knew. God is good. She is with him now, so she is at peace.'

'Edie was on about it earlier.'

'Yes, she is not as tough as she would like us to believe, little Edith.'

'I'm not so sure about that. There's times I could murder . . .' The word died on Cathy's lips. How could she have said this, with Mam lying murdered?

Mrs Schiffman leaned forward and patted her hand. 'I know what you mean.'

Chapter Four

Cathy

MAGGIE WAS ENERGETICALLY TIDYING. 'That's how she copes,' Cathy thought. 'She works.' Maggie straightened up and looked around her. 'Thank God they've all gone. They mean well, but . . . anyway, Mrs S. is right: get our Stella out of here as soon as Edie's got her ready. Edie too, if she'll go.'

Cathy nodded but her mind was not on going out. 'Why would anyone hurt Mam, Mags?'

Her sister was looking at her, almost pityingly. 'You know why, Cath. She always was a sucker for a good-looking man. I expect he picked her up and . . .' She shrugged.

'Was she . . . ?' Neither of them liked to put their fear into words.

'I expect so, but it won't do to think about it. We've got to think about managing, Cath. Keeping this place, and our Stel at school. Just keep thinking about that.'

'We've got our wages . . .'

'For now.' The interruption was staccato. 'There'll be men flooding home soon, wanting their jobs back. Our factory will go. Munitions won't be needed any more, so that'll be my £3 13 shillings a week up the spout. But don't think . . .' Her words died as the two younger girls came back into the room.

'There now,' Mags said firmly, 'our Cath's going to take you out to see . . .' She hesitated over the word 'celebrations' . . . 'to see what's happening. I'll stay here and make sure there's something to eat when you get back.'

The notion of something to eat failed to bring a smile to either face. 'You coming too, Edie?' Cathy said, trying to sound encouraging.

'No, thanks.' The stuffing had been knocked out of her, Cathy thought, but she didn't persist. It wouldn't do Stella any good to have Edie moping along behind them. It was a relief to get out into the open air and shepherd Stella down the street towards the bus stop. Inside the shelter she put an arm round her sister. Stella's thin body was shaking, and she drew her close. 'It's going to be all right, Stel. You'll see.'

'How can it be? I don't believe it, Cath, I don't believe it, and I don't want it to be all right, anyway. I want Mam.'

'I know, chick. We all want Mam. But she's gone, Stel, and we can't change that. We'll manage – like we did when Dad died. You just have to trust me and Mags, and be brave. Because that's what Mam wants us to do.'

She used the present tense deliberately, so as to sound positive, but as they boarded the bus her own fear rose up in her throat, almost choking her. It wasn't all right, not all right at all. 'We're none of us able to stand on our own two feet, not even Maggie. So what will become of us all?' she thought.

The bus was filled to bursting with happy people. The odour of alcohol hung in the air, but nobody minded. It wasn't a day for minding, as far as the passengers were concerned. Outside the bus windows pavements were full of scurrying people, some wearing bunting around their necks or waving Union Jacks. There were Yanks too, plenty of them, and here and there a Pole or two, small and handsome and distinctive in their maroon berets. No one collected their fares, not even when a seat came free. Cathy slipped into it and pulled Stella on to her knee.

'Are you going to the palace?' the man sitting in the

window seat next to her asked.

'I was thinking about Trafalgar Square,' Cathy replied.

He shrugged. 'Same difference. They've got loudspeakers everywhere. People are dancing and singing. Of course, you'll get the royals at the Palace . . . sooner or later. You won't get into a pub, mind. Not that you'll want to with the kid. They say supplies ran out in the night. The Yanks are calling it worse than Prohibition. And the price of flags! Seven bob for a bit of rag on a stick. I'd shoot profiteers'.

Cathy smiled politely, and tried to work out whether the stop for Buckingham Palace would come before or after Trafalgar Square.

'You got anyone in the Forces?' The man looked genuinely interested.

'I did . . . we did have. Our Dad. He wasn't in the army, he was a fireman. He was killed in the Blitz.'

'Ah! Well, never mind. At least it's over now. And don't feel sorry for them Japanese. Shrivelled up they say, but they asked for it. Birds dying in the air . . .burned to a cinder.'

'Excuse me.' Cathy was shoving Stella to her feet. 'We're getting off here.' They were only at Holborn, but she'd had enough of conversation, especially about death. The only thing she had wanted to say was, 'Someone killed my Mam last night,' and that would never do.

The clippie was in the arms of an RAF sergeant, but she put up a hand to ring the bell. The bus slowed and she said, 'Watch your step,' before turning back to her new boyfriend.

The streets were crowded and noisy. A lot of people were blowing whistles, and a man with a tray was selling them: 'Victory Whistles 2s 6d!' The crowd was loud and boisterous, and everyone was friendly, hugging anyone who came within reach; but for Cathy it lacked the joy of VE Day. That had been magic, especially when the blackout ceased and she saw London again lit up like a Christmas tree. This was just loud.

'Perhaps it's just me,' Cathy thought. 'Perhaps I'll never know joy again.' She glanced at Stella – at least she wasn't crying now – and felt the coins in her pocket. Yes, she had enough. 'Come on, our kid. Let's see if there's a café open, and I'll buy you a lemonade.'

On the counter in the café, a wireless set was tuned to the BBC. They listened to the newsreader as they sipped their drinks. 'There is joy and celebration around the world as nations celebrate Victory in Japan day. After days of rumour and speculation, US President Harry S. Truman broke the good news at a press conference at the White House at 1900 hours yesterday. He said the Japanese Government had agreed to comply in full with the Potsdam declaration, which demands the unconditional surrender of Japan. Supreme Commander General Douglas MacArthur will receive the official Japanese surrender, arrangements for which are now under way. Later, in an address to a crowd that had gathered outside the White House, President Truman said: "This is the day we have been waiting for since Pearl Harbour. This is the day when Fascism finally dies, as we always knew it would."'

'Why is it all about Americans?' Stella asked.

Cathy shrugged. 'It's just the way they are, Stel. You know, bigger than life. Got everything . . . chocolate, nylons, tins of fruit.'

'They have better uniforms as well,' Stella said. She smiled a wan smile. 'We call them cissies at school.'

There was silence for a while, and then she spoke again. 'Do you remember when Mam knew that Yank?'

'Jerry?'

'Yes. I used to be scared she'd marry him, and we'd all have to go and live in America.'

Cathy smiled, but looking at her sister she knew what they were both thinking. If Mam had married Jerry and gone to America, she would still be alive today.

It was tea-time when they got home, and Maggie had fishcakes and chips waiting. Afterwards they sat together to hear the King speak, willing him to get the words out, and relieved when he did. 'Our hearts are full to overflowing, as are your own. Yet there is not one of us who has experienced this terrible war who does not realise that we shall feel its inevitable consequences long after we have all forgotten our rejoicings today.'

'He did well,' Maggie said, when he'd finished.

'Yes. He's a good king,' Edie said, and looked faintly surprised when no one contradicted her.

Chapter Five

Cathy

Cathy was awake before dawn, but she lay still, anxious not to wake her sisters. Edith was grinding her teeth again, but Maggie slept soundly. 'Thank God for our Mags,' Cathy thought. If anyone could get them out of this, she could. But the minute she thought that, she felt ashamed. How could she be thinking . . . worrying . . . about the future when Mam was dead, lying in that cold, grey place?

Today there was going to be a post mortem. The young policeman had told them that, and Mrs Schiffman had explained. 'It's very respectful. But they need to find out how she died. That way they find who did this thing.' She had spoken very softly, and her eyes had been watery. 'She cries a lot,' Edie had said once. 'On account of all her lot, killed in the gas chambers.' Mam had hushed her then, but not before she had widened Stella's eyes by adding, 'They pulled all their teeth out for the gold fillings in them.'

Edie was hard, Cathy thought. Mam had never said so, but it was true. Maggie was practical, and would sort things out. Edie was hard, and would come out on top, whatever happened. Which left her and Stella, who must be protected at all costs. She herself was going into work today, but if Mr Hopkins was in charge he'd send her home when she told him. Mrs Hopkins was made of sterner stuff. 'That's life,' she would say. 'Now get them pots washed.' A little chuckle rose in Cathy's throat at the thought of Mrs Hopkins in full flow, but she suppressed it. If the worst came to the worst, she could ask for a raise. There was still a shortage of kitchen help, and surely women coming out of the services wouldn't want to skivvy?

The room was light now, and she slid from the bed. Outside the window, the street was still quiet. Everyone recovering from last night, no doubt. Beyond the street one or two structures were still intact, but she knew there were areas of rubble there, and sites where rosebay willowherb had taken over. The Germans had been after the marshalling yards and the US billets that lay beyond them, but their aim had been poor, and more often it had been terraced houses that were hit. Especially the Barrington Road area, now overgrown and derelict. She had played there three years ago, before she left school and went to work. The bomb-sites had been irresistible. Sometimes a wall still existed, with pale patches where pictures had hung. There had been water tanks and flooded basements to explore. She leaned her forehead on the cold window-pane and remembered the plop as the pebbles made as they dropped them into the dark water.

She had played more with boys than girls then, because she was tall for her age. Some gangs had ruled 'no girls allowed', but her lot had accepted her without a word, while other girls were condemned to picking golden rod and the lupins that had sprung up wherever there was open ground.

Behind her in the bedroom, Mags was stirring. 'What time is it?'

'I don't know. Early. Go back to sleep.'

But Mags was already up, reaching for the red cardigan that served as a dressing-gown. 'Get the kettle on, our Cath, and let's see what we can scrape together for their breakfast. We need to get our Stella back to school.'

In the end it was easy enough to get Edie and Stella off to work and school. 'They're glad to get away from it all.' Mags was munching on dry toast as she spoke. 'I'm not going in to work today. They won't be pushing for production now, and I'll explain tomorrow. But you should pop round the Queen and tell them you need time off.'

They were still at the table when a knock came at the door. Mr Hopkins stood on the step, a cardboard box in his arms. 'We heard, Cathy. Terrible. Terrible! We're not expecting you in for a day or two.' He thrust the box at her. 'The wife thought you might need a few things. It'd be more, but you know rationing.' With that he was gone, in a red-checked blur of embarrassment. Cathy recalled her earlier bad thoughts about Mrs Hopkins, and felt her eyes prick. Mags was already exploring the box. 'Milk – get the kettle on again, Cath. Digestives, two packets. Tea, sugar, lard . . . and a bottle of sherry. That'll come in handy.'

They sat either side of the kitchen table and drank tea, silent at the thought of the enormity of what lay before them. 'How much do funerals cost?' Cathy asked at last.

Mags shrugged. 'Search me. A lot. When Dad was killed, I remember someone telling Mam at least she wouldn't have a funeral to pay for, because he was insured. As though it cost a lot.'

'What are we going to do?'

'I wish you wouldn't keep saying that. It's bloody irritating, if you'll excuse the language.' If Mam had been here, she would have slapped Maggie for swearing. 'I'll wash your mouth out,' she would have threatened. Cathy looked at her sister and knew she was thinking the same thing. 'The Government pays for air-raid casualties to be buried, I know that. They give a grant.'

'Mam wasn't killed in an air-raid.'

'She died because of the war. She wouldn't have been out if it hadn't been VJ night.' But they both knew Mam had gone out most nights. 'There's always been murders, Cath, war or peace.'

The silence was broken by a knock at the door. 'Mrs S.,' Mags said. But it was not their neighbour, it was the young policeman – not in uniform this time but still with a formal air.

'I'm not here in an official capacity,' he began pompously. Then he cleared his throat and started again. 'I thought you might be worrying about the . . . well, the funeral expenses, and that sort of thing. So I looked it up.'

He was glancing from one to another, until Mags waved an imperious hand. 'Spit it out, then.'

Cathy winced. 'It's very kind of you to bother,' she said and gave her sister what she hoped was a warning glare.

'There is a procedure,' he said. 'Paid for by the local authority.'

'You mean a pauper's funeral? Our Mam's not having that . . . you don't get even a coffin, just a shroud, and then chucked in an open grave.'

'They don't do that in this authority,' the young man said swiftly. 'It's Bethnal Green uses shrouds. Here there is a coffin. Yes, it's a communal grave.' He was staring at Cathy, whose eyes had indicated horror. 'But it's nicely done.'

'What's the alternative?' Mags sounded cold, but Cath knew what the conversation was costing her.

'I'm not sure about that. In normal circumstances there is no alternative: if you can't pay yourself, you take what the council offers. But if the death is by enemy action, there's more: a coffin, a hearse, bearers, and a coach for the mourners. And they make the graves look a bit more individual.'

'It's still a mass grave. I'm not having our Mam in a mass grave.'

'You'll have a bit of time to think,' he said, still looking at Cath. 'They won't release the body until after the post mortem. Not even then, if there's complications.'

'Will it be before the trial?'

He coloured up at Maggie's question. 'There may not be a trial. Unless there's some sort of breakthrough.'

'You mean you won't catch the man who did it?'

He was shaking his head. 'London was wild that night. No one was taking notice, no one was in their own place. It's like looking for a needle in a haystack.'

'He means well,' Cath said when the young PC had gone.

'I suppose so.' Mags's tone was grudging. 'But he's only the first of the nosey-parkers.'

'We've told the police everything we know.'

'I don't mean the police. There'll be the pension people about the money. And about our Stel.'

'What about her?'

'She's still a kid, Cath. She needs a mother – that's how they'll see it.'

'They? The council, you mean?' Mags nodded. 'She's got us, Mags. We're her family. You're her next of kin, being oldest.'

'But I'm not twenty-one, Cath. Not an adult, not in their eyes, anyway. And besides . . .' There was silence for a moment and then her head came up. 'I might not always be here.'

'What d'you mean?' Suddenly Cath felt fear, greater even than she had felt at news of her mother's death. 'You're not ill, our Mags? What are you saying?'

It came out, then. The soldier Maggie had kept quiet about because it was no one's business but hers. 'He'll be demobbed soon, and we mean to get married and go north. I love him, Cath. He lives in Durham. There's jobs there, in the pits, and he has rights after five years of war.'

Tears came, from both of them, an odd mixture of joy and guilt on Maggie's part and joy for her sister and terror on Cathy's.

Mrs Schiffman found them weeping, and sought to comfort them. 'I know why you cry. For the loss of a mama, and for the cruel way you lost her. One bad man. But so many people have died in this war, so many. The war killed your mama, think of it like that. One more victim of a cruel war.'

Chapter Six

Cathy

'SEE!' MAGS SAID, AS they got ready for work. Cath looked up from tying her shoelace. 'What?'

Mags gestured at the wireless. 'They've just said one million to be demobbed by the end of the year, and another million let go from munitions. That's my wage up the spout.'

'You'll get something else.'

'Oh yes, two million people let loose on to the Employment Exchange, and I'll waltz into something else? Still, I can't worry about it now.' She was twisting her headscarf into a turban and tucking in the ends.

'Anyone there?' The voice was followed by a little rap on the door.

'God, it's Mrs S. We haven't got time now – well, I haven't. Still, she might see Stella off to school if our Edie falls down on the job.'

But Mrs Schiffman had not come to see to Stella. 'It's sorted,' she said triumphantly, holding out an envelope. 'There's a collection in there from the good people around here. And from the public house.'

'How much?' Again Cath winced at the brusqueness of her sister's tone.

'Not enough, but the good undertaker will accept it, and wait for the rest of his money. Everyone is on your side, *lieblings*. And there's the Lord Roberts Workshops, too. Mr Hopkins knows them, and he says they might help, on account of your papa dying in the war. If not, he says, there'll be someone else. He'll see to it.'

'Thank God,' Mags said, as they clattered down the stairs, leaving their neighbour to see to Stella and Edie, who was, Mags had decreed a few moments before, 'a lazy, selfish little sod'. Now, though, she was in better humour. 'What a relief. I was stumped, I'll admit it, Still . . .' She stopped short at the sight of the man lurking outside the door. It was the young policeman again.

'He's after you, our Cath,' she muttered, but as they came face to face with him all she said was, 'You again! Can't stop.'

He fell into step alongside Cathy as they made for the Queen's Head. 'I was just passing. No news, I'm afraid.'

'I've got some for you,' Cath said triumphantly, and told him about Mrs Schiffman's solution.

'That's grand,' he said, obviously relieved. They were outside the pub now and she turned towards the alleyway.

'I don't suppose you'd like to go to the pictures one night?' he said. 'Well, not now, obviously, but . . .' His voice tailed off.

'Eventually,' Cath said firmly. 'Eventually. That would be very nice.' She didn't really mean it – she found the idea of going to the pictures with any boy a bit embarrassing – but the pleased expression on his face made her feel guilty. If he asked her again, she would have to go, after all he'd done for them. But just the once.

The pub kitchen smelled of frying onions. 'Sausage and mash today, Cathy. Watch this gravy for me.' Mrs Hopkins was trying to make Cathy feel this was just one day like any other, but then couldn't resist adding, 'Just do what you can today, till you get your mind back.' She looked flustered then. 'I don't mean that . . . I mean . . .'

'I know what you mean,' Cath said. 'And thank you for the things you sent.'

Her employer was still looking flustered. 'Least we could do. It'd've been more if these were normal times. Hitler's got a lot to answer for. Now, don't take your eye off that gravy. It's the last of the onions, and God knows when we'll get more.'

As Cathy stirred and waited for the bubbles that signified thickening, she felt an easement. At least, inside the Queen's Head the world was not rocking on its axis. All the same, before the day was out she would have to ask for more money. Twelve shillings and sixpence had been OK for a start, but she knew what she was doing now. She was eighteen, not a kid, and she ought to be paid accordingly. Not that she'd get the kind of money Maggie got – factory work paid well. Perhaps she could get in there too . . . except that munitions factories would be closing now, as Maggie said.

She saw the brown goo begin to bubble, and turned off the gas with a satisfying plop. After that it was stir and fry and serve and wash and stack and rub down benches, and not much time to think at all.

That night Stella was sent off to visit Mrs S., who was already primed to keep her occupied until bedtime. 'Welcome home, Edie,' Maggie said as the younger girl walked through the door. 'We don't want any argument: you've got to divvy up your tips now . . . and don't say you don't get them, because we all know you do. At least eight customers a day, threepence from each of them, that's two bob a day.'

'Threepence each, our Mags? You must be mad! Half of them don't tip the shampooist, just the stylist, and them as do only give a penny or twopence.'

'Two bob a day for three days, Edie. If you want to eat, that is. You can keep the other three days for yourself, if you're greedy enough.'

Mags's tone was scathing, but Edie was defiant. 'If Mam was here you wouldn't dare do this. Asking me to get money out of thin air.'

'Six bob.' Mags was implacable. 'Cath got a raise today: five bob, and she's tipping up the lot.'

'She gets a proper wage, I don't. Tips are what I live on.'

'Aha!' Her sisters spoke in unison. 'So you admit you get them!'

'And,' Maggie continued, 'any more argument and I'll recalculate how many customers a day . . . eight seems an under-estimate to me!'

'All right,' Edie said, 'but it's still not fair.'

Any feeling of satisfaction Cathy had gained from besting Edie was dissipated by the time she went to get ready for bed. Edie had moved in with Stella now, and Mags was still clearing up in the kitchen. Cathy went to the window and looked out over the crowded streets once more. In less than a week her world had changed.

'I've grown up,' she thought. 'Last week I still felt a child – safe. Now I've grown up, and I don't much like it.' The days of skating on the Ashey in borrowed skates, 'hopping on' bumpers if a rare car entered the neighbourhood, skipping the alphabet to stop on the initial of the boy you fancied . . . they were all gone. From now on it would be debt and responsibility. Still, she suddenly remembered the rhyme a Polak girl had chanted in the playground. Polaks, the children of foreign Jews, were full of rhymes and stories, and this one had stuck: '*You die if you worry, you die if you don't, so why worry at all? It's only worry that killed the cat, anybody can tell you that.*'

She repeated it to herself as she climbed into bed, and then remembered her prayers. She hadn't kneeled to pray since she was a little girl, but since Mam had died it had seemed like a good idea. The lino was cold to her knees so she kept it brief. 'Please God, take care of us all, and especially Mam. Don't let Mags go away, not yet, anyway. And make it a nice funeral. For Jesus's sake, Amen.'

Chapter Seven

Cathy

A T TIMES IT HAD seemed as if the house would never cool. Officials had seemed to spring up out of nowhere, shuffling papers, talking about things like the War Pensions Act and 'entitlements'. In the end, it had been as bad as they feared. Mam's money ceased on her death, and there would be 'provision' for Stella only until she left school. 'Provision spelled P-I-T-T-A-N-C-E,' Maggie had said bitterly, and the man had had the grace to look ashamed. After that there had been the WRVS woman, who had looked dubious at the idea of Stella's staying put.

'We can look after her,' Cath had said desperately. 'We always have.'

'Are you sure?' The woman had had a mean little mouth and fussy little hands that hovered over her notebook all the time. Mags had settled it: 'She's staying put,' she said. 'I'm as good as twenty-one, so I'm her guardian.'

The woman looked dubious. 'Technically, you are still a minor . . .'

'Yes, but . . .' Cath produced her trump card, 'we have someone to look after us all. Mrs Schiffman downstairs – she sees to us. You can ask her.'

When the door had closed on the green uniform, who was going down to talk to Mrs Schiffman, Maggie had put her arms

round her sister. 'Well done, Cath. I was within an inch of
clocking her one.'

'And a nice mess we'd've been in then,' Cath said wryly.

Mrs Schiffman must have done them proud, because the
woman came back to say, sniffily, that Stella could stay put 'for
the time being'.

'And knobs on to you,' Maggie said when the door shut
behind her.

Later on they had another visitor, an unexpected one. It was
their mother's former employer, Mr Shepherd, who came
bearing gifts. 'It's not a lot, but every little helps, they say.' He
had brought £85, collected from their mother's former
workmates, and supplemented by him. They thanked him
profusely and genuinely. 'We never expected it,' Cath had said,
and he had shaken his head.

'She was well thought of, your mother. Never let things get
her down. She'll be missed. There's six of the girls who'll be
there at the funeral today. I'd have let off more if I could, but
you know how it is.'

'If that's all . . .' Maggie had risen to her feet, her eyes on
the clock on the mantel. It was nearly time.

'I'll see you out,' Cathy said, half-ushering, half-pushing the
man towards the door, where the hearse and a single car were
already waiting. Mrs Schiffman was waiting, too, black
mantilla in place, gloves on her hands.

'Nice,' she said, looking them over. 'She would be proud of
you.'

When the undertaker signalled time, they squeezed on to
the back seat, and Mags pulled down the tip-up seat opposite.
'Move over, Edie, and make room for Mrs S.' The older woman
stepped inside and took her place, and the cortège moved
slowly past neighbours who lined the kerbs, heads bent.

'Look,' Edie said, 'even the Polaks have turned out.'

Cathy felt her cheeks burn. Mrs Schiffman wasn't Polish,

but she was a foreigner, and it seemed disrespectful to use the word 'Polak' in front of her. 'Shh,' Mags said, but Edie was not to be shushed.

'I only said . . .'

'That's your trouble, lady.' Mags's interruption was swift. 'Now let's have a bit of peace until we get to church.'

They sang 'O Love that wilt not let me go' and 'All things bright and beautiful', which had been Mam's favourite. The vicar spoke about tragedy and the suddenness of death, but Cathy kept her eyes fixed on the flowers that rested on the coffin. She had written the card at Mags's instruction: 'because you've got a good hand, our Cath.' It said: '*To a loving mother from her grateful daughters*', and then their names in Cathy's best copperplate.

'He's here,' Mags whispered when it was time to walk down the aisle.

'I know,' Cath said, trying not to look at the young policeman in the second back row. The inspector was there, too, and another man who looked like a policeman.

And then they were back in the car and moving towards the cemetery in Tower Hamlets; and suddenly the finality of parting reduced them all to silence.

The cemetery was grey and quiet, ancient stones and neglected graves with here and there a newly turned plot or a splash of colour from flowers. Their grave was a reddish gash in the earth, and Stella turned away, shuddering. The vicar murmured something, and then threw a handful of earth on to the coffin they had lowered down on ropes. 'They do this every day,' Cath thought. 'It doesn't mean a thing to them, because it's all in a day's work.'

They walked back to the waiting car in silence, and no one spoke on the journey home.

'Well, you done her proud,' Mrs Essex said, as they ate sausage rolls and little sponge cakes provided by the undertaker. They had each had a glass of sweet sherry, even Stella, and now there was tea in plenty, sweet and hot.

'Mrs S. has been a big help,' Cathy said.

Mrs Essex was having none of it. 'That's as may be. Some of us think foreigners should take a bit of a back seat sometimes. Hardly here five minutes, and they're running the show.'

'She's a refugee,' Cathy said, genuinely shocked at such unfriendliness, especially today.

'Well, that's as may be, an' all. She's German. Fifth-column, some of those "refugees" have turned out to be. Getting everyone's sympathy, and sabotaging things on the sly.'

'I don't see Mrs S. blowing up railway lines.'

'Never said she did – but she's not too old to signal, to move her black-out and guide them in. Lost everyone in the gas-chambers? Never seen her near the synagogue, if she's so Jewish. They're taking over London: Polaks, Choats, coloureds. They've got gypsies down Hind Grove, and they're a law unto themselves. Living by dropsy, the lot of them.'

Cathy knew what Choats were. Unlike the Polaks, they were English-born Jews, but all of them were involved in trade, which was where the dropsy came in. Back-handers were an essential part of any business – Mr Hopkins had said so many a time.

'Well, Mrs Schiffman is a real refugee,' she said as firmly as she could. 'And she used to be a ballet dancer. I've seen her photos.' She could tell a retort was forming on Mrs Essex's lips, but enough was enough. 'Anyway, I've got to get round and make sure everyone's got tea.' And with that she made her exit.

The mourners stayed till the last of the food was gone. 'Like locusts,' Mags said bitterly, as they cleared the empty plates. 'I fancied one of those cakes tonight.'

'They were awful,' Edie said. 'I had two, but you could tell they were made with liquid paraffin.'

'Why did you have two then, greedy pig?'

'I wasn't going to see them go to strangers.' Edie's brows lowered. 'Not when I was paying for them.'

'Oh God!' Mags's eyes were raised to heaven. 'We'll never hear the last of our Edie's tips. They're like the loaves and the fishes, paying for everything.'

What Edie might have replied, they were never to know. Stella began to sob, quietly at first and then more savagely, and all three sisters flew to comfort her.

Chapter Eight

Cathy

IT WAS QUIET IN the Queen's Head kitchen, apart from the sound of soup bubbling on the stove. 'We've got more onions,' Mrs Hopkins had said when Cathy arrived at eight a. m. 'Strings of them. So it's onion soup, and keep your eyes shut while you're peeling or else they'll smart.'

Cathy knew better than to ask where the onions had come from. They most certainly hadn't been obtained legally over the greengrocer's counter. It was the same with most of the food that came through the pub kitchen: they had an allocation at the controlled price, but little that was worth having came through the proper channels. Lorry-loads of food, cigarettes, and whisky were stolen every night, and sold on the black market at inflated prices. Everyone grumbled at what they had to pay for stolen goods, but they paid just the same. When you were hungry, you didn't think too much about right and wrong.

As she alternately peeled and wiped her eyes with the back of her hand, Cathy thought about how lawless London had become. And not just stealing – the year had hardly begun before there were queues at the Old Bailey to see a GI, a deserter, and an English girl who should have known better, tried for the cold-blooded murder of a taxi-driver and the attempted murder of another young girl. Then there had been 'Irish Molly', strangled in an air-raid shelter, and a dozen or more others. No one had been found guilty. Had one of those murderers killed Mam? Or had it been some nice-faced man who could even now be sitting in the bar next door, laughing and talking as though he hadn't a care in the world?

She switched her thoughts, then, and got on with peeling and chopping and washing pots, and making sure they were ready for the dinner-time rush. Whatever London had become, she was stuck with it, so no point in dwelling on misery.

It was a relief when four o'clock came round, and she could escape from the steaming kitchen into the open air. If she hurried, she would meet Stel coming from school. She was half-way down Whitechapel Road when a figure loomed up beside her. 'Oh, it's you,' she said, at the sight of the young policeman. And then, aware that she had been a bit ungracious, 'It's a lovely day, isn't it?'

He agreed that it was a lovely day, and then cleared his throat. 'You all getting on all right?'

'Yes,' she said carefully, 'we're OK, if that's what you mean. Except our Stella, who's still in a bad way. Well, we're all . . . you know . . .'

He was nodding. 'I know. I've seen a lot of it in the past few years. Grief – it takes people different ways, but it always takes it out of them.' He cleared his throat again. 'I was wondering . . . well, if you need cheering up there's a good picture on at the Palace tonight. Betty Grable in *Pin-Up Girl*.'

Cathy felt a surge of relief. She had a ready-made perfect excuse, one that was truthful, at that.

'I'm going to the pictures, sorry. We're all going. We're going to see *Blithe Spirit*. They say it's a laugh. We thought it would be good for Stel.'

'I see. Well, another time.' She was peeling away as they came to the corner and he suddenly screwed up his courage. 'I'll ask you again, if that's all right? My name's Paul. Paul Steele. Well, I told you that the other day, but you might have forgotten, with everything that's going on.'

'It's perfectly all right to ask again, Paul Steele,' she called as she crossed the road, but she knew in her head that answer would be the same. She wasn't ready for a boyfriend – never would be, unless things changed. They had to stay together as a family if they were to survive. An uneasy memory of what Mags had said about her boyfriend reared up, but only for a second. Mags hadn't mentioned him again, and wouldn't desert them, not now. The school came in sight and she hurried to pick out her sister, and link arms with her for the journey home.

They had faggots and chips for their tea, and then set off for the picture house, Maggie and Cath in front, Edie and Stella behind. 'The play's been running for years up the West End,' Edie called. 'They were talking about it in the salon today. It's about a ghost . . .'

'We don't want to hear what it's about, Edie, thank you.' Mags was firm. 'If we know what it's about, we can save the one and threepences.'

'All I'm saying is it's about ghosts . . .'

This time the older sisters spoke in unison. 'Shut up, our Edie. Now!'

They trooped into the magnificence of the picture house and settled down for a treat. Rex Harrison played the husband and Constance Cummings was his wife. At least, she played one of his wives. The other one was the ghost that wanted him back. 'She's got a really husky voice,' Edie whispered.

'Shut up,' Cathy said fiercely.

A demented old lady, a medium, was played by an actress called Margaret Rutherford. 'I'm sure she's a man,' Edie whispered. This time Cathy took hold of her sister's knee and pinched till she heard a stifled 'Ouch'. That should shut her up.

'Did you think she was good-looking?' Mags asked on the way home.

'Which one?'

'Elvira . . . well, I know she was green, but underneath?'

'That was make-up. Did you notice when she flopped down on the settee and her skirt came up you could see where the make-up ended. She was attractive, but the other one was better looking. Classy.'

They walked on for a moment, and then Cath plucked up courage. 'Do you believe in that . . . ghosts and everything? People coming back?'

'No, Cath, I don't. And I don't think we should go there with our Edie's ears flapping. Let alone Stella's. But Madame Arcati was a scream. Mad as a hatter.'

They were on home ground now and their steps quickened. 'We need to talk after they go to bed,' Mags said as home came in sight.

'I don't like the sound of that.' Cathy was as crestfallen as she sounded. They had been to the pictures, which had cost a few bob. The fact that Maggie had allowed it, even suggested it, had given her confidence. If they could afford four seats at the pictures, they must be flush. 'We need to talk' meant that they weren't.

'I don't see how we're going to manage, Cath.' Stella had been tucked up, and Edie was sitting up in bed putting rags in her hair to get the curls she craved. Mags shut the door carefully and sat down. 'It's not the rent and food on the table, we'll manage that. It's the other things. It's treats like tonight, and clothes and . . . well, make-up and nylons, and . . . you know what I mean.'

Cathy resented the fact that tonight's treat was rapidly losing its good effect, but she struggled to find something constructive to say. 'I expect I could get a job with better money. Maybe not now, but . . .'

Her words died away as a strange sound came from the bedroom. Mags was first at the door, Cathy behind her. 'Don't look at me!' Edie was all injured innocence, hand still entangled in the rag she was winding into her hair. A scream rent the air.

'Stella's having a nightmare,' Cath said.

For once Maggie seemed uncertain. 'Shall we wake her up?'

'I said those faggots were off,' Edie said.

Both sisters turned on her. 'Shut up,' Cath offered. Mags was more forthright. 'One of these days you'll open your mouth, our Edie, and I will swing for you.'

'I only said . . .' Edie was innocence personified.

'One more word, Edie. One more word!'

Cath had advanced on the bed. Stella was whimpering now, and she put out a hand.

'Stella? It's me, Stel. Cathy. It's all right, you're home now.'

Stella's eyes opened and widened as she took in her surroundings. 'It was Mam, Cath. Mam came back, like Elvira. She was here, she had her arms round me.'

This time Edie was not to be restrained. 'I said that picture was creepy, all about ghosts. Now . . .'

Her words were drowned as Mags advanced upon her and tried to smother her with the eiderdown.

Chapter Nine

Maggie

THINKING ABOUT IT NOW, Maggie couldn't remember why she had kept Joe a secret. Perhaps she had wanted to keep him to herself, not wanted him to be drawn into the bosom of the family, with everyone questioning him and, maybe, telling tales about her when she was younger. Whatever the reason, she had not said a word at home while Mam was alive, and if she couldn't speak out when everything had been normal, how could she tell them properly about him now?

It had begun in the blaze of flags, fireworks, and floodlights that was Victory in Europe night, 13 May 1945. She had been in Whitehall to see Churchill in his siren suit and Homburg hat waving from a balcony that someone said was the Ministry of Health. They had sung 'For he's a jolly good fellow' until they were hoarse, and then Winnie had conducted them in 'Land of Hope and Glory'.

She had been with some of the girls from work, and afterwards they had made for Piccadilly, where the licensing laws had been suspended for the night. 'We'll serve till it runs out,' one landlord had said. 'And then, bugger me, we'll turn water into wine if we have to.' Here and there, men and women in uniform were carried shoulder high by total strangers through cheering crowds. Maggie had been caught up in the magic of it, drunk without alcohol, thrilled with the feeling that no more bombs would rain on London, and all the men would soon come home.

Her legs were tired by the time they wound up in Trafalgar Square, driven from Piccadilly by the AFS coming to douse the bonfires. She made no protest when an arm came round her and drew her close to a serge uniform. Everyone was singing – 'The White Cliffs of Dover' and then 'We'll Meet Again'.

She had cried at that, and the man had turned to her for the first time. 'Lost a sweetheart?' he said gently, and she had shaken her head. 'My Dad,' she said. 'He died in the Blitz.' He had drawn her close, and she had buried her face in the rough serge and remembered that Dad's navy uniform had felt the same.

'I'm Joe,' he had said later, and when she told him her name was Margaret he had said, 'Then I'll call you Meg.' He came from County Durham, and had been a builder's labourer until he was called up. His dad was a miner, his mother was a wonderful cook and homemaker, and he had a sister called Mavis.

After that, they had seen one another at every opportunity. He had been overseas for most of the war. Now he was stationed in Shoeburyness, which was not that far away, but he could come to London only when he had leave, and sometimes, even then, he went home to see his family. When he kissed her, Maggie felt her knees grow weak. Sometimes he would cup a hand round her breast, very gently, and she liked the feeling.

'Have you ever thought he might be married?' one of the girls had asked one day, and the suggestion had shocked her. How could anyone think such a thing? In the end she had told him what had been said, and he had laughed till he almost cried. Afterwards, he had teased her unmercifully until, when he saw she was upset, he had shown her his paybook and his army status: single; next-of-kin, father.

Now Maggie came to with a start as the buzzer for the tea-break sounded.

'All I think about is sugar,' someone said, as they collected their tea. 'Great dollops of it. I won't put it in anything, I'll just eat it.'

'It's butter with me.' The speaker was an older woman. 'Lovely creamy butter from the Maypole, slapped on with a knife. Not spread. Just plopped on everywhere till you can't see the bread.'

'Oranges,' a girl opined. 'Jaffas, big ones. Or bananas, lovely yellow ones . . .not those awful brown things they sent in food parcels.'

'I liked those,' one girl said. 'Lovely and sweet.' She giggled then. 'We used to get them in parcels sent from dad's cousin in Ireland. You know what they looked like, brown worms. My bother put two of them on the carpet once and Mam thought the dog had crapped.'

'What a waste,' a woman said, but the first speaker shook her head. 'We ate them afterwards, don't worry about that.'

'All we talk about now is food.' Maggie sipped her tea before she continued. 'It's nylons I want, and skirts with plenty in them so they don't bite your knees. And patterned china . . .'

'It's pay packets I want to keep seeing,' another girl said gloomily. 'I mean, they can't keep this place going much longer. The war's over. They don't need shells.'

'They'll make something else. Kettles, pans . . . they'll still need workers.'

'Yes, and there'll be ten ex-servicemen queuing up for every job. They won't want us.'

'Put a sock in it, Freda,' someone said. 'I'm crying into me bleeding tea. Did anyone hear Anne Shelton last night?'

The talk turned to safer waters, then, until someone opened her *Daily Express*. 'I see they've got that Tokyo Rose.'

'Tokyo who?'

'You know. Like Lord Haw-Haw, only Japanese.'

'Hope they shoot her. And Tojo.'

The newspaper owner swooped triumphantly. 'Too late. It says here General Tojo, Premier of Japan, shot himself in the heart. They've saved him, though, so he'll likely hang as well.'

'Hanging's too good for them.' A woman wiped tea from her mouth to continue. 'They've starved men and beheaded them. Women as well, and kids probably. They should've dropped more of those bombs on them.'

There was a murmur of agreement, and then the talk turned to German war criminals and what was to be done with them. 'Trials are too good for them, my man says. Put them up against a wall and shoot them, that's what he'd do.'

At that point the buzzer sounded, and it was time to go back to their lathes. As she turned on the power and heard the hum, Maggie thought about Joe's letter. 'Not long now, Meg.' He was the only person who called her Meg, and she liked that. 'I long to hold you in my arms and love you properly.'

She had offered him sex more than once, but he had refused her. 'Not when I might not make it, Meg. Any bairn of mine's going to have a dad.' She had promised to take precautions, without knowing where the hell she would get them; she had even begged for the right to show how much she loved him. But he had been firm. Now the war was over and he was safe, so he said that they could love properly. She felt happiness flood through her at the thought that she would see him tonight – until the memory of how she had hidden the truth from her sisters intruded. They thought she was going out with the girls, and so wouldn't be home until bedtime.

She would have to come clean eventually . . . either that or give up Joe and any prospect of happiness, which was unthinkable. They couldn't manage without her wage – couldn't really manage even now. It was scrape from one day to another, and if it weren't for hand-outs from Mrs S., who had little enough herself, life would be grim.

She made a real effort to banish worries. Tonight she would

be with Joe. They would find a pub and huddle together in a corner until it was dark enough to melt into some alleyway and hold one another close. Did she love him? How could you tell? She couldn't imagine life without him, that was certain. But did she love him more than Cath or Stella? Even Edie, come to that? They were flesh and blood.

'I can't leave them,' she thought despairingly. 'Not while they're still kids.' Even Cath was a kid, earning buttons in a pub kitchen and not old enough to serve in the bar where she might get tips. 'It's not fair,' Maggie thought bitterly – and then drew down a curtain on any future further than the next eight hours.

Chapter Ten

Maggie

SHE REACHED OUT AN arm to the clock. Five to six. On a weekday she would have to slide from the bed and start getting ready for work – but today was Sunday. She stretched cautiously. Mustn't wake Cathy, asleep beside her. Nothing short of rifle fire woke Edie in the morning; and Stella was now sleeping better, thank God.

Maggie decided to allow herself another half-hour before she got up, time to think about the day ahead. It was her last day with Joe, for a while at least. He was being posted back to Germany. 'I've put in for demob, Meg, on the grounds that I'm needed back in Belgate in the pit. They're desperate for miners now that the Bevin boys are done. They'll take their time – the army grinds slower than mills of God – but it'll get there. I never wanted to go down the hole, but now it seems like a good idea. I want you to come back to Belgate with me, Meg. We'll have to live in at first, until I find a place. But I still want you with me, as my wife.'

She had felt torn by his move to get a speedy demob. Half of her wanted him home for good, half of her didn't want decision time, and that's what it would be. She thought of her sister's faces if she said she was going north. Cathy would look stricken, Stella would dissolve into tears, and Edie would immediately try to work out where advantage lay for her.

Things were better now in some ways. They had ceased to wait hourly for news of their mother's killer. Paul, the young policeman, called regularly, and promised the case was on-going, but they all knew the real reason he came. 'He's soft on you, our Cath.' Even little Stella had said it, but Cath was having none of it. Just as well. They couldn't both go off. 'None of us can go off,' she thought.

Except that once she lost her job she'd be a liability not an asset. The country was in a mess, one way and another. Some people were losing their jobs, and others playing ducks and drakes with theirs. Today 6,000 troops would be unloading food ships in British ports because 43,000 dockers were on unofficial strike for a minimum wage of twenty-five shillings a day. A day! And dockers got perks as well, everyone knew that. Besides, fancy boycotting food ships when everyone was hungry! It was scandalous. At least the dockers in Cardiff had relented and unloaded a cargo of oranges. Oranges! Just to hold one would be nice, never mind the juice. They must be getting into the shops now, but they never appeared on top of the counter. Like everything else worth eating, they were under it.

Maggie made her excuses over the breakfast table. 'It's the girls from work. Well, I think they think we won't be together much longer, so we might as well make the most of it.'

'Again? Where are you going?' It was Edie, nosey as usual.

'Round and about. Nowhere special. A drink somewhere and a bite to eat. I won't be late, and Mrs S. is bringing the meal up.' Of late they had shared Sunday lunch with Mrs Schiffman. They provided it for three weeks and she for the fourth, to keep the rations fair.

'Will you manage, Cath?'

''Course we will. You get off and enjoy yourself. I'm taking Stella up the market later on.'

Maggie called on Mrs S. on her way out. 'It's really good of you, Mrs S. I worry if I leave them for long.'

'Don't worry, they are good girls, and Catherine . . . well, she is special. A jewel. But I will keep an eye on them, so off you go. Enjoy. You have been good since your mama went. The best.'

What would the older woman think if she knew there was a possibility she might stop being the good sister and leave them all in the lurch? But guilt evaporated at the sight of Joe's smile, the feel of his hand, big and rough closing round her own. 'Let's make the most of today,' she said.

They walked in the park until nightfall, taking dinner and tea in the café near the band, walking the paths in between until they found a seat without onlookers where they could embrace to their heart's content. Autumn was welcome for more than the falling leaves that rustled under their feet. It gave them a cloak that folded around them and provided for intimacy. When dusk fell and strollers had left the path, they climbed a fence and lay down on a bed of leaves. Sex was painful at first, but Joe was a gentle lover. There had been others before her – she knew that from the skill with which he brought her to a climax when he was done, and dealt with the French letter, so that she was never embarrassed. 'One day', he said, 'we won't need these. Ten children, Meg. Five of each.' And she laughed and told him to find another mug. But she had loved the idea all the same.

They lay together for a long while, feeling warm and satisfied, and not in the least anxious to separate. 'I've done it,' she thought. 'I've crossed the Rubicon, no going back.' Virginity was one of the few things at which you never got a second chance. But she had lost her virginity to him, and he was the best man in the world, so it was all right.

She was shivering as they adjusted their clothes and got ready to leave the park. 'What time do you have to be back?'

'There's a lorry back to camp picking us up on Southampton Row at eleven. That'll get us back to camp by midnight, if he puts his foot down. If not, he'll plead a puncture. They can't put us all in the chokey. Anyway, they're not so strict now it's peace-time. They just want to keep us quiet until we're demobbed.'

It was quarter to eight, she could see that from the watch on his wrist as they walked under a street lamp. She took a deep breath. 'Do you want to come back home and meet the girls?'

He looked suddenly pleased, and then anxious. 'If you're sure it's all right . . . with them, I mean?'

'It will be,' she said, with a certainty she was far from feeling. Then suddenly she thought of Cathy's face. Cath would know the significance of her bringing him home. 'On second thoughts,' she said, 'I think I'll keep you all to myself for a little bit longer.'

In bed that night she thought about the possibility that she could be pregnant. She felt a little sore between her legs, and aware of that area as she had never been before. Joe would stand by her if she was, that much was sure. A lot of single women had had children in the 1940s. Someone on the radio had said it was because young men wanted to ensure their genes lived on if they died. All the same, it was still shameful to have a child out of wedlock. Some girls had been forced to hand over their baby for adoption . . . even been threatened with being sectioned, for the madness of getting herself into the situation in the first place, if she didn't. Some families took the baby in as their own; still others threw girl and baby out. No wonder so many women risked the dangers of back-street abortion. A few married the probably unwilling father of the child, and thereafter had a life of hell. And one girl she knew had had the baby and been forced by her employers to start work again the next day or they would have turned her and the baby on to the street.

'That would never happen to me,' she thought. 'I have Joe and the girls.' Except that she couldn't have them both.

Chapter Eleven

Maggie

A s MAGGIE CHANGED INTO her overalls, the other girls could talk about nothing but the morning's meeting, at twelve sharp in the canteen. 'It's the sack,' one woman said bitterly. 'What else would it be?'

'We knew it was coming,' Maggie said, trying to sound resigned. In truth, she felt sick to her stomach. What would happen to them all without her wage? She'd get dole, but that would only be enough for one person to exist on. Perhaps the bosses would understand that she had responsibilities. And what if she were pregnant? She couldn't regret loving Joe, but it had been crazy to take such risks. She fought down panic, and forced herself to concentrate. If they were going to keep anyone on, it wouldn't be those who did faulty work.

She tried to remember what Joe had said in this morning's letter. 'They say demobs will depend on three things. Compassionate reasons, age, and length of service. That means the older men who were in from '39 will get first crack at it. But I still stand a good chance if I go to the pit. Me dad says they're desperate for men, with coal being in such demand.' He had gone on, then, about the unfairness of a system that would class someone who had been a filing clerk for the duration getting the same eligibility as someone who had slogged through Burma or Europe; but had then forgotten all that in details of what he would get on demobilisation. 'They say you can keep your boots. And you get a suit . . .I'm having pin-stripe. You get shirts, underwear, even a hat.' He had sounded like a little boy in toy shop.

'Penny for them?' The foreman was at her side, eyeing her sympathetically. She laughed, and said her thoughts weren't worth a penny, but she couldn't work out what his expression had meant. Was she for the chop? Was that it? Again panic threatened, and she quelled it. They would manage because they had to manage: it was really as simple as that. It would be more than three years before Stella was earning, and at least three more before she could stand alone. Joe had finished his letter with 'Not long now, love, until we're together,' but sooner or later she would have to tell him the truth. He would understand. He would get on well with the girls, teasing Stella, and being nice with Cath. Even Edie would be charmed into behaving herself. Maybe they could all move to Durham? If he really loved her, he would realise she couldn't leave them behind.

The meeting, when it came, was as they had expected. The boss thanked them profusely for all they had done for the war effort, and to boost production. Then came the bad news: the workforce was to be reduced, starting at the end of the month. At first it would be voluntary: anyone who wanted to go could do so. After that it would depend on length of service. Some of the women had been there before the war; others, the majority, had started in 1941, when war work became compulsory. Maggie had been there only since '43, one of the late-comers.

She felt the weight of her worries bearing down on her. It was as though everything that could go wrong was going wrong. Easement came at four o'clock when she went to the lavatory and found, to her relief, that her period had started. That was one less thing to worry about, at least.

No one talked much through the afternoon, not even in the

tea-break. They were all eyeing up their chances, apart from one or two who had only come because they had no choice, and couldn't wait to leave. The mood among the girls had changed, and not for the better. 'We were all friends once,' Maggie thought. 'Now we're eyeing one another and thinking "Will it be her or me?"' It was a relief when the buzzer went for home time and she could move into the fresh air and think about the evening ahead. They were having fish and chips tonight. A treat, and no pans and pots to wash.

All the girls were at home when she let herself in, but she could tell at once that something had happened. 'They're closing Mam's case,' Cathy said flatly. 'An inspector called round just after I got in. He says it will remain on file, but unless there's some fresh evidence they can't do anything.'

'Fresh evidence?' Edie said. 'That means until someone else gets murdered?' No one contradicted her.

They sat round the table, even the joy of fish and chips eroded by their news. 'It's as though Mam didn't matter,' Edie said quietly and again seemed surprised when no one contradicted her.

In the background the wireless was spilling out news. The dock strike was over after seven weeks, so food supplies would be easier, but that seemed not to matter. After the meal had been cleared away they tried to settle. Edie was curling Stella's hair with tongs she had taken from the heart of the fire. 'That stinks,' Cathy said as the smell of burned hair assailed their nostrils.

'Don't blame me,' Edie said indignantly. 'If we weren't poor we could all have permanent waves and never need tongs again.'

Maggie sighed. 'If we weren't poor, Edie, I can think of a hell of a lot of things we'd need before we went in for perms.'

There was nothing decent on the wireless, and they were beginning to look at the clock and long for bedtime when a knock came at the door. It was Paul Steele.

'Can I come in?' he said, already stooping through the doorway. 'I won't keep you long. I know it's late.'

They looked at him expectantly, but no one spoke until Edie said, 'Go on, then.'

He had removed his helmet and now he passed it from one hand to another. 'Well, I know the governor, my boss, the inspector, came today to say the case is closed. It is, officially. But I told you we wouldn't let go till we found the perpetrator, and I just wanted you to know we . . . I . . . the Force doesn't let things go.'

'Thank you,' Maggie said, a bit at a loss. 'I think we knew you'd do what you could, but it's nice to hear it said all the same.'

The door had hardly closed on him before Edie was mocking him. 'He thinks he's Sexton Blake. He's only a common copper. And we all know he only comes because of our Cathy.'

'That's enough.' The weariness of the day hung heavy on Maggie. She couldn't be doing with nonsense. 'I've had a hell of a day, Edie, and if you want to be nasty when someone tries to do right by this family, you can shut up. He's a good lad, that one, and if he fancies our Cath he could do worse. She could do worse. I'm off to bed, and if one of you could shift to set things out for the morning I'd be grateful.'

'Just all talk about me as though I wasn't here,' Cathy said, but she said it absent-mindedly, as though her thoughts were elsewhere.

Maggie was glad that Cath didn't follow her to the bedroom. She couldn't explain how she felt. How could you tell sisters you loved that you felt trapped by their very existence? It was a long time since she had kneeled to say her prayers, but tonight she did so. It was brief. 'Please God, sort this out, because I can't, and that's a fact.'

Chapter Twelve

Maggie

IT SEEMED STRANGE TO be hanging her clothes in her locker for the last time. 'I could do this in my sleep,' she thought, 'and now I'll never do it again.' Tomorrow there would be no six o'clock alarm, no shivering at the bus stop, no clocking on. And no pay packet on Thursday. She felt a shiver of fear at the thought, and dismissed it instantly. She mustn't give way today, not in front of the others.

She hadn't chosen to do factory work. She had tried for the Wrens, in spite of Mam saying that only toffs got in. In the end, she hadn't even made it into the ATS. 'Bloody snobbery,' Mam had called it, but she'd looked relieved all the same. So it had been munitions, fifty-five hour weeks, ten-hour days, until they found out that fatigue led to mistakes, and reduced it to forty-eight hours. The work was monotonous and repetitive, but while the war had teetered on a knife edge no one had minded. Most of the women had someone away, and each shell seemed somehow to make them safer. It was only lately that it had seemed a bit pointless. One or two girls had tried to dodge fastening their hair inside a scarf, and there had been ructions over time-keeping.

'I won't miss night shift,' Maggie's neighbour said, as she started up her lathe. 'It's bad enough in here in day-time . . . the noise and the smell. But when the blackout was up you could feel yourself dropping off, it was that airless.'

The blackout! It seemed a long way off, and yet it had only been a few months since the illumination of Big Ben that had ended the blackout in London.

Maggie began the monotonous drilling, and tried not to think about how soon Joe would be home, demanding an answer. Last week at home they had barely scraped by. Without Edie's tips they couldn't have paid the undertaker's instalment . . . not and eaten as well. And next week it would be worse, with her getting coppers on the dole instead of a proper wage. They would just have to pull their horns in, all of them. No more picture-going, not even a night at the Palais – not that she'd done that since Joe. But Cath should have a life, a night at the Strand Ballroom or up Hammersmith. Paul Steele would take her there like a shot, but Cathy was having none of it. She had her head screwed on, had Cath. Once you got in with a man, heartbreak was practically guaranteed. Except that without them there was no happiness.

Maggie was relieved to have her reverie broken by a tap on the shoulder. It was the foreman. 'Word with you . . . in the office.'

She switched off her machine, wiped her hands, and followed him to his cubby-hole.

'I might have a place for you,' he said, when he had closed the door. 'Not sure yet, but it's possible.'

'I'd be ever so grateful.' Even to her own ears, it sounded like crawling, but she didn't care.

'Of course,' he said, staring down at his desk, 'one good turn deserves another.'

She felt her mouth dry. 'What do you mean?'

'Well, I scratch your back . . .'

Maggie sought for words, but could only repeat, 'I don't know what you mean.'

'Well, I'm nice to you, you're nice to me.'

'I'm always nice, Mr Bullen.'

'Of course you are. That's why I want to keep you on.'

'How nice do you mean?'

'I think you know.'

'Do you mean "drop your knickers" nice?'

'Something like that. I'll need an answer by tomorrow.'

She wavered, but only for a while. Even for her sisters some prices were too high. 'I can tell you now. You can shove your job.'

He was moving to open the door. 'As you wish.'

It was a relief that the buzzer was going for tea-break. If she'd had to start that bloody machine feeling the way she did now, she'd have lost a finger for sure.

'All right?' The other girl's face was anxious. And knowing.

'I'm OK,' Maggie said. 'But Bullen . . .' her words tailed off.

'Offered to keep you for dropping your knickers?'

'You as well?'

'Everyone under twenty-five, chuck. Now get this tea down you. We're going for a drink at home time. Bit of a knees-up.'

'I would love to,' Maggie said, and meant it. 'But I've got to get home for our Stella.'

On the bus home she thought about the foreman's offer. Should she have said yes, put up with it to put food on the table? A lot of women had done that down the years. For a few seconds she wondered if it was too late to change her answer, but then she remembered his hands on the desk . . . fat fingers, hairy on the back, with dirty broken fingernails. 'There has to be another way,' she thought, and got up a stop early so she could stand on the rear platform and feel the wind on her face.

When she got in, the table was already set and there was a cake on a glass stand in the centre. 'Mrs S.,' Cathy said by way of explanation. 'To celebrate.'

'Celebrate what?'

'Your new job.' Edie couldn't wait to blurt out the news.

'Our Cath's got you a new job at the pub.' Her outburst earned her an elbow dig from Cath.

'Shut up, Edie. It's true, though, Mags. Behind the bar, and in the kitchen where necessary.'

'What's the money?'

'By negotiation, Mr Hopkins says, but it'll be better than nothing.'

The tears came then, to be soothed away with cheese on toast and slices of Polish cake. 'And we're going to the pictures,' Stella said through a mouthful of crumbs. Mrs Schiffman was treating them all to *Brief Encounter*. 'Even me,' Stella said. 'Not in the one and nines, but the back stalls, so the next best thing.'

The film seemed slow. 'Not a patch on *Blithe Spirit*,' Cathy whispered half-way through. But Mrs Schiffman hung on every word that came from Trevor Howard or Celia Johnson's lips. 'She's crying,' Edie whispered half-way through, and Mrs S. wept into a lace-edged hanky until it was wrung out.

She had cheered up by the time they emerged into the darkness. 'Look at the street lamps,' she said. 'Isn't it wonderful? No more darkness. And Christmas coming, a peace-time Christmas.' They walked on, their neighbour between them, in a mood of happy contemplation.

It didn't last. When Edie and Stella had been packed off to bed, the two older girls sat either side of the table.

'Spit it out, Cath. I know there's something.'

'The money won't be that much, Mags. But there'll be tips over the bar.'

'That's OK. Like you said, better than nothing.'

'Oh, and there's a letter for you, from Joe, I think. It came after you left this morning.'

Maggie waited to open it until Cath, too, had gone to bed.

'Dear Meg,' it began. 'Good news! My demob's through. I leave this place next month, there's a week or so at Aldershot, and then home. Let's get married, Meg, as soon as you can arrange it. I want us to be together for ever. I think about it at night, imagining you beside me. Even snoring. And with your curlers in.' She put up a finger to flick away a tear. He'd be talking about her teeth in a jar and a wooden leg next.

When she had read to the end she folded it carefully into its envelope. She kept thinking of Mrs Schiffman, crying her way through a love story. She and her husband had escaped from Germany when it all went wrong for the Jews, but he hadn't lasted long once they got to England. That was real sorrow.

She crossed to the door of Stella and Edie's bedroom. Only the sound of easy breathing – both girls were asleep. She moved back to the table and reached for pen and paper.

'Dear Joe,' she wrote. 'I'm sorry if I've misled you, but there's no question of my marrying you.' She didn't give reasons – how could you say, 'I have to see to my sisters'? He would give her arguments, try to talk her out of it, but there was no other way. When she had signed it 'Sincerely, Meg', she licked the envelope and put it aside for posting. Then she made up the fire, put out the light, and made her way to bed. She didn't cry. It was too bad for tears.

BOOK 2
1947

Chapter Thirteen

March 1947
Edie

'IT SAYS HERE FOUR million workers were made idle by the power cuts.'

'If you're going to read the paper out loud, Edie, read something cheerful.' Edie took no notice. She had spent a penny on a paper when she went to get some bread. That's what was biting Cath, but she'd have to put up with it because Edie needed to read the news so she could talk to clients. She went on reading aloud: 'It says troops used flame-throwers to clear drifts in Dorset . . . and they let men out of jail to clear roads.'

'We know all that, Edie. We lived through it, remember? No coal, no electricity most of the time . . . not even a bloody lift in John Lewis. And we saw the snow, miles of it.'

'Language!' Cath was glaring, and Edie indicated Stella with a flick of her head. Inside her, though, jealousy stirred. Stella, Stella, must protect little Stella. 'She's only three years younger than me,' she thought, 'and yet I have to tip everything up, and she gets all the treats.'

As if she had read her thoughts, and to make things worse, Cath pushed a mug of tea across the table. 'Take that to our Maggie, but if she's asleep leave it beside the bed.'

'Why isn't she up, and why is it always me?'

'I'll do it,' Stella was up and seizing the mug.

'Greaser!' Edie said, and was pleased when she saw Stella's

cheeks flush crimson.

'God, you're a bitch, our Edie.' Cath waited to speak until Stella was beyond the bedroom door.

Edie wasn't taking that lying down. 'I need to be a bitch in this house. If you don't stick up for yourself here, you've had it. And if Mam was here to hear your language, you'd catch it. Mags is as bad, always going around biting people's heads off. And now . . .' she rose to her feet in what she hoped was a majestic way, 'I'm off to work to earn the money that keeps this place going.' She had seized her coat and bag and was at the door before Cath could get out more than an outraged 'Huh!'

On the bus Edie thought about the breakfast. Mags was usually there, sorting everything. Why not today? Come to think about it, she had been funny yesterday – ever since that letter had come at breakfast time. Something was up, and Cath knew about it. That was why tea had been sent in to her. As her stop came into view, she got up to leave. She would find out tonight, one way or another.

'Morning, Edith. On time as usual.'

Mr Edward was twinkling at her. She smiled as sweetly as she could. 'I like coming to work, Mr Edward. You know that.' Slipping into her white overall with its blue piping, she reflected on men. Pushovers, every one – even when they were bent as a five-pound coin. All she had to do was butter them up, and they were putty. She slipped off her snow boots and slid her feet into her white heels. Then she checked her hair in the mirror, licked her fingers to smooth a stray eyebrow, and went forth to greet the clients.

She had those same clients divided into categories. Rich bitches who thought you were there to wipe their boots, but tipped well. Bloody little upstarts who tried to lord it over everyone but were no better than she was herself: they would tip as though they were dispensing riches, but it was a threepenny piece if you were lucky. Then there was the bunch that gave no trouble and tipped, and the ones who couldn't afford anything but a once a year perm. The last three categories she treated civilly, especially if Mr Edward was in earshot. But she reserved her energy for making sure the first bunch rewarded her as she deserved.

'You've got lovely hair,' she would say, massaging the shampoo into their scalps until they almost purred. 'Now, let me get you a lovely warm towel instead of this damp one.' That was always good for a bit extra. All things considered, she had been right to hold out for a better class of salon. Mam had urged her to work nearer home, but she had wanted something more. If you were going to get on, you had to shake the East End off your shoes. Better sooner than later.

Most days she just shampooed or prepared trays for the stylists, but lately Mr Edward had introduced hand massages for some clients. She liked doing hand massage: it meant she could give her own hands a good going over with the cream, and she could also get a good look at their rings. The rich ones sometimes had rings on every finger. Well, almost. She liked diamonds best, solitaires set in platinum, but rubies were interesting. And more expensive, according to Mr Edward, who was a fount of knowledge about anything to do with jewellery or luxuries in general. 'Emeralds, Edie, that's the stone. Green for jealousy. Ooh, I do like a little bit of that in a relationship.'

Once or twice, as she worked, she looked up to see his eyes on her. If he wasn't a poof she'd have thought he was after her. As it was, she gave him her most charming smile. Wasted on him – except that it paid to keep all men sweet, bent or straight.

During her coffee break she continued to think about men. She particularly liked the Yanks, although she would never marry one. Some girls swallowed all the tales of Cadillacs and swanking around Palm Beach. Not her. You could be dirt-poor in America – she'd read about some GI brides going over to find they were living in log-cabins with an outside lav.

But Yanks were all right for now. She had met Marvin at the Hammersmith Palais, and he was good for nylons and the occasional tin of fruit, which she could always sell at work. If her sisters hadn't been so mean over the tips, she might have shared it out at home, but why should she, when she was already putting food on the table?

Yanks were different from English lads. Take that daft PC who was always hanging round after Cathy – if he knew how to spoil a girl like the Yanks did, Cath might've taken a fancy to him, because he wasn't bad-looking. Instead, she seemed hardly to notice him, and he hadn't the spunk to move on. Marvin knew how to spoil a girl, all right. He'd even walked her into the Savoy once for a drink. That had made people sit up. All the same, he had thought all English girls were tarts, and she'd made him pay for that. He'd had to say please a few times before he got as much as a feel. Which was all he got. Every time she went in a lav and saw the notices on the door about VD, her blood ran cold. She might give in to him one day, depending – but he'd have to use the rubbers he was always talking about. In her opinion he was as green as grass, but you couldn't be too careful.

By home-time she had a satisfactory amount of coinage, and she divided it into three. Two parts for her, and one for home. But today that one part amounted to more than she was supposed to tip up. She subtracted the largest coin, and added it to her own store.

She scented an atmosphere as soon as she let herself into the flat. 'What's up?' she said, but no one answered. Stella was quiet, but that was normal. Cath never looked up, except to say, 'There's tea in the pot,' and Maggie was . . . well, that was a puzzle and no mistake. Half the time looking like she'd won the pools and the other half looking as though she was going to burst into tears.

'What's up? I know there's something!' she said again,

sitting down at the table.

'Nothing,' Cath said, 'except the usual. Where's the rent coming from? Our Stella's shoes are done, so she needs a new pair. And we're a month behind with the funeral payments. Any suggestions?'

'It's not that bad, Cath.' Maggie was looking anxiously at Stella. 'No worse than usual, and we always manage somehow.'

'Well, some of us manage, Maggie. Others just swan in and out, as carefree as the birds.'

'I know you mean me, Cath. In spite of the fact that I tip up more than my share.'

'Please!' Cath had risen to her feet. 'You don't know the half of it, our Edie. Some people have made sacrifices you can't imagine.'

'Well, more fool them. And as I can't get any peace, let alone a bit of tea, I might as well get ready and get out of here!'

She hadn't been looking forward to seeing Marvin tonight, might even have dropped him, but anything was better than this hell-hole. Before she started to get ready she put her share of the tips into the hidey-hole she had established in the bedroom. It was mounting up nicely, and every time she counted it she felt good. That was her escape route from this crumby place. 'One day,' she told herself as she made up her face. 'One day!'

Chapter Fourteen

Edie

'YES, IT'S SERIOUS, ISN'T IT?' The plump body bent over the sink quivered with indignation. 'Serious? The world's gone mad. The war, of course, it's all the fault of the war.'

'I couldn't agree more, Mrs Percival. Is that water all right for you? Can't have you shivering, can we?' Indistinguishable sounds were coming from the bent head. 'Let's have you up, now. And a nice warm towel.' Mrs Percival was a fat fool, but always good for a two-shilling piece.

'I read it in the paper,' the woman said when she was settled in front of the mirror, Edie's fingers soothing her damp hair. 'Things have come to a pretty pass when the Government has to act. Marriage guidance? I'd give them marriage guidance. They say there are 50,000 divorces a year. Disgusting!'

'Disgraceful,' Edie agreed. 'Marriage should be for life, that's what I believe.' Privately she felt that marriage was a trap for suckers, but it wouldn't do to say that. 'I'll just go and tell Stephanie you're ready.' She kept her hands at her sides. It didn't do to look too eager.

'A little extra,' Mrs Percival said, scrabbling in her bag. 'You're such an intelligent girl.' It was half a crown. Half a flaming crown! Things were looking up. She thanked Mrs Percival profusely, and sped away in search of the next sucker.

'Good girl,' Mr Edward said, as she passed. 'I want to

speak to you later.'

She spent the rest of the day worrying. Surely he wasn't going to demand a share of the tips? It was bad enough Mags and Cath leeching on her, let alone a queer. She kept reminding herself that he had said 'Good girl'. You wouldn't say 'good girl' and then say 'hand over'. Well, you could – but he wouldn't. Whatever you could say about him, he wasn't greedy with money. He spent a fortune on the salon, and uniforms, and even their shoes. Some places made you supply your own shoes.

When at last she was closeted with him in his office, his words took her by surprise. 'I've been watching you, Edith. You're a pretty girl – if you weren't, you wouldn't have got in here. But you're more than that. You know how to work, and you're greedy for money. Oh, I see how you winkle money out of people. Well, why shouldn't you? So take that "Not me, Mister" look off your face. You're not in the dock – just the opposite.

'I've got plans, Edith, big plans. I'm tired of hair, and there's a revolution coming. Women don't want sets any more, they want the Rita Hayworth look – roaming all over the place as though it never saw a comb. Or else they buy Amami and do it at home. There'll always be money in hair, but only for those who expand. I'm buying the place next door, as soon as the War Damage is finished with it. It's going to be a beauty salon. Everything from eyebrow-plucking to massage, facials . . .we'll go big on them . . . manicures, pedicures, and waxing. That's going to be big, too.

'This is going to make my fortune, and I want to take you along with me. I want you trained and in there, Edith . . . we'll have to change your name to something posh . . . French perhaps.' He talked about his heroine, Helena Rubinstein. 'A shopkeeper's daughter, Edith, no better than you or I, and one of the world's richest women now. All through beauty.' He held out glossy book. 'This is her life story. Read and learn, Edith, read and learn. She's the first self-made female millionaire because she understands publicity. Remember that, publicity is essential. That, and word of mouth. Keep them happy. She was practically self-taught . . . no real training. But you're going to get training, lucky girl.'

On the bus home, Edie kept wondering if she was dreaming, but the paper in her bag gave details of the place where she would be taught all these new treatments. And she would be called Edwina. They had decided on that eventually, which meant she wouldn't have to change her name much. Edith/Edwina: hardly a change at all, but much more stylish. But, hard as it would be, she mustn't say anything at home. Not a whisper, not yet, and she'd have to keep the Rubenstein book well hidden. They would only expect more money from her if they knew she was getting on. She thought of the wages Mr Edward had floated in front of her – not now, but eventually. My God! She had to stand a full two minutes outside the door to compose herself before she went in.

She sniffed the air as she closed the door. 'Faggots and chips again. God, I loathe faggots.'

There was no sympathy. 'Pass them over here, then,' Cath said. 'Our Maggie's going out, and I'm working, so you'll have to stay in with our Stella.'

'I can't. I'm going out, too.'

'You're not. And don't argue, Edie. If you won't pitch in, you can pack your bags. And if you act up in front of Maggie, I'll kill you.'

Edie ate her meal greedily, one eye on the clock. She didn't really want it, but if Cathy did, it had to be put away.

'It's your turn to wash up,' Cath said firmly.

'It's not, and, anyway . . .' She was about to repeat that she was going out when Stella interrupted. 'I'll do it, Cath.'

'You will not. It's share and share alike around here, and you did it last night.'

'What about our Maggie, then?' said Edie.

'She's going out, and even if she wasn't, it's your turn, so get cracking.'

Maggie looked strange when she came back onto the room. Dressed up and tense – and 'That's my best coat!' Edie said.

'Yes.' Cath was firm. 'Although where you got the money to buy it, no one knows. But neither Maggie or I have got a best coat, and she needs it tonight, so she's borrowing it. Conversation closed.'

'She's bigger than me. She'll stretch it.'

No one answered her. Maggie went out, still jittery, and Cath was close on her heels. The sooner she was out of here herself, the better.

She waited until there was no chance of either of them coming back for something forgotten, and then she pushed back her chair. 'I'm going out too, Stel. You'll be all right, and Mrs S. is downstairs. I'll be back before the others, and don't you say a word. Not a word, Stel, or else.'

She came back into the room when she was ready. Stella was listening to the radio.

'Where's our Mags gone?' Edie tried to sound casual.

'I don't know. With a boy, probably.' Stella didn't seem interested.

'Our Maggie doesn't do boys, Stella. Something's up.'

'Well, I don't know. And you're supposed to stay in with me.'

'I'm supposed to do a lot of things, Stel. Keep your mouth shut. I'll be back in no time.'

On the bus she saw Paul Steele. He looked different somehow. Chunkier. Quite handsome, in a way. She swayed along the aisle and sat down beside him. 'Bunch up, room for a little one.'

He was smiling at her in a bemused kind of way. He really was a bit wet. Must be if he fancied Cath. Still . . . 'We haven't seen you round for a bit. Our Cath's missed you.'

'Really?' He perked up at that straight away. She gave him one of her best, slow smiles and batted her eyelashes, but he was getting up to get off. 'Tell Cath I was asking after her.'

Silly bugger. Didn't recognise a brick wall when he saw one. Perhaps Cath was . . . for a delicious moment she contemplated Cath's being queer. Women were sometimes. But no – Cath was too boring to do anything so interesting. How did women have sex with women? She was still thinking about it when she jumped off the bus into Marvin's arms.

Chapter Fifteen

Edie

SHE LOVED HER ROOM at Madame Carter's. Everything matched – turquoise velvet curtains, a turquoise carpet with a thick pile. There wasn't an inch of linoleum in the entire house. The bedspread was eau-de-nil and so was the chaise-longue. That was what Madame Carter called it, although it was really a settee with only one arm.

But even if it had been a dump, the room would have been better than home. Ever since she that evening had come home late to find Cath already back with Stella, they had gone on and on at her . . . both of them. Useless to point out that Stella had come to no harm. When she had got lonely, she'd gone downstairs to Mrs S., so nothing spoilt. The Jewish lady was always glad of company.

Anyway, Edie was here now on her course, and loving it. It was a huge house. Downstairs was all treatment rooms, everyone a different colour. Upstairs, which was two floors, was Madame Carter's home. One woman and eight rooms, if you counted two bathrooms! And that was another thing – she had her own bathroom, of green marble, floor to ceiling. Well, it looked and felt like marble. There was even a tiled floor, and the towels were as thick as cushions. If only she could stay here for ever. Still, if she paid attention, she too could be a Madame one day.

She thought about home: what would they be doing now? Sitting round the table, talking about money. No, not money –

debt. When she was a Madame . . . not that Madame Carter hadn't been a bit of a disappointment in some ways. She talked posh, but there was a twang in there somewhere: Yorkshire or Lancashire, something like that. But she knew her stuff, and she had style. Black hair taken back into a little bun, a bit like a ballerina. A white overall that fastened on one side, and lovely nails: no polish, but perfect ovals with white cuticles. That was pencil, one of the assistants had explained.

Edie had just stood around watching the first day, or fetched towels, or glasses of water with a slice of lemon in them. That went on the client's bill – iced water, two shillings and sixpence, even though it was straight out of the tap. The second day she had been allowed to try massage on selected clients, but first she had practised on one of the assistants, who had grunted pleasure or told her off if she got it wrong. Edie had told that girl she was grateful to Madame Carter for giving her the opportunity to learn, and the girl had laughed. 'Don't be too grateful. Your boss is paying through the nose for this.' That was fair enough, Edie thought. She would make Mr Edward a fortune once they set up the salon, especially with iced water at two and six a glass. She had sat at a desk like a schoolgirl to study massage oils and creams, and had a book full of coloured pages that showed you where muscles were, and how to apply pressure. She was getting the intensive course, which was four weeks of twelve-hour days, and only Sundays off. It was a bit of a steal, really.

As time went on she would do more and more on clients, and Madame Carter would get paid for them, even though she was also getting paid by Mr Edward. Tomorrow it would be feet. Edie had seen some awful feet in the last few days: bunions and hammer toes, even on women who looked really smart with their shoes on. She slipped her own foot out of her shoe and wriggled her toes. She had pretty feet. She was quite pretty all over. Not as pretty as Stella, but miles better than Cath or

Mags. And when she could afford to buy good clothes . . . she thought of the women swanking in and out of Madame Carter's in furs and suede and something called cashmere that looked like wool but made all the staff ooh and aah. The women all had rich husbands and they all seemed to know one another. They would lie in the steam room, and talk to one another across the spaces – Roger this and Humphrey that. Pampered, that's what they were: pampered kids, who'd married husbands who could afford to keep up the pampering.

Suddenly Edie remembered her Dad, which was odd because she hardly ever thought about him. If he hadn't been killed in the war, would her life have been different? Probably not. He had been a porter in Covent Garden before he was a fireman, so they had probably been better off on Mam's widow's pension. She stood up and walked across to the cheval mirror. Behind her, the room was a concoction of turquoise and pink. She put up her hands and scraped her hair back in an imitation of Madame Carter. It suited her, because she had good features, but she'd love to dye her hair. You didn't get anywhere with mouse. But she didn't want to find a rich husband. 'I want to make my own money,' she said aloud to the mirror. All her life she had been bossed around. When she was rich, no one would ever again tell her what to do.

She turned away from the mirror, went back to her seat and took out Marvin's letter. He had been posted to Burton Wood. Nearly crying, he'd been, about leaving London. So she had let him have it for a leaving present, and he had really cried then, with gratitude. It was there in his letter. She smoothed it out and read it again.

'My darling Edie, We got here last night. It's OK. One barracks is like another, I suppose. But I miss you, Edie. I'll come up to London as soon as I get a furlough, or could you come down here? I'll send you money . . . first class on the train. Oh, Edie, that last night I knew I wanted to be with you for ever. I've written to Mom and Pop. I know they'll love you when they meet you. I want to take you back with me. We'll need to get married . . .'

She read on for a little while, and then put the letter back in the envelope. It didn't do to close any doors until you were sure. That's why she would ring the pub tomorrow, and keep Mags and Cathy sweet. She'd tell them about the marble bathroom: let them suck on that and see how they liked it. She snuggled down on her eau-de-nil bedspread and opened her book.

Helena Rubenstein had been born in Poland, which was a surprise. She'd been christened Chaja, so she must have changed her name when she got on – 'just like me,' Edie thought. She had been the eldest of eight children born to a shopkeeper in Kraków. Somehow she had arrived in Australia in 1902, with no money and little English. What she did have was style, that and a lovely milky complexion. Soon she found enthusiastic buyers for the jars of beauty cream in her luggage. When those jars ran out, she began to make her own from a grease, chemically known as lanolin, which she got from the fleece of sheep, and to disguise its pungent odour, she experimented with lavender, pine bark, and water-lilies. In other words, she mixed perfume and grease . . . so that was how it was done. Within five years, her Australian operations were profitable enough to finance a Salon de Beauté in London, and a multi-million-pound career was launched. Paris and New York followed, and that was where she still was, rolling in money. Her favourite saying was, 'There are no ugly women, only lazy ones'– but, from the look of her picture on the cover, she was no oil painting herself.

As Edie put the book aside and switched out the bedside lamp, she reflected on the fact that Helena was always referred to as Madame Rubenstein. Madame Jackson didn't sound quite right, so it would have to be Madame Edwina. That had a ring. Contented, she drifted into sleep.

Chapter Sixteen

Maggie

S HE LOOKED AT THE clock: there were still a few minutes to spare. She closed her eyes and tried to quell the feelings welling up inside her. How had it all wound up like this? Life was supposed to be easy: you worked hard at school, you grew up, you worked hard at a job you liked, and then you met the man of your dreams and became a wife and mother. That's what the story-books told you. What they left out was the bloody uphill struggle, the pitfalls not of your own making, the sheer bloody grind of it all. Had she ever believed the hearts-and-flowers version? That night she'd met Joe, when London was alive with relief and joy, had she believed it then? She tried to remember but couldn't.

She'd had one letter from Joe in reply to the letter she had written in 1945. That he was hurt was apparent in every line. If that was the way she wanted it, he wrote, so be it. There would be no pleading from him. She had regretted not being truthful about her reasons then: he might have had pity, and given her time to sort things out at home. Not that there had been any sorting out possible. Two years on, they were still just scraping by from day to day. When Stella left school, it might be easier; but back in 1945 that had seemed years away. Now there was a faint glimmer of hope of their hanging on till then – except that when Stella was bringing in a wage, her government money would stop. You couldn't win.

And there was nothing in the news to cheer anyone up. As if the harsh winter hadn't been enough, icebergs off the Norfolk coast which had never been seen before, the power crisis had been so bad that the Prime Minister, Clement Attlee, had declared 'an emergency of the utmost gravity', and had appealed to everyone to save fuel. A few times they had all gone to bed when they came home from work, just to keep warm. It was summer now, but somehow Maggie felt as though things had never warmed up. And all the time there was the struggle to find decent food, never mind afford it. Last week the milk allowance had been reduced to two and a half pints a week . . . not even milk to put in your tea, now. And newspapers were so thin at four pages you could read them in seconds. 'Did we win the war?' Cathy had asked last week, and she wasn't far wrong.

Maggie turned her thoughts back to today. Joe's second letter had come ten days ago, out of the blue. 'Dear Meg, I don't know if this will find you. Perhaps you've married and moved on, who knows? But on the off chance that this does reach you, I want you to know my feelings haven't changed. I've been back home for eighteen months now – a free man, you might say, but forget any idea of Hail the Returning Hero. Civilians seem to begrudge us coming home with a gratuity. They talk about it as though it was thousands. Mine was £78 16s 2d, and a new suit. For five years out of my life! Civilians say they did war work too, but at least they slept in their own bed every night. Still, I'm not writing to bellyache, but to ask if we could meet up. I'm making good money at the pit, and London doesn't seem like the far side of the moon, as it did before the war.'

Maggie had waited two days to reply, and had confided in no one. In that time she had weighed the possibilities in her mind. Could she ask him to wait longer? Would he be willing? That she still loved him, she had no doubt. That she would be glad to leave the pub behind was certain. But how could she tell her sisters that her weekly contribution to the pot would cease? It made the difference between starvation and existence, which was what their lives were . . . except for Edie's. She swore she was tipping up everything, but clothes and shoes and make-up seemed to grow on trees for her. Maybe she could contribute a bit more, if it came to the push. 'I want to be with Joe,' Maggie thought. 'I want that more than anything else in the world.'

So she had written back, and agreed to a meeting. They had met the first time at King's Cross station. He looked strange out of uniform, but more handsome. 'You've filled out,' she had said, and then blushed at the inadequacy of that for an opening remark. He had taken her to the pictures to see *Singin' in the Rain*, a wonderful film with Gene Kelly dancing through puddles as though they weren't there. But all Maggie had been conscious of was the feel of the broad shoulder next to hers, and later, after she'd finished her ice-cream, his big hand enveloping hers.

Tonight they were meeting again at the station, and he was staying for two more days. She had told Cathy, or, rather, she'd had it wormed out of her. But Cath could keep her mouth shut.

She put on Cath's skirt that evening, but found it uncomfortably tight around the waist. She squeezed a finger inside and tried to ease it. She would have to stop eating leftovers at the pub, tempting as they were. She applied one of Edie's lipsticks, and then pressed her lips together. In the mirror her eyes were sparkling. 'I love him,' she thought. 'God help me, I love him.'

Joe took her arm to hurry her through the crowded station. 'Where are we going?' she asked, and received, 'You'll see,' for an answer.

The hotel was little more than a house in a side-street. Only the glowing 'City Hotel' above the door set it apart from its neighbours. 'Don't say anything,' he said to her as they entered the narrow hall. A few minutes later they were alone in the room he had booked. 'Is it all right?' he said anxiously, looking at the bed with its rust-coloured coverlet.

'It's lovely,' she said, and began to unloosen her coat. They made love fiercely at first and then more gently, afraid it would end too soon.

'I love you, Meg.'

'I know you do?'

'What kind of an answer is that?'

'The only one you're going to get, Joe Harrington.' And then, as his breath grew more laboured and his thrust more fierce, 'I love you too, Joe . . . I love . . . love . . . love . . .' The end was lost in a tumbling fulfilment.

He had brought her some chocolate, and a packet of fig rolls. 'You used to talk about them – "Wait till the war's over, and we can get fig rolls again."'

'Did I say that?' For no reason tears were pricking her eyes. They'd thought it was all going to be wonderful once the war was over: milk and honey; jubilation. Well, they had had their night of jubilation, but peace had turned out to be a let-down.

'Come back north with me, Meg. There's room at home now our Mavis has gone, and me Mam and Dad'll love you. Besides, I'll get a pit house by and by. When . . . before . . . bairns come along, if that's what worries you.'

'I can't leave London, Joe. Not now, not yet. I need to see the girls up . . . Stella's still at school.'

He had listened quietly as at last she outlined her dilemma, but she could see he wasn't really listening. He knew what he wanted, and nothing was going to put him off getting it. It was what she wanted, too, but, in her case, it wasn't that simple.

'We could manage . . . send them a bit sometimes.'

'You can't feed people on "a bit sometimes". I don't earn much, but my money makes the difference. I couldn't just leave them, not like that.'

'What about us, Meg? What about me? Don't I deserve something? Don't I matter?'

She shushed him then in the only way she knew how. They were moving together, moaning in unison, when she remembered the French letters unopened on the bedside table. They had remembered the first time, and then forgotten. For a moment she started to tense and draw away, but then she relaxed. She was tired of managing life. For once she was going to let it take its course.

Chapter Seventeen

Cathy

NO ONE COULD TALK about anything but the announcement, from Buckingham Palace, of the engagement of Princess Elizabeth to Lieutenant Philip Mountbatten. It was like a fairy story, and the country was in desperate need of some good cheer. Stella was entranced. 'He's so handsome, and he fought in the war . . . and she looks so happy!'

Edie had become an authority on the subject. 'He's a Prince twice, Greece and Denmark. Don't ask me why, but he is. His mother was German, but he's also a great-great-grandchild of Queen Victoria, so that's all right. He's got no money because his father's lot were thrown out by Greece years ago. He slept in an orange box – it's true, it says so here. His parents have split up, and his mother's now some kind of a nun. Earl Mountbatten brought him up, sent him to school and everything, so he's well connected. That's why he's called Mountbatten, he changed his name. All the papers are saying they met when she went to his naval college, but it's not true: they met at Princess Marina's, who's married to the Duke of Kent. I love that woman, she's got such style. He served right though the war, invasions and everything. A proper hero. And it's no use your tongue hanging out, Stella. He's spoken for, and if he wasn't, I'd be having him.' They were discussing the wedding in the pub kitchen now, even though the wedding in

Westminster Abbey wasn't to be until November. 'She'll make a lovely bride,' Mrs Hopkins said, 'and the dress'll be magnificent, you can rely on the royals for that.' Cathy carried on with the order she was dealing with, trying hard not to feel resentment. Even if she could afford a new dress, she wouldn't have the coupons to buy one. Princess Elizabeth wouldn't have any complications like that.

She had carried the last of the pasties through to the bar when she saw the girls in a corner booth, giggling together over halves of some kind of beer or lager. She felt a sudden outrage: no older than her, and in a bar, and drinking. 'I'm jealous,' she thought ruefully. Jealous because they could afford to sit and drink at in the middle of the day, while she was dishing up hotpot and pasties, and washing score upon score of greasy plates. She moved closer, anxious to hear what was so funny and get a better look at their clothes, which were very stylish.

'She won't take anyone without ballet training. I've brushed up on my entrechats, I can tell you. You've got to be tall, and look posh. Apparently she's very demanding. But the pay is huge, and there are all sorts of perks. One girl got given a diamond bracelet.'

'And Paris!' The other girl feigned a swoon. 'I'd work in Paris for buttons. Why do they call her Miss Bluebell?'

'Search me, but they say she's a fantastic woman. Her husband was a Jew, and she kept him hidden all through the war. Her girls are called Bluebell Girls. I mean, if you're one of them, you're treated like royalty.'

'So why is she looking for girls now . . . and why here? They've got dancers in Paris, surely?'

'Of course they have, silly, but she prefers British. I mean, that's why Bluebell Girls are special – they're British bluebells, if you know what I mean.'

'It sounds marvellous. What are the details?'

'Well, it's Wednesday nine-thirty sharp at the Caxton Street rehearsal rooms. I'll go if you go. We could share a flat. They call them apart-e-mong in Paris.'

Cathy carried plates back to the kitchen and clashed them into the sink. 'I will be here for the rest of my life,' she thought, 'fishing bits of pastry and gristle out of the washing-up water.'

Paris. She rolled the name round in her mind. 'April in Paris'. It was July, but who cared? Suddenly she dried her hands, and went back into the bar to eavesdrop further.

'Mind, they say she's a tartar: you've got to keep up if you work for her. Look at the way she stood up to the Germans in the war. She came from the Folies Bergère, of course, so that's the standard she wants. That's where she created the Bluebell Girls . . . but this new show will be at the Paris Lido. It's on the Champs-Elysées, just think about that. The Lido only opened last year. And they call Paris the City of Light, did you know that?'

Cathy tried to make it look as though she was clearing the next table, but when all the dishes were lifted and the table wiped she couldn't move away. She couldn't bear to lose a single word.

'So I'll see you Wednesday, nine-thirty sharp. You'll need ballet shoes and a leotard. Oh, and she's a stickler for proper behaviour, so mind your Ps and Qs.'

The other girl nodded. 'I'd still like to know why they call her Miss Bluebell?'

'Who cares? She's a fantastic woman, and she's got fantastic jobs to offer. Real money! What else matters?'

Back in the kitchen, Cathy recalled every word of their conversation. 'She won't take anyone without ballet training.' 'You've got to be tall.' 'The pay is huge.' 'It's on the Champs-Elysées.' 'You'll need ballet shoes and a leotard.' 'Real money!' 'Wednesday nine-thirty sharp at the Caxton Street rehearsal rooms.'

Paul Steele was lurking outside when she left, and fell into step beside her. 'Fancy the flicks tonight?' Last time they had gone to the pictures, he hadn't tried to kiss her. He was getting the message.

'OK,' Cathy said. 'But I can't afford the one and nines.'

'I'll pay.'

'No,' she said firmly. 'I pay for myself or I don't come.'

'OK,' he said. 'How about we go in the one and nines, and I pay the difference?'

She could hardly make him sit at the front. 'OK,' she said grudgingly. 'What do you want to see?'

'*Singin' in the Rain*. It's on at the Odeon. One of the blokes at work has seen it and he says it's fantastic. You know Gene Kelly, he's good. And Debbie Reynolds and Cyd Charisse.'

'She's a ballet dancer, isn't she?'

'Well, there could be ballet in this, for all I know.'

They parted on the corner, promising to meet again at a quarter to seven. Mags was tonging her hair when Cathy got home. 'Table's set. No sign of Edie yet, but Stella's in the bedroom doing her homework. Tea's in the oven – toad-in-the-hole, I'm afraid. Sorry.'

'As long as its not faggots. When I'm rich, I will never eat a faggot again.'

Maggie smiled but only weakly.

'What's wrong?' Cathy struggled out of her coat and moved towards her sister. 'Nothing. Nothing. I'm just being daft.'

'I know you, our Mags. Something's up. You'll have to tell me in the end, so don't string it out.'

There was a moment's silence, and then it came. 'I think I've fallen wrong, Cath. We didn't mean it to happen, but I think I'm six weeks gone.'

At that moment Edie erupted into the room. 'I hope the tea's on the table. Can't stop. Got a date. Please tell me there's some hot water . . .'

Her words tailed off as she took in her sister's expressions. 'Oh, God. What's happened now?'

Chapter Eighteen

Cathy

SHE HAD TOSSED AND turned all the previous night, trying to work out how Maggie could be set free to go with Joe. It had to happen, if for no other reason than that they couldn't cope with a baby, another mouth to feed. Maggie had hinted at 'doing something about it'. They both knew what that meant: a trip down to Mrs Leaky, and a dirty knitting-needle. Their eyes had met, and there had been a mutual unspoken agreement that that was unthinkable. And then it had come to Cathy: if they had more money, enough to make up for the loss of Maggie's wages, they could manage. If she could get one of those jobs and go to Paris and earn the 'huge' money those girls had talked about, that would do it.

For a moment, the thought of being alone in a strange city made her swallow convulsively, but then she remembered Mrs Leaky, and braced up. If only Mam had been here. In the dark, lying still in case she disturbed Mags, she let tears wriggle down her cheeks and settle in the folds of her neck. At the pictures Paul had promised her they were still looking for Mam's murderer. 'He'll slip up, Cath. They always do. He'll do it again, but this time he'll be cocky, leave clues, and we'll have him.' The thought of her mother's murderer out there somewhere in the city made even Paris seem safer. She had watched them dancing last night in the film, Cyd Charisse waving around long strip of silk. That had been complicated, but Debbie Reynolds in *Singin' in the Rain* was just an ordinary girl. Anyone could dance, really, if they tried.

Now, with the younger girls gone off to work and school, and Maggie still in bed, she went downstairs, took a deep breath, and rapped on Mrs Schiffman's door.

'Come in, Catherine, come in. I've just made tea . . .'

She stammered excuses. She had had Mrs S.'s tea before, black with lemon, and once was enough. She cleared her throat. 'You were a dancer once, Mrs S. A ballet dancer?'

Mrs Schiffman put down her cup. 'What makes you ask that?'

'You showed me a photograph once, of you in the shoes and everything.' She lifted a curved arm. 'With your arm up like this.'

'I wasn't a dancer, not professionally. But I went to ballet class, with my sister.' She was quiet for a moment, and Cathy did not interrupt her. Her sister had died in the gas chambers with the rest of the family, that much she knew.

'Well, it was all a long time ago. Gracious times. The ballet mistress was French . . . we had to call her Madame. She wore black and had a cane. When you got out of step she slammed it on the floor, hard. We didn't like that.'

A picture was growing in Catherine's mind, of two little girls from a nice family going hand in hand to have dancing lessons. And now one was dead, and the other lived alone in a tenement in a foreign city. What a bloody life it was.

'We had a good life, then.' Their neighbour was talking to her, but she was staring, as though into the distance. 'There weren't that many Jews in Germany . . . less than one per cent, my Afrom said. They thought they were good citizens, they loved the German culture and language. They were doctors, scientists, artists. My father made violins that went all over the world. He had a factory, he employed people. When bad things first started, he said we would be safe: we were contributors to German success.'

She smiled then. 'He didn't realise that Hitler had only one goal, one dream: to make the Jews leave Germany. It began as soon as he took power. I was married then, but we lived near to my family. It only took a few weeks, and then the Dachau concentration camp, near Munich, opened. It was for Communists and Socialists, my father said: anyone considered an enemy of the Reich. A few weeks later they were standing outside Jewish-owned stores and businesses in order to prevent customers from entering. And still my father said, "It won't happen to us." Even when they said Jews could no longer be civil servants or work for the government . . . and that was when my Afrom said it was time to go. After that . . .' She threw up her hands, 'writers could no longer write, musicians could not play . . . they burned books.'

'Were you afraid?' Catherine asked, and then felt foolish. How could you not be afraid in that situation?

Mrs Schiffman didn't answer. She just carried on reciting what was obviously a familiar tale to her. 'We left in 1935, when the Nuremberg Laws were passed, stripping the Jews of their citizenship and forbidding non-Jews to marry a Jew. They even banned Jews from universities. That broke my Afrom's heart.'

'Did he teach there?'

'He was a physicist. But when we came to England he became a pawnbroker. It was a way of making a living. We had a little money, but it is nearly gone now. Like my family, the foolish ones who thought they would be safe.'

'What about your neighbours . . . and your friends?'

'What neighbours? What friends? They were the people who pointed out where we lived or worked. They spat upon us in the streets. Hitler used the Jews as a scapegoat, blaming them for all Germany's problems. Jews who had fought for Germany in the First World War were stripped of their medals. When we decided to leave, we needed a permit. Afrom had a friend who got it for us, but we had to pay him.'

'At least you got here,' Catherine said uncomfortably.

'Only because we had money. Most countries refused to accept more Jewish refugees. Great Britain said you could come only if you had money, or a job to go to. But no university had room for Afrom, so we set up the shop in Earle Street.'

'You never had children,' Cathy said.

'Afrom said it would not be safe. We might have to run again. In 1939 he said the Nazis would come here. I think it broke his heart.'

'Was that when he died?'

'They said it was a heart attack but I knew his heart was broken. I sold the shop for a song, and I came here.'

'I'm glad,' Cathy said. 'You've been a godsend to us these last few years.'

'And you to me, Catherine. Especially the *liebling*.'

'Our Stella? She thinks the world of you.'

Mrs Schiffman was rising to her feet. 'I think we need a little comfort.' The drink was warm and grasped the back of Cathy's throat. 'Now,' Mrs Schiffman went on, 'what was it you wanted before I let my mind wander?'

Cathy drained her glass. 'I want you to teach me some ballet.'

The story came out then: the audition, the money, the need to be tall and ballet-trained. 'Let me see what I can remember,' the older woman said.

For the next hour they moved around the little sitting-room, Mrs Schiffman as nimble and agile as a bird, Catherine mimicking her as faithfully as she could. 'Watch the arms, Catherine. It's in the arms.'

At last Mrs Schiffman collapsed on to her chair.

'It will be better tomorrow . . . we have a few more days

until the audition, you said?'

Cathy nodded. 'Yes. Wednesday morning, nine-thirty sharp.' Her heart was thudding in her chest now, and she took another deep breath. 'There's something else . . .'

Stella was in alone when she got back from work that evening. 'Maggie's gone out,' she said dolefully. 'She said you'd do the tea.'

'And I will, if you cheer up. What's the matter, chick?'

Her sister shook her head. 'Nothing.'

'It's not nothing, Stel. It's something. You can tell me.'

'I want to know what's up with Maggie? And don't say there's nothing wrong, Cath, because I heard her crying.'

'OK, I'll be honest with you, Stella. You're grown up now, and we shouldn't be keeping you in the dark. You know about Joe?' Again Stella nodded. 'Well, he loves Maggie and she loves him. And that's why they have to be together.'

'Here?'

'No, not here. Can you imagine his great long legs stretched out in this room? No, Maggie will have to go and live with him in Durham.'

'It's a long way away!' It was almost a wail.

'It's not, Stel, it's a train-ride. We'll go up there, and he'll come down here. Anyway, she hasn't gone yet. Now, help me get the tea on before misery-guts gets in.'

Mention of Edie's nickname produced a smile. So far so good.

'Is that bacon?' Edie's nose was twitching as she came through the door.

'Looks like it. Half a rasher each, and don't touch our Maggie's bit. She'll get it later.'

They ate eggy bread, with the delicious crispy bacon not much more than a dot on top.

'Lovely,' Edie said, wiping her mouth and noisily pushing back her chair.

'Holy smoke, she's pleased with something for a change. Write that down, our Stella. It might not happen again.'

'Be sarky, it doesn't worry me, I'm off out. I'll be late back.'

After the table was cleared, the dishes washed, and Maggie's tea put under a plate to warm up later, they played cards and listened to 'Monday Night at Eight O'Clock'. At nine Stella allowed herself to be led to bed, school clothes laid ready for the morning, hair brushed with a sisterly hand. 'You won't be at school much longer, Stel.' Cathy had meant it as an aside, no more, but she felt her sister stiffen.

'Have I got to leave?'

'No, not until the time comes. You'll want to leave then, believe me. No more tellings off, no detention . . . only I'm forgetting you're a good girl. Not like me.' She tucked Stella in and kissed her cheek. 'We'll always take care of you, Stella, wherever we are. You know that.'

But alone in the now silent room, Cathy felt misgivings. Could you care for a fourteen-year-old from a distance? Edie would be less use than nothing, and Mrs S., however kind, wasn't family. But there was no other way.

'Sit down,' she said when Maggie came through the door, strain showing on her face.

'I've got your supper heating up over a pan, and then we need to talk.'

When Maggie had finished eating she outlined her plan. 'So you see, you could go to Durham, I'd send money home, and Mrs S. will make sure the other two are all right here.'

Maggie pushed her plate away. 'Have you gone stark raving mad? Bad enough one of us going, but two? Leave our Stella to Edie?' She threw up her hands. 'Anyway, I'm not going to get upset, because the chances of you getting to Paris are so slim they're non-existent.'

Chapter Nineteen

Cathy

T HERE WERE SEVENTEEN GIRLS in the rehearsal rooms when she got there, all of them clutching bags that presumably held ballet shoes. When one of them opened her coat, Cathy saw that she had a leotard on over black leggings. One by one the girls went off, and there was the distant sound of a piano playing. The girl would come out, usually looking disappointed, even tearful, but occasionally smiling broadly and waving aloft a paper. Twice Cathy took fright: how had she dared to come here on the strength of a few hours' tuition with an ageing lady who had only been an amateur? But she sat down again each time. At least she had to try.

At last it was her turn. She entered the room, slipping out of her coat as she moved. Two people were there, apart from the pianist, a man smoking a cigar and a woman in a blue coat, a chiffon scarf at her neck.

'Name?' the man said.

'Catherine Jackson.' She was slipping off her shoes as she spoke.

'Experience?'

She took a deep breath. 'None. But I can dance.'

He was rising to his feet. 'Sorry, I think you've misunderstood. This is a . . .'

The woman had raised her hand. 'Let Miss Jackson show us

what she can do.'

He was remonstrating with the woman and Cathy heard something about ballet shoes. The woman shook her head, and raised a hand to start the music. The pianist started to play and Catherine lifted her arms. 'The arms tell the story,' Mrs S. had said. 'Remember, it's in the arms.' She threw herself into the dance, trying to forget that anyone was watching, pretending she was dancing for the mirror in the bedroom as she had done for the past couple of nights. At last the music ended, and she stood, arms at her sides.

'Thank you,' the man said. 'But . . .'

The woman interrupted him. 'I'll take her, Pierre. She's got character. I can teach her to dance, but you can't teach character. And she's the right height.'

It was only when she had picked up her shoes and left the room that Cathy realised the woman had not been French. Her accent was Irish.

As she went up Caxton Street, she felt a curious mixture of elation and fear. She had done it – but she had also lied. Lied about a lot of things. What if they found her out? What if she couldn't do it, and they sent her home with her tail between her legs? The woman's words rang in her ears: 'You will be extra-special, the *crème de la crème*.' She had known what that meant. Mam had said it once about some posh dressmaker. '*The crème de la crème.*' And the money! She would be earning three times what she picked up at the pub. If she lived carefully, she could send money home . . . and save. She would need to save in case it all went wrong.

She was outside the pub door when Paul loomed up beside her. 'They said you were coming in late. There's nothing wrong, is there?'

She couldn't resist it. 'No, Paul, there's nothing wrong. Something's gone right, for a change. I'm going to Paris, to work at the Paris Lido. I'm going to be a dancer.' As soon as she said it she regretted it. He looked at first disbelieving, and then he began to laugh. 'Yes,' he said, 'and I'm Sexton Blake of the Yard.'

'It's true, Paul. I've just auditioned. Here . . . here's the paper telling me everything about it.'

He took it from her and ran his eyes down it. When he looked up, his face was stricken, and she put a hand on his arm. 'Don't worry, I'm not going just yet. And it won't be for ever.'

'I don't understand. I thought . . . well, I hoped . . .'

Here it was, the moment she had been dreading. 'Paul, I like you. A lot. Since Mam . . . well, since then you've been really kind but . . . I'm not ready. You're a friend.'

He was biting his lip, and she struggled to find words that would comfort without giving him hope. She was saved by Mr Hopkins poking his head out from the tap-room door. 'Are you working today, Cath?'

'I've got to go,' she said, and scurried inside, ashamed of her own cowardice.

The Hopkinses were also inclined to disbelieve her at first, but were understanding when she explained. 'You're a good worker, Cath. We'll miss you.' They promised to do all they could to help with her move, and oohed and aahed when she described what her life in Paris would entail. 'Fancy that!' Mr Hopkins said. 'A slip of a girl like you on the Paris stage. But watch what you're doing, Cathy. Keep your hand on your halfpenny, if you know what I mean.' Which brought forth a shocked 'Father!' from Mrs H.

They didn't really care that she was leaving, Cathy thought, as she stirred and chopped. Nor would they care when Maggie said she was going too. They were good people, but they were also business people. London was awash with women displaced from war work and looking for jobs. She would be replaced in the twinkling of an eye.

Maggie was coming down the stairs when she reached

home. 'I got it!' Cath said. 'I leave in two weeks' time, and I'll be able to send plenty of money home, Mags. It's going to be all right. So tell Joe you're on your way.'

There were tears in her sister's eyes. 'Are you sure, Cath? I'll never forgive myself if you come to harm. How will you manage in a foreign country? You've never been out of London.'

'That's all taken care of,' Cath lied cheerfully. 'You live in a hostel, all the girls together, and they do everything for you. I'll be lucky if I see anything of Paris. And it won't be for ever, Mags. Just till our Stella's working.'

She sent her sister on her way comforted, and then knocked on Mrs Schiffman's door.

'I did it!' she said, flinging her arms round the older woman's neck. 'I did the arm movements just like you showed me, and they lapped it up.'

The other woman's eyes at first widened, and then grew misty. 'Catherine a ballerina. Who would have thought it?'

Cathy smiled and nodded. 'All thanks to you. I'm not going to be a ballerina, though, more like a chorus girl; but it's all above board. Posh, even. There were loads of girls there, but they didn't have character, she said. So . . . are you still happy about the girls moving in?'

They sat for a few moments in the quiet sitting-room, discussing arrangements for Edie and Stella to move downstairs and share expenses. They had talked about it during their dancing lessons, and it had seemed the ideal arrangement. Mrs Schiffman was running out of money, and a shared rent would be a bonus for her. The girls would have someone to keep an eye on them, and the older woman would have company.

'It's going to be a big change for you,' Cathy said at last, thinking of how Edie could play up when the mood took her.

'I'll manage.' Mrs Schiffman clasped her hands to her bosom beneath the cameo brooch. 'It will be new life in this house. For me and for them. And it will help us all: one home is cheaper than two.'

'Our Edie can be a handful. And she will bully Stella if she gets the chance.'

But Mrs Schiffman was not to be put off. 'Good for you, good for me,' she said. 'You wait and see.'

When she went back upstairs, Cathy made no move to get the girls to bed even though she could see Stella beginning to droop. It was twenty past eleven when Maggie came in.

'We've got something to tell you all,' Cathy said then, and outlined the plan. 'So there'll be no heat and light bills, and shared rent. You'll still be living in the same place, same house . . .'

She tried not to sound pleading, but the silence that greeted her was getting her down. She had expected resistance, but it was not forthcoming.

But then Edie spoke, quietly and with venom. 'Live with that old cow? Over my bleeding dead body!'

Chapter Twenty

Edie

SHE POURED THE PERFUMED oil into her cupped palm and drizzled it over the naked back on the bed in front of her. 'How's that?' she said as she began to massage. The client gave a satisfied sigh as Edie began to tap her spine, increasing the pressure as she moved downwards. One day she would be the one on the bed, having her every whim gratified. 'It isn't fair,' she thought, and felt the woman flinch beneath her probing fingers. Murmuring an apology, she went on massaging, but her mind was not on her work.

She had tried every trick in the book: sulking, refusing food, throwing tantrums, even packing her bags – but her sisters hadn't given an inch. Bitches! As long as they could go off and get what they wanted, they didn't give a bugger about her and Stella. 'You'll be all right with Mrs S.' – that's all they said, over and over again. 'You'll be all right with Mrs S.' Edie knew what that meant: rules and regulations in someone else's house. It had been bad enough with those two bossing her about, never mind a stranger.

She felt her eyes prick, and blinked away a tear. Mustn't display emotion in front of clients, even when they were stark-naked face down on the couch. She would just have to find a way to afford a place of her own. Stella seemed to feel all right about moving downstairs – well, she was just a kid, and couldn't see what was coming. And Mrs S. was a better alternative than going to Durham with Maggie – Edie had laughed out loud when Maggie had suggested that.

'Joe won't mind,' Mags had said.

'Well, I bloody would,' she'd replied. She'd heard about Durham: pits and coal-heaps and people hanging around on corners. No life. Nothing like London.

'There now, Mrs Parker-Lane,' she said, giving one last flourish from bottom to top. 'You just lie there and relax. I'll be down in reception when you're ready.' This one was always good for two and six when she'd had her feet done, and a back massage. Mr Edward had said the woman's husband was a broker, whatever that was. Something to do with insurance. Filthy rich, anyway.

She left the softly lit room and sped down to the reception desk. 'She's had the works, all the extras.' A young man was sitting in one of the gilt chairs. 'Who's that?' she asked in a low voice. He had lovely clothes on, and what looked like handmade shoes.

'He's come to collect your client, she's his mother apparently. He's a bit of a cissie, if you ask me,' the receptionist said.

Cissie or not, he looked fanciable. Edie walked across to him. 'Your mama will be down in a minute.' For a moment she wondered if she had overdone it: where had she got 'mama' from? But he was smiling up at her with eyes like a puppy. 'I'm Edwina,' she said and held out her hand.

When he had gone, she thought of how easy it had been. 'I hope I see you again,' he had said as he followed his mother to the door. She had smiled and nodded, while silently saying, 'You surely will.' The car, she could see through the glass door, was long and low and expensive. It would have leather seats and a cigar lighter. Perhaps even a cocktail cabinet in the back. 'I'll ride in that,' she thought, and hugged the idea to herself. His name was Tim, he had said, which was short for Timothy. She would never call a boy Timothy. For a moment she contemplated bearing his children, and having someone on hand to give her massages whenever she wanted them. Except that she didn't want to be dependent on a man: she wanted to make her own money. Oodles of it, like Mr Edward. Still, he had her name and the number of the salon . . . and he would ring or lurk outside in the long, shiny car. She knew that for a fact.

Edie went back to the reception desk and began to get ready for her next client.

This one was young and unmarried, but she was having her legs waxed, a massage, and a facial. How was she affording that? Her clothes were lovely, too – crepe de Chine, and fine wool. One day she would have a wardrobe . . . wardrobes . . . wall to wall, and carpets you sank into when you walked on them. Whenever she had a spare moment, she read the magazines in the waiting room, cover to cover. When the time came that she could afford it, she wanted to know how to build a lifestyle. She'd seen people get money, before, and ~~blue~~ it on trash.

BLEW

She went through the afternoon in a daydream, sometimes imagining a bachelor life in which she was ruler of her own fate, and sometimes imagining what it would be like to be Mrs Tim, with some rich idiot to pay the bills. But she stayed alert enough to flatter and cosset every client, and to make sure she extracted the maximum reward for her pains.

'Tea's in the oven,' Cathy said, peering out from the bedroom door when she got home. 'We're going through Mam's things. We can't leave it any longer, Edie, not now we're moving out.'

'I don't care. It's horrible, going through her things.' Edie felt as though she were going to cry, and bit the inside of her cheek to stop it.

'We don't like it either, Edie. That's why we left it so long. But it has to be done. They're nice things, and they'll fit you.

Get your tea, and then . . .'

'No, thanks.' Edie tried to inject as much contempt as she could into her words. 'I don't want cast-offs.'

Mags appeared in the doorway. 'They're not cast off, Edie, they were Mam's things. We thought you'd like them. They won't fit me or our Cath, or we'd have had them like a shot.'

Edie felt an uncomfortable lump in her throat. 'I know. It's just . . . well, they'd make me sad, that's all. Give them to our Stella.'

'They're not suitable for Stella, Edie. She's still at school.'

'Well, keep them for her, Cath. I can't . . . I won't . . .bloody well leave me alone. I don't want me tea, now. Satisfied?'

Mags was through the door then, folding her arms around her. 'I know, Edie, I know. It's all too much for you. Leave it to me and Cath. Get your tea, like a good girl. It's meat pie that Mrs S. made, and the pastry's lovely. It's going to work out, Edie – for everybody, you'll see.'

'If you play about with that pie and waste it, I'll murder you,' Cath said. 'There's good meat in there, Mrs. S.'s ration, and the meat ration's just been cut again. So don't you dare waste it.'

'And now holidays abroad are off, and no motoring for pleasure,' Maggie added. 'It's getting worse.' Suddenly Edie started to laugh. 'No holidays abroad, can't use the car for pleasure? Well, that's us buggered, for a start.' Her sisters were laughing so heartily at her heartfelt tones that they quite forgot to rebuke her for swearing.

Edie let herself be cuddled after that, and even sat down to have Maggie place her plate, hot from the oven, in front of her. 'There now,' Maggie said comfortingly. 'It's going to be all right.'

Edie lifted the first forkful to her mouth. It was going to work out all right, that was certain. Because she was going to make bloody sure it did.

Chapter Twenty One

Cathy

SHE HAD ALWAYS known the goodbyes would be painful, but it was worse than she had thought. 'We'll keep in touch, Mags. There'll be the telephone. I can ring you at the pub till you go to Durham, and then you can ring me from a phone box. I'll send you a number.' Maggie was staying on in London for few weeks to oversee the transfer of their things to Mrs Schiffman's rooms, and settle the girls in.

'What'll happen if our Edie finds somewhere else to live?' Cathy had asked, and Maggie had rolled her eyes.

'Good riddance! Mrs S. and Stella will be better off without her. Anyway, you see to yourself, and leave them to me. And don't forget what I said . . . if you find it's not what you thought, or you're unhappy, or homesick, just get on the ferry. We'll manage, and we have Joe now – he'll help.'

There had been a pause, and then Maggie spoke again. 'Of course, you could always marry your policeman, and wipe that love-struck expression off his face.'

Cathy had smiled, and passed it off, but she felt sad about Paul. 'Come back, Cathy,' he had said last night, 'when you've got it out of your system. I'll be waiting.' The trouble was that she liked him, liked him a lot. But somewhere in her head there was this idea that love should be magical: you should feel something change inside you. And she didn't feel anything like that for Paul. If she was honest, what she really felt was gratitude, because he had always looked out for them, right from the beginning.

The worst farewell of all had been to Stella, who had clung to her till Mrs S. had gently pulled her away. 'I have to go, Stella, because we need the money. I couldn't make that kind of money here . . . you know there aren't enough jobs to go round. But I'll be back. I'll be back often. And I'm not going for ever, just for long enough for everything to work out.' She had been about to say, 'You've still got Edie,' but pulled back just in time, because being left with Edie wasn't much consolation.

Cathy cried on the way to the station, where she was joining the others, but she dried her eyes long before she got there. She didn't want to be seen as a cry-baby.

'Catherine? Hello, glad to meet you. I'm Marcelle, and I'm with you until we get to Paris.' She was ticking Cathy off on a list clipped to a board. 'Stay with the others until I round up the last two, and then we're off.'

She was glamorous in a trenchcoat and beret. 'She used to be a dancer,' one of the girls whispered. 'Got too old.'

The woman didn't look a day over thirty-five, but when she paused to light up a thin brown cheroot, Cathy saw that her hands were thin and blue-veined, and that there were lines around her eyes. Was that what happened to dancers when they grew too old to dance – they became shepherds for new, younger dancers? It didn't seem a glorious end to a career. But she would be back in London long before she was thirty-five. She had never dreamed of being a dancer, until the chance to make some money dropped into her lap. It would do for now . . . and if it didn't work out, she could always go home.

As they travelled to Harwich she grew fascinated with Marcelle. Old or not, she seemed unbelievably glamorous. She smoked her long, thin, brown cigarettes, and had a throaty laugh like a cat's purr. 'She's not French,' a girl whispered. 'She likes to think she is but she's no more Froggy than I am.'

The girls chattered and laughed as the journey proceeded. One or two were less forthcoming: they did laugh, but their laughter was forced. 'They're scared, like me,' Cathy thought. But the ferry crossing was so choppy that all thought was banished except the will to survive. She vomited again and again, until she was sure there could be nothing left to leave her stomach. Some of the girls managed not to throw up, but they all looked distinctly green. 'Oh, God,' one whispered to herself, if no one else, 'if I'd known it would be like this, I'd never have come.'

Even when they were back on dry land, Cathy could feel the ship moving beneath her. Her first moment on foreign soil, and all she wanted to do was lie down!

It was dark when the train reached Paris, but it was right that it was called the City of Light, for as they left the Gare du Nord and journeyed to their destination the buildings twinkled around them. London had seemed big, but Paris was vast. 'Ooh, the smell,' one girl said, as they climbed down from the charabanc. The air was redolent of something. 'Cigars,' someone said. 'Spices,' said another.

They were spending the night in a small hotel. 'Four to a room,' Marcelle said. 'It's just for tonight. Tomorrow we'll get you all into your permanent accommodation. Mostly that will be two or three sharing an apartment, quite near to the theatre. Tonight you can relax, and there's food and a glass of wine. Get off to bed, though, as soon as you can. I'll be here in the morning, and there'll be a tour of Paris, if you want it. Tomorrow's the last day off you'll get for a while, so make the most of it.'

Cathy could feel her eyes drooping, but the thought of going upstairs alone was intimidating. Besides, Marcelle was outlining the route tomorrow's tour would take: 'We'll go to the Champs-Elysées first . . .' she was rattling off names, the Moulin Rouge, Sacré-Coeur, the Trocadéro . . . And then someone was shaking her. 'Come on, sleepyhead, let's get you to bed.' The clock on the wall told her it was too late to ring Maggie, who would have been home for an hour or more by now. A wave of longing to be back in the flat, her sisters around her, swept over Cathy, but she quelled it. There could be no turning back.

She found herself in a small hotel room, almost completely filled by two double beds. 'We'd better introduce ourselves,' one of the girls said. 'I'm Joyce.' The other two were called Norma and Elaine. They were friends, so they opted to share a bed. 'That leaves you and me, kid. Hope you don't snore,' Joyce said cheerily. She poked the bed. 'Mattress a bit hard, but horrible long thin pillows. It'll be like sleeping on a brick. Still, which do you want, left or right?'

It turned out that Norma and Elaine came from Reading, and Joyce from Bolton. They had all been dancing in London for the past year or more. 'So you're experienced?' Cathy said, a small knot of anxiety forming inside her. What if she showed herself up?

Joyce was on to it like a flash. 'Don't worry, kid. No one expects you to be Pavlova. Let's face it, we're there to please men . . . look around you. We're none of us hard on the eye. If we had been we wouldn't be here.'

'But I thought being a Bluebell Girl was . . .'

'Something special?' Joyce's interruption was instant. 'It is. That's why I came: so as to get on. But that doesn't mean we're in the *corps de ballet*. You'll be fine.'

As she undressed, turning her back on the room full of strangers, Cathy felt confused. Was she really here to attract and please men, or was she here to do something artistic? They took turns to go down the corridor to the bathroom, which had a strange thing like a little lav as well as a bath and a proper lav, and then she climbed into the high bed. The pillows were, as Joyce had suggested, extremely hard. She settled down to work out her worries, but before she could even begin she was asleep.

Chapter Twenty Two

Cathy

O UTSIDE THE NARROW WINDOW she could hear a shutter rattling, and, quite near, a cat was meowing. An hour ago there had been faint music, an accordion, playing a tune she knew, because she'd heard it on the wireless back home. '*J'attendrai*', that was its name: 'I will wait for you.' Jean Sablon was the singer . . . on the record, anyway. She moved gingerly on to her other side, anxious not to wake Joyce, asleep in the narrow bed opposite. She was glad she was sharing a flat with Joyce: confidence oozed from her, and she was sleeping like a baby while she, Cathy, lay awake. Apart from that first day off after they arrived in Paris, they had been rehearsing ever since, and it had been a terrifying process.

'One, two, three and . . .' She went through the moves in her mind. 'One, two, three . . .' and then kick, every leg having to rise at exactly the same speed as all the others in the line. That was the hard part. Now her muscles ached in places where she had never thought muscles existed. Her feet were sore, and, for some unknown reason, even her eyes felt tired. She closed them now and squeezed her lids together. Perhaps they would feel better today.

Down in the street, someone coughed. She reached out and felt for her little clock. In the moonlight she could see that pointers stood at ten to two. Two o'clock already, and she hadn't closed her eyes. They were due at the Lido at eight sharp. If she didn't sleep now she'd be a dead body in the morning, and never mind one, two, three.

She must have slept then, because suddenly it was morning, and Joyce was shaking her awake. 'Brew's up,' Joyce spoke between lips clinched around two hairpins. 'Got to get a move on, Cath, or we'll get a rocket.'

Ten minutes later they were out in the narrow street, wiping toast crumbs from their mouths and buttoning as they went. The rue Camborne, where their flat was situated, led on to the rue Lamennais, and thence to the rue Washington. This morning it was practically deserted as the two girls hurried towards the Lido. A few moments later they were in a narrow side street, and turning in at the rear doors of the club. Alec was already at the piano, sorting sheet music.

Cathy had warmed to Alec at once. He was kind and courteous, and when she had stumbled over steps he had lifted his hands from the keys and given her time to recover. She had confided this to Joyce, but it had met with a sharp retort: 'Well, don't go fancying him, chuck. He's as bent as a two-pound note.' Seeing Cathy's puzzlement she had elaborated. 'Bent . . . you know?' Still meeting with a blank, she ploughed on. 'He's not, you know . . .' And then, in desperation, 'He does it with other fellers.'

Cathy had tried to look knowledgeable, as though meeting queers was an everyday occurrence. She had heard them talked about, but now she was face to face with one and she wondered what all the fuss was about. Alec seemed disconcertingly like other men, and if he wasn't going to try anything on with her, that seemed like a distinct advantage. Joyce had also informed her that Alec was a Jew. 'Another refugee,' she said. 'He used to live in Stuttgart.'

'How do you know that?' Cathy had asked in wonder. Joyce had arrived at the same time as her, and yet already seemed to know everything. 'You've never even talked to him, not properly. No more than me, and you know the ins and outs.'

But Joyce had only laughed and tapped her nose with a forefinger.

They had all hoped they would be taken through their paces by Madame Bluebell herself, but she had yet to make an appearance. Rehearsals were taken by the man who had been at the auditions. His name was Pierre, and he was a hard taskmaster, shouting if they got out of step and forcing them on when they flagged. 'You are Bluebells,' he would yell. 'Hold your heads up! Be proud!'

They rehearsed all morning, and then collapsed on to chairs as coffee and croissants were wheeled in. The hot pastries were split and filled with what looked like wafer-thin beef.

'Horse,' Joyce opined, killing Cathy's appetite stone dead. One girl turned out to be a mine of information about Miss Bluebell. 'I know all about her. My sister was with her up until she married, that was before the war. She says she's OK really, if you pull your weight. And she's had a hard life. She was born in Dublin, but she never knew her mam and dad. An Irish priest gave her to some old woman, who took her to Liverpool. Liverpool's choc-a-bloc with Irish. She got in a dance class there, and never looked back.'

'How did she get to Paris?' Joyce asked.

'She got in a precision dance troupe and went to Germany. She was there for ages, and then created her own group called the Bluebell Girls. She was only twenty-two.'

'How old is she now?' someone asked.

'Well she started the Bluebells in 1932. She was a dancer at the Folies Bergère before that.'

'So she's in her middle thirties,' someone said.

Their informant nodded. 'She's worn well, hasn't she? Considering she went all through the war, and had to keep her man hidden because he was Jewish. The Gestapo had her in more than once, but she didn't crack.'

'I bet she collaborated,' someone said. 'They all sucked up to the Germans, even Maurice Chevalier, so I bet she did.'

She was silenced by a hum of disapproval. 'She's putting food on our plates, mate, and don't you forget it.'

After that it was more rehearsing, and costume-fitting. Joyce was enamoured of the scanty costumes that seemed, for Cathy, to show far too much flesh. Once the feathered headdresses were in place, however, Joyce's enthusiasm waned. 'They weigh a ton. How're we supposed to keep our heads tilted while we're carrying all that?'

But Pierre was giving no quarter. Once they were all kitted out it was back to 'One, two, three, kick', until necks and feet could take no more and he called a halt.

They adjourned to a bistro, a dark, poky place full of men muttering into glasses of beer. Cathy accepted the glass of wine Alec proffered, and tried to enter into the conversation. Alec was filling her in on plans for the Lido show, and Cathy was interested, until she spotted the phone booth just outside the bar area. 'Could I ring England from there?' she asked.

Alec nodded. 'You'll need a lot of francs, but you can do it.'

Cathy had the number of the pub in her purse. Tonight was Maggie's last shift: tomorrow she would be gone to that unknown place called County Durham. With Alec's help she negotiated the dialling, and heard Mr Hopkins's familiar voice. When Maggie came to the phone, Cathy could tell she was worked up. Within minutes both girls were in tears.

'Be careful, Mags. And write to me. And tell Edie to take care of Stella. And, Mags . . . yes, yes, I'm all right . . . it's you . . .' A clean white handkerchief was waved in front of her face, and she received it gratefully. 'Oh Mags, I'm glad you're going to be with Joe but I wish . . .'

When she put down the phone, she dried her eyes. She had

wished to turn back the clock, and be home with Mam at the stove and *ITMA* on the wireless. And that was something that could never come again.

'I know,' Alec said sympathetically. 'But at least you've got your family. They'll still be there when you go back.'

She wiped her nose. 'Did yours . . . ?'

He nodded. 'Yes. All gone. Come on, I'll buy you another drink, and you can cry into your beer.'

His hand on her elbow was comforting. Perhaps she was going to manage after all.

Chapter Twenty Three

Maggie

THEY CAUGHT A BUS at Victoria, and settled in two seats at the back. 'It's a long journey,' Joe said, 'but they stop every now and then.'

He looked anxious, somehow, and she put out a hand to reassure him. 'It's going to be all right,' she said. He had bought her two newspapers, and a precious bar of chocolate. Who could ask for more? But as London fell away, and then receded, she was less sure about the future. What did she know of pit life? Joe had tried to explain, but it had become a blur of strange words like 'tub-loading' and 'marrer', which turned out to be another word for workmate. They would live with Joe's parents at first. 'But we're down for a pit house. It'll not be long.'

He didn't sound sure, though, and Maggie's terror at the thought of what lay ahead steadily mounted. How would she cope in a strange house, full of strange people who probably didn't want her there at all? Joe was a good-looking lad. There might have been other girls . . . one other girl . . . whom his mother had favoured. And now she was blundering in, spoiling everything, a cuckoo in the nest.

She opened the first newspaper and sought some light relief, but there was precious little of that on offer. Pages and pages of Attlee's crisis plan. Life in Britain wouldn't be worth living shortly. She turned to Joe, intending to ask him how things could still be so bad two years after they had won the war, but his eyes had closed and he was breathing easily. Let him sleep.

She turned back to the paper. Lots and lots of detail about the coming royal wedding. She turned hastily away from all that. It was bad enough to be planning a wedding on a shoestring, with no clothes and nothing much else, but to be constantly exposed to speculation about whether the royal bride would wear silk or lace was too much. Nor could she derive much satisfaction from pictures of Christian Dior's autumn collection, which was expected to be less controversial than the spring one. When would fashions like that be within the reach of ordinary women? Never.

They were out in the country at last, and she tried to get more comfortable in the narrow seat. She was aware of the baby now, and the thickening around her waist was solid beneath her hand when it rested on her belly. If only they'd been more careful. She could have gone to Belgate, then, with her head held high, not crept there like a scarlet woman. As they passed the sign for Luton, she wondered whether it might have been different if her mother had lived. She could have been open about Joe earlier on, and that would have helped. But her mother had been murdered. Out of all he possible victims in London that night, it had to be her mother. That brought a new terror: what would Joe's family think of someone who fell wrong without a ring on her finger, whose mother was a murder victim, and whose sisters were scattered to God and good neighbours?

She felt tears come at the thought of Stella's face when they had parted. Stella had not cried or made a fuss: there was just a dumb resignation about her. 'She is losing us all, one by one,' Maggie realised, and only the thought of her duty to the baby within her stopped her from leaping from her seat and walking back to London.

They passed Doncaster, and she must have fallen asleep then for suddenly she was being shaken awake, and it was dark outside the bus. A motorbike and side-car were waiting inside the bus station.

'This is Dave. Dave, Meg,' Joe said. She held out her hand as Dave muttered, 'Pleased to meet you.' She had heard about Dave, Joe's marrer. No one had mentioned a motor bike. She climbed into the side-car, her case on top of her, and then Joe was on the pillion, and they were off. She closed her eyes at the first corner, and kept them shut until all motion had ceased.

'All right?' Joe was pushing back the hood.

'Yes,' she said faintly, and started to struggle free.

The family were lined up at the door. Father, mother, a sister, and a brother. Dave went off in a squeal of brakes, and introductions began.

'There's tea on. You must be famished,' Joe's mother said, once they were inside. But her tone was far from warm. They ate leek and bacon pie, the pastry melting in the mouth, washed down with warm, sweet tea; and then Mrs Harrington was rising to her feet.

'I expect you'd like to see where you're sleeping?' There was a pause and then: 'And before you say anything, our Joe, she's in your room, and you're in with your brother.' Joe made a sound of protest, and she held up a hand. 'You won't share a bed in this house, not till you're wed. It's bad enough, as it is. We've got to keep some standards.' She turned to her husband: 'Isn't that right, Alf?'

Alf's eyes rolled skyward as though he was begging some unseen Deity to rescue him. No one else said anything, so Maggie followed her future mother-in-law up the narrow stairs, her heart sinking with every step. It was bad enough to be in a strange place, but to be alone tonight, her first night away from home!

When Mrs Harrington had given her a towel and closed the

curtains, she spoke: 'Come down when you're ready,' and with that she left the room. Maggie crossed to the window and parted the curtains. Outside, the street was narrow, the houses opposite so tiny they could have been doll's houses. But it was the huge shape behind them that drew her eye. That must be the pit-head, silhouetted against the night sky. It looked dark and sinister. 'What have I done?' she thought, and pulled the curtains together.

When she went back downstairs, conversation was stilted at first, until someone mentioned the royal engagement. 'Prince Philip's like a Greek God,' Joe's sister Mavis said in reverent tones.

'That's because he *is* Greek.' Joe sounded none too keen. 'A lad at the pit says he's German as well. He says the whole royal family's German, when it comes down to it.'

There was a chorus of disapproval, led by his mother. 'The King was good in the war. And the Queen went round all the bomb-sites, I saw it in the Pathé news at the pictures.'

Joe was not giving way. 'I bet she won't have a cardboard cake, and have to borrow a dress to save clothing coupons.'

There was a sudden silence, and Joe coloured as he realised what he had said might be insensitive.

'We'll all get a day off,' Mavis offered. 'My boss says we'll get a day off to go and cheer. And there might be a street party – they're good, those. I stopped up until two o'clock for the VE one.'

Maggie sat on for a little while and then she pleaded fatigue after the journey and went upstairs to her room. Five minutes later, there was a tap at the door. 'It's me, Joe.'

She opened it a crack. 'You better go back down. Your Mam'll not like you being in here.'

'I know. I'm sorry. But it won't be for long. We'll see about the wedding tomorrow, and then we'll have a house before long. Our own place.'

She assured Joe that all was well, but when she had shut the door she went back to the bed. It was too bad to cry, and that was a fact. She must have sat for ten minutes or longer, unsure whether to go to bed or to pick up her bag and make for London, on foot if necessary. And then there was another tap at the door. He was back to see her! But it wasn't Joe, it was Mavis, who had married a year ago. She was carrying a brown-paper-wrapped bundle.

'I'm sorry about me Mam. Her bark's worse than her bite – she'll come round. Joe told me about your Mam and your sisters, and I know this must be a wrench. Anyway, I'd better get back, or there'll be ructions.' She laid the parcel on the bed. 'I thought you might not have a dress for the wedding. This was mine. Is mine, I'd like it back. But it's yours for the day, and there's a veil and some satin shoes. It's nothing grand but . . . well, I like it.'

When she had gone Maggie did cry, but this time they were tears of relief.

Chapter Twenty Four

Edie

EDIE TILTED BACK HER chair and surveyed the salon. The refurbishment had made a world of difference. Pink and grey with mirrors. Mr Edward had given her a free hand, and she had used it. 'We've done amazingly well,' he had told her. 'Better than I had expected. You've a real head for business, Edwina.' She had smiled to herself. If he had known quite how good her business head was and how much she had managed to siphon off from the profits, he might not have been so pleased.

It was fair enough, though. He couldn't have opened the salon without her, and if he'd brought in a trained beautician he'd have had to pay twice what he had paid her in the beginning. Now she was on a share of the profits, and in a little while she would think about getting a salon of her own. First, though, she must get out of Jubilee Street and find her own place. The problem was Stella. She hardly ever saw her sister now, not since she'd taken up with Timothy. But she had given her that lovely broderie anglaise blouse last night, so that should do for the time being.

Stella would do well when she left school. You couldn't fail, with looks like that. Edie looked at herself in the salon mirror: she was good-looking, but not beautiful. Stella was beautiful, but she didn't have a lot of personality. 'I've got that in spades,' Edie thought, and gave a little sigh of satisfaction. She leaned forward to examine her face. It was funny how they were all different: Maggie had a nice face, and a bit about her, but she wasn't a beauty. However, Cathy was . . . and she had gumption as well. That young policeman had been all over her. Remembering the policemen, Edie remembered her mother, and blinked away a tear. It was no use crying, she'd learned that early on when Dad just went out whistling and never came back. People died and the world went on.

All the same, she would look out for Stella, for Mam's sake. If she got a place of her own, an apartment, somewhere on the river, or up in Hampstead, or in Barnes . . . she closed her eyes on a picture of magnolia walls and long, low settees with scatter cushions like the ones in *House Beautiful*. Of course, if things progressed with Timothy, his parents would buy him a house. A town house, double-fronted. Nothing less for a pampered only son. That was the trouble – he had been so indulged that he was spineless. His love-making was . . . she sought for the right word and found it: pathetic. It was like doing it with a child. She had thought the boys at school were inexperienced, but at least they had initiative; they pushed for what they wanted. Forcefully, if necessary. Timothy was so pathetically grateful.

She sat upright and regained her common sense. He was also well bred, filthy rich, and would be even richer one day. And he would be here in five minutes, so she had better get a move on. There was a timid knock at the door, and the junior put her head into the room. 'I've cleared up, Miss Edwina. Is it all right if I go now?'

Edie bade the girl goodnight. She was a pleasant enough kid, but . . . a thought had struck her. Once Stella left school, she could come and work here. The girl could go, and she herself could train Stella up. Keep an eye on her. That would make up for not living with her. It was all working out. Now that she had Mags and Cath off her back, she could work everything to her advantage.

She kicked off her shoes, and put her feet up on the desk. Mr. Edward was not a controlling presence; nowadays he was hardly a presence at all; but he was still the boss on paper. She could hire and fire now, but everything had to go through him. She ordered supplies, but he signed the cheques. 'More than anything else in this world, I want to be my own boss,' she said aloud. That would make up for all the years of being the third one down. Stella had been the baby, to be indulged by everyone. She had been the misfit, the one who had to do as she was told. Well, that would end eventually, was already ending. And about time!

The Daimler was at the door when she came out to lock up. 'Let me.' Timothy sprang forward. She handed him the keys so he could do his masterful bit and lock up the salon, then settled back into the Daimler's leather upholstery and thought of the night ahead. They were going to the American Bar at the Savoy, which was rapidly becoming her favourite place.

They sat there, sipping champagne, nibbling the tit-bits that came with it, talking now and then, but mainly watching the other customers. The place was full. Still a lot of Yanks – would they never go home? She had fancied them once, got her first pair of nylons from a GI called Mario Angeli. That was before Marvin. Now she could see that they were common. They lacked what Timothy had – class.

'I thought we might go back to Cheyne Walk?' he said tentatively. His parents were in Bermuda, so the house was empty except for the servants. 'We might,' she said. 'Can we have some more champagne?' She was not in the mood for sex tonight. Besides, better to keep him wanting. She leaned forward and put a hand on his knee, smiling as she felt his muscles contract at her touch. Perhaps they would go back for a while. He was quite sweet really. Like a puppy.

Later on, she lay passive while he laboured above her. If she gave him any encouragement, he would come too quickly, and she would be left unsatisfied. She closed her eyes and thought about Cary Grant, who was her very ideal of a man. Imagined it was him inside her now, thrusting, pushing. She put up her hand and caressed Timothy's back, ran her hand down to his buttocks, cupping them, pulling him into her, and then, as desire rose, she started to move, slowly at first then quickly, quickly, until her scream came in duet with his groan of release.

Afterwards, while he stammered with gratitude, she thought about Stella. She could never really desert Stel. She was her baby sister, after all.

Chapter Twenty Five

Maggie

S HE WOKE WHILE IT was still dark, and listened to the footfalls in the street. First men going in to night-shift, then men coming off back-shift. Or was it the other way around? She would never get them right. A tiny flake was winnowing in a shaft of lamplight: she knew what it was, because Joe had explained it to her. 'Subsidence,' he had said when she noticed flakes of plaster falling from the ceiling. He had pointed to the jamb of the door. 'See how it's warping? We're living over the hole, Meg, the great tunnels they've dug over the years. Now the ground is settling. They come in every now and again and shore things up, but the pit always wins in the end.'

There was a sudden creak, and then Joe was there, a huge shape looming above her, moving gently into the bed. He smelled of toil, and when she touched his cheek she could feel bristle. 'You'll need to get a wash,' she said into his ear.

'Impertinence,' he whispered back. 'As if I wouldn't get a wash for church.'

'Chapel,' she said. 'Get your facts straight.'

'By God, you're bossy. I've let myself in for it, all right.'

And then he was loving her, gently because she was bigger now. 'I love you, Meg. Do you know that?'

'I wouldn't be here if I didn't, big soft lump.'

'I know what you're giving up for me, Meg, and I wish to

God you could have family there today. But I'll make it up to you. We'll get the house straight first, and then we'll be able to afford to travel up and down . . . and they can come here. For good, if they'd like.'

She felt her throat constrict with love for him and for love of all she had left behind. 'I know,' she said. 'I know.'

He left her then, silently, before the house woke up, and her wedding day began. When she sat up, she reached under her pillow. The letters were there, one from Cathy bearing a Paris postmark, and another begun by Stella and finished by Edie. Cathy wrote of their parents, and how proud they would have been on the wedding day. Stella spoke of her disappointment at not being a bridesmaid, but promised to think of her all through the ceremony. Edie was to the point: 'Make the best of it, Mags. You're getting a ring and a house and a bit of security. We're all wishing you the best, and would be there if we could. There'll be presents when we see you, so let us know what you'll need for your new place.'

She closed her eyes and held the letters against her lips, until it was time to put them away and start the day.

Mavis insisted on bringing her breakfast in bed, and then carrying in a bowl of warm water. 'You'll never get in the bathroom with that lot hogging it,' she said. 'It was easier when we had a tin bath in front of the fire. No one could lock you out of that.'

They talked of the new house, of when she and Joe would get one, and whether or not it would have a bathroom. 'They're fitting them as fast as they can,' Mavis said, 'so even if you have to wait for one, it won't be for long.' When she had washed from head to toe, and wrapped herself in her dressing-gown, Mavis came back to do her hair. 'You can't have a hairdresser in the family and do your own,' she had said, when they were discussing the day. Now she took Maggie's brown locks up in a sweep, and fixed the silver circlet in place. The veil would come later.

Her face looked back at her from the mirror. 'You look lovely,' Mavis said and Maggie knew that she did. The dress had been let out at the seams to accommodate her bulge, and she stepped into it as it lay in a circle on the floor. 'That's it,' her soon-to-be-sister-in-law said, and began to draw it up and slip the sleeves over her arms.

Joe had been banished from the house, so only her future father-in-law was waiting when she came downstairs, Mavis following behind.

'By, thou's a bonny lass,' he said. 'I wish it'd been your own Dad here for you, but I'll do me best.' He was jingling coins in his massive hand with the strange blue flecks that showed he was a miner. Joe had explained, 'You get many a nick down there, and coal dust gets in. When it heals over, it leaves a little blue mark.'

'Stop rattling that change, Dad,' his daughter said, 'you'll be rid of it soon enough.' Maggie wondered what the change was for. Perhaps he paid the driver of the wedding car on the spot?

They went out of the front door, a door that was only opened on ceremonial occasions, for the life of the house went in and out at the back. There was a crowd of neighbours at the gate, and a horde of expectant children. 'There you are,' Mr Harrington cried, and flung the handful of coins towards them.

'It's to bless the bride,' Mavis said. 'And here's the sweep for luck.' The sweep was there, complete with brushes, nodding and smiling and tipping his hat to the bride. 'Good luck, lass,' someone was calling, and then she was stepping into the car and the tears could no longer be contained for they were tears of joy. 'Eeh, lass, don't take on,' Mr Harrington said, anxiously, searching in his pockets for a handkerchief. 'Our lass'll go light if you turn up at the church a wreck.' His face paled suddenly. 'You're not having second thoughts, are you? Say if you are, and we'll turn straight round.'

'No,' she said. 'I'm not having second thoughts.'

'Thank God,' he said, sitting back. 'She'd have killed me if you'd said yes.'

And then they were at the chapel, and she was walking between rows of smiling people, and Joe was there, smiling but obviously strained, and the music ceased, and the wedding service began.

Chapter Twenty Six

Cathy

They had been dancing in front of an audience for weeks now. Cathy had felt the thrill of applause, and begun to lap it up. It made up for all the sweat and pain and blisters, although her toes would never be the same again. Bit by bit, the magic of Paris was creeping over her. Alec had been her guardian angel, filling her in on all that had happened there in the two years since the end of the war. He had tried to explain why the Communists seemed to hold sway everywhere. 'They were the heroes of the Resistance,' he told her. 'Always the boldest, so now they are worshipped.' The Communist papers *L'Humanité* and *L'Avant-garde* were on sale every Sunday morning, and there was an array of important rallies and meetings organised by the Communists which left Cathy bewildered.

'They're be-bopping,' she told Alec in astonishment, when they went to one of the Saturday-night parties. All she had ever heard about Communists suggested they were stern and unbending, but these Communists appeared to be carefree young people like her. Sometimes, though, there were pitched battles between the anti-Communists and the *gendarmerie*, and riot squads had to be called in. 'In war, they were united,' Alec said. 'Now they are scrabbling for power, determined, each one of them, to come out on top.'

One night, after the show, Alec took her to a club called Les Lorientais, where he promised her the best live jazz in Paris was played. 'They played during the Occupation,' he told her, 'in secret – but it kept the music alive.' It was a strange, exotic place, and Cathy gave herself up to the wonder of it all.

But Paris, however exotic and interesting, was not what she had imagined. For one thing, food was in even shorter supply there than in London. Everyone, or so it seemed, operated System D, which meant doing whatever you needed to do to stay alive and out of trouble. Miss Kelly, who looked after the dancers, made sure they got enough from the black market to keep them going, but there was still grumbling about the unfairness of the system. There had been unfairness in Britain, with the rich seldom going short, but here, in Paris, there seemed to be one rule for the poor, another for the rich, and a third for the Americans.

Joyce had soon decided she had had enough. 'The money's good, chuck, but the rest of it's crap. "Gay Paree"? There's more fun in Bolton in one night than you get here in a week.' Cathy would miss Joyce, but the thought of being in the apartment . . . she liked calling it that, even if it was only one room . . . alone for a while appealed. Another girl would move in in a few days, but for a while she had the place to herself.

She was growing close to Alec. She had told him about Mrs Schiffman and how good the Jewish lady had been to them. 'And you to her,' he had said approvingly. He had told her of his own desire to get to Israel eventually, but the fiasco of the *Exodus* had almost convinced him that he would never get there. He had told her the story: how an underground Jewish organisation in Palestine, intent on helping Jewish immigrants enter Palestine, had renamed an old ship *Exodus*. 'It's from the Bible,' he told her. 'The Jewish exodus from Egypt to Canaan?' She had nodded as though she understood, but in reality she didn't. The ship had been deliberately chosen because of its derelict condition, so that the British would be forced to let it through the blockade in case it sank. It left at night with more than 4,000 passengers, and arrived at Palestine's shores in July. The British navy had tried to board it, but the *Exodus* had been purposely fitted to make boarding impossible. There was a battle, and two passengers and one of the crew died. Several dozen others were injured before the ship was taken over, and the would-be immigrants sent back. 'So you see,' Alec said resignedly, 'they will never let us reach the Promised Land.'

Cathy thought about him as they walked home. One day, she was sure, he would get to his promised land. He was quiet but determined; he would find a way. In her bag she had two brioche that Alec had bought for her, together with a few inches of wine in a dark bottle. She had thanked him profusely, without mentioning that the wine she had tasted in Les Lorientais had almost put her off alcohol for life. When she got home she would have a little feast, and then write a letter to Mags.

Alec walked with her as far as the rue Camborne. From there it was only a few hundred yards to her door. She bade him goodnight, and watched as he turned down the side street and was soon lost to view. She liked this walk through the deserted streets. Sometimes there would be a stray cat to come up and purr round her ankles. Occasionally a man, homeward bound. Tonight, though, the streets were deserted.

She was almost home when she heard the sound of scuffling, and then a groan. Someone was cursing. She recognised '*Cochon!*' and then '*Boche*'. '*Boche sanglant!*' – the words almost spat out. She stood still, and then, afraid, ducked into a nearby doorway. Two men suddenly loomed up, running, brushing past too fast for her to be frightened.

She waited for a while, afraid they might come back, but after a while she walked slowly on. And then, in a pool of light spilling from a window, she saw the body on the cobblestones.

She halted. What if he or she was dead? Suddenly, and horribly, she thought of her mother – had she lain like this in another deserted street, with people ready to turn and leave her there?

Horrified, she moved forward. The man, for a man it was, was groaning. She bent down and touched his arm. 'Are you all right?' It was a silly question: his face was bruised, almost pulpy in places, and blood was streaming from his nose. 'Lie still,' she said. 'I'll fetch the police.'

The bloodied head shook from side to side. 'Please, no police.' He was speaking English, but he was a foreigner – not even French. *Boche*, that's what they had called him. It meant German, she knew that much.

'Are you German?' she asked, feeling her sympathy evaporate.

He was nodding. 'I'm sorry. Please don't let me hold you up. It's late, I just need a few moments. and I'll be on my way.'

She straightened up and stood, uncertain. German or not, he'd had a beating. 'You won't get far in that state,' she said at last. 'My place is just over there. You can get cleaned up, and I'll make you a drink. Then you'll have to go.'

He was struggling to rise, and she could see he was going to refuse her offer, but his strength failed him and he sank back to the ground. 'It's no good,' she said. 'Now, let me help you up and off this street before they come back, whoever they were.'

She was thinking of Mags as she half-supported, half-carried him to her door. '*Don't do it, our Cath*': that's what Mags would have said. And, as she tried to haul him up the stairs to her landing, she wished she'd taken her sister's advice.

Chapter Twenty Seven

Cathy

S HE HAD THOUGHT HIS stumbling was due to the beating, but once they were in the lighted room she could see that he walked with a decided limp; and as she began to bathe his bloodied face the wet cloth revealed a puckered scar running from the side of his eye up into his hairline.

'This is kind of you,' he said again and again. And then, 'I'm sorry to inflict this upon you.' He saw that she had noticed the scar. 'Italy,' he said, 'Monte Cassino.' His English was surprisingly good, and at last she told him so. He smiled then and thanked her. 'I was one year in your city of Oxford. Before . . .' He hesitated . . . 'in 1938.'

She cleared away the bowl of water and the towels, and brought out the brioche. 'You should eat something,' she said. 'And I have some wine. Or I could make you some tea?'

He smiled again. 'English tea! That sounds good, but perhaps a little wine. And then I must go. You must sleep.' The clock on the bedside table said two-fifteen.

'Where are you staying?' she asked.

'In the rue Victor Hugo. I came to this quarter to search for an old friend, who was my comrade once. We may have fought on different sides, but I wanted to know if he had come through. I didn't find him, but I did find a bar . . . a bistro. It was pleasant to sit there listening to the music, and I thought they might have news of him. I stayed too late. When I left, I thought I could find a cab but . . . I think they followed me. They must have realised I was German. They robbed me, but they also repaid me for much wrong, I think.' He looked at her ruefully. 'I don't blame them. And you, you're English. Don't you hate all Germans?'

'My Dad died in the London Blitz,' she said quietly. 'That's hard to forget. But . . . the war is over. Here . . .' She held out the glass. 'You can't go out as you are. You need to rest. And if they robbed you, have you got the price of a cab?'

He was struggling to his feet. 'I can't stay here, you need your sleep.'

'And I'm going to get it. There's two beds. My flatmate isn't here tonight. You can have that one. In the morning we'll get you back to rue Victor Hugo, one way or another.'

'You are very kind. And very brave. And also, perhaps, very foolish.'

It was her turn to smile. 'I'm none of those things. And I'm not daft either. You couldn't attack a feather, the state you're in. Now drink up, and tell me a bit about where you're from.'

He threw back his head to laugh, and she felt a sudden thrill of emotion. He was handsome – but it was something else. 'He is kind,' she thought. 'I think he is a kind man.' And when he smiled, she felt a strange feeling in her stomach. She longed for him to smile again, although she could see that smiling with his wounded face made him wince.

He talked, then, of his home, a house which sounded more like a castle above the Rhine. 'It has many windows,' he said. 'When I was a boy I tried to count them. I gave up at one hundred and twelve. And there is a ghost, they say, a lady who prowls the corridors crying for her lover.'

'Poor lady,' she said.

'The town below is called Badesheim,' he continued. 'In summer you can row on the river, and the swans will come and circle your boat, hoping for bread.'

'It sounds beautiful.'

'It is. Its history goes back to Roman times, and there is a wonderful main street which is lined with wine bars. We make the wine, you see. The banks of the Rhine are lined with vineyards.'

He talked on for a while but she could see he was tiring. 'Get some sleep,' she said. 'You can tell me more in the morning.'

He smiled, and again she felt a strange sensation, half pleasant, half disturbing. 'My name is Gunther,' he said. 'Tell me yours?'

'I'm called Cathy, and I come from London. That place you blitzed.'

'I know the bombing was bad. We had it in Germany too.'

'But . . .' He held up a hand to interrupt her.

'But we started it? I know that. Most Germans know it now – now that it's too late. I defended my country because it was my country, not because I thought my country was in the right. But enough of war . . . you are tired and I am too. But before we try to sleep tell me . . . what were you doing alone in the dark?'

She told him, then, of her sisters left behind in England. Of Miss Kelly, and the audition, and Mrs Schiffman, and life at the Lido.

'You are a very brave young woman,' he said when she had finished, and she felt her cheeks flush. They should have tried to get to sleep, but somehow they were held there, in the little room with the ticking clock, and light from the lamp holding them in a charmed circle. He talked of the war, of the battle at Monte Cassino where he had received his wounds, of his capture by the Americans, and his relief that the war was over. 'I didn't kill anyone . . . at least, I tried very hard not to kill someone. But in war you never know.'

When she plucked up courage to voice her own feelings of revulsion at Germany's crimes, he did not argue. 'My country was led by madmen, Catherine, but that is no excuse. Few of us were brave enough to make a stand, so the rest of us must share the blame. Now Germany must win back her good name, but it will take a long time.'

It felt unreal to be here in a small room in a strange city with a man she had only known for an hour or two, and yet she felt . . . she searched for the right word . . . she felt at peace.

He chuckled when she talked of her sisters, and his voice softened when she spoke of her mother's death. 'That was very terrible. Senselessness is always harder to deal with, because it is just that – senseless.'

When at last they both fell silent, she turned back the quilt on Joyce's bed and he lay down, wincing a little as he did so. 'There now,' she said, and turned out the light before slipping into the opposite bed.

She lay for a long time, almost pinching herself in disbelief at the night's events. What would Mags have said. '*A man! A German! My God, our Cath, you've gone mad.*' She smiled in the darkness, listening to the even breathing from the other bed. In the morning she would slip out for milk and fresh bread before she woke him. And then . . . but the then was lost in sleep.

Chapter Twenty Eight

Cathy

S HE WOKE EARLY, IN spite of her late bedtime. She had drifted off to sleep, thinking of how she would care for him in the morning, but when she woke to sunlight streaming into the room the bed opposite was empty. She lay between sleep and waking, trying to work out whether or not she had dreamed it all, and then Gunther loomed up suddenly at the side of her bed. 'I made some coffee. I thought you'd want to sleep, since I kept you awake so late last night.'

He sounded guilty, and Cathy sat up in bed, glad that she had not divested herself of her clothes the night before.

'Thank you,' she said, taking the cup. The coffee was hot, but not sweet enough, and she made a little moue of distaste. 'Sugar?' he asked. 'I wondered.'

When he had brought her the sugar she drank the coffee gratefully. 'Did you sleep?' she asked, and received a nod in reply.

It was awkward trying to wash her face and hands in the confines of that small room in the presence of a stranger, but neither of them wanted to venture on to the landing yet. In a little while the last tenant would have clattered off to work. 'Right,' Cathy said, when she had spruced herself up as best she could, 'I'm going for bread. I won't be long.'

She sped back from the *boulangerie*, arms full of warm

bread, and they ate either side of the narrow table, bread and butter, boiled eggs and more coffee. As they ate he told her the reason why he had come to Paris.

'I have this friend, his name is René Marceau. We met as boys, a long time ago in Bavaria. His mother was a distant cousin of my father, and we shared holidays sometimes. I was . . . I am, fond of him. He was with me at university in Munich, and later in Oxford and then . . . well, as you know, our worlds diverged. We wrote at first, until letters became impossible. We disagreed. He told me what Germany was doing, but I chose not to believe him. I haven't heard from him since April 1940. In May that year, Germany went into the Netherlands and Belgium, and the French moved forward to support the Dutch and Belgian forces. I believe René was with them, but I never heard from him again. He lived in the rue Maricot. I thought I might find him back there, but the house is gone. That was why I went in search of drinkers. I thought they might know what had become of him.'

'And you had no luck?' He was shaking his head.

'I'll ask around,' Cathy said. 'Someone at the Lido may have heard of him.' He was shy, she knew that now, but his eyes, blue and searching, were warm when they met her own. She wanted to reach out and touch his hand, but that would be fatal.

They sat for a little while in silence. She could see that he was not at ease in a strange situation, and yet he seemed reluctant to depart. She was afraid to speak in case she broke the spell. She had never been alone with a man like this, the walls around them a shield, the sun streaming in at the window a blessing. 'I want him to stay,' she though. 'Not move or speak. Just be here forever.'

But like all spells, it had to end some time. 'I must go,' he said, rising to his feet.

She crossed to her handbag, lying on the chair. 'You'll need money for a cab.' He shook a vehement head, but she would not be over-ruled. 'Don't be foolish, Gunther. You're still weak and you need a cab. I'll come down with you to the rue Camborne, we'll find one there.'

He took the notes when she pressed them into his hand. 'I will repay you, I promise.' He was fumbling in the inside pocket of his jacket. 'Take this. It's the one thing those thugs missed. My grandmother gave it to me when I was a child, and I've carried it ever since. It's the Rhine at Badesheim – I told you about the swans last night. I will reclaim it one day. In the mean time, it is a . . . how do the French say . . . *un reconnaissance de dettes* . . . an IOU.'

'I can't take this. It's valuable, it's gold.'

'Perhaps. But it's also my honour, my promise. You wouldn't begrudge me that, Catherine?'

She took it then. It was round and fitted in the palm of her hand, chased on one side, smooth enamel on the other, white swans sailing on a blue river.

She walked with him to the rue Camborne, and saw him safely into a rickety cab. 'Take care of yourself,' she said.

He leaned forward and kissed her temple. 'Thank you, Catherine. I will be in touch. I want to know what happens to you in the future.'

'Who knows what'll happen?' she said awkwardly. For a reason she couldn't quite fathom, she was embarrassed by his words. But his face was sombre as he drew the door to.

'Lucky Catherine,' he said, 'not to know what happens next. I fear my life is quite planned out.'

She watched until the cab disappeared, and then she walked back to the apartment, all the while wondering if it had really happened or if, at any moment, she would awake and find it had not. And what had he meant by 'quite planned out'? She passed the rest of the day in a daydream, not wanting to tidy the apartment because that would dispel the memory of what had gone before.

That night, when she arrived at the Lido, she asked Alec if he had ever heard of a René Marceau. He nodded. 'I know of him. I've heard people talk about him.'

She had not expected it to be as easy as this. When Gunther contacted her, she could tell him, even lead him to his friend. 'Where is he, Alec?'

'I'll take you to him later.' He turned away then, intent on his preparations for the night ahead, and she saw that for now, at least, the subject was closed.

After the show, he took her arm as they left by the stage door, but they did not turn in the direction of the bistro they usually visited.

'Where are we going?'

'You'll see.' He was being deliberately mysterious, and she knew better than to push him. At the corner he hailed a cab and handed her inside. When they got out, she could see the Arc de Triomphe in the distance, but he was turning away, down a side street. 'There,' he said, pointing to the wall. A slab was let into the stonework, gleaming new against the old, dark stone.

She tried to read the inscription. '*Ici*'. . . that was 'here': but what did the rest mean?

Alec saw her hesitation. '*Ici est tombé René Marceau pour la libération de Paris 24 Aout 1944.*' He translated: 'Here fell René Marceau for the liberation of Paris, 24 August, 1944.'

Chapter Twenty Nine

Edie

S HE CAME INTO THE room quietly, throwing the towel from hand to hand because it was too hot to hold. On the couch the client lay inert under the pink blanket. Edie waved the towel in the air to cool it: if she put it on too hot, there'd be ructions. She looked at the chair where her client's handbag sat. Crocodile – that would have cost a pretty penny. And matching shoes beneath. That was the sign of a lady. Real leather or skin, and matching.

'There now.' She laid the warm towel over the face with its eyes closed. How lovely it must be to just lie there like a big, dead cow and have someone baby you. 'This is to open the pores and let all the impurities out.' It would need more than a hot towel to improve that complexion. As she poured the massage oil into her cupped hand she reflected on the unfairness of life: Mrs Sturridge was fat and forty, and definitely not fair, and yet there were diamond rings cutting into her fingers and her clothes were obviously made for her. You'd never get a fit like that in Oxford Street, not for that figure anyway.

She soothed and pummelled by turns, taking care to caress the ear lobes from time to time. That always improved the tip. The pointers of the watch on her wrist moved so slowly that twice she held it to her ear to make sure it was ticking, but at last she could anoint the eyes with a lighter cream, and apply the final touches to the flabby face, and say the magic words, 'There now. All done.' She got a satisfactory two-shilling piece for her pains, and the customer also bought two products, which meant bonus points for Edie.

In the staff-room she brewed herself a pot of tea. Fifteen minutes before her next client. A pedicure, which she hated. Most feet were ugly. Some, where they'd crammed their toes into too-tight shoes, were positively disgusting.

Another girl erupted into the room, kicking off her shoes as she went. 'Let me sit down. My legs are throbbing. Throbbing!'

'Put them up,' Edie said, sympathetically. 'That's fresh tea.'

'Ta,' the girl said, raising her feet to the chair opposite.

'She's expecting me to pour her tea,' Edie thought. 'Who does she think she is?' The girl was older than her but that didn't count. She was the one Mr Edward depended on – she had been in at the start. 'Well, help yourself,' she said, as gracefully as she could, and watched as the girl levered herself to her feet.

'How's your sister? The one that's in Paris, lucky devil.'

'She's fine . . . well. I mean, Paris – she couldn't be anything else. She's seen it all . . .'

'She's at the Moulin Rouge, isn't she?'

'No, the Paris Lido. It's in the Champs-Elysées. The main street. She's the head dancer.'

Edie had sometimes got into trouble for lying at school, but it was different now. There was no one to sneak on her. She threw in a bit about Maggie's four bedrooms on the Durham coast, and then put down her cup. 'Back to the treadmill,' she said.

Her next client was Timothy's mother, and who knew what little gems of information she might glean if she was subtle? She prided herself on her subtlety. All the same, she would have to be careful. It wouldn't do for them to find out too soon, and put a spanner in the works. Timothy was scared of his parents, that much was obvious. She collected Mrs Parker-Lane from the pink and silver waiting-room, and wafted her into the treatment room. 'Let me take your coat. Oh that feels lovely. I love sable.'

'It's mink, actually. Not that it makes a difference.'

She was down for a pedicure and a back massage. 'Feet first,' Edie suggested brightly, anxious to get the worst over first.

'No,' Mrs Parker Lane said firmly. 'Massage first.'

'Just as you please,' Edie said. She would get her own back when it came to the deep massage. If you used your thumbs properly you could inflict a fair amount of pain and pass it off as knotted muscles. 'There now, that's better.'

In the end, she decided to go easy. Wouldn't do to make a bad impression. She was careful in the pedicure too, clipping and filing as gently as she could. When it was over she helped Mrs Parker-Lane with her shoes and handed her into her coat. With luck, she might get two and six. Even five bob. To her amazement, the woman was holding out a note . . . not ten bob, which would have been amazing, but ten pounds!

'What's that for?' Edie winced at the quaver in her own voice.

'Well, not for your expertise, my dear. You massage like a badly trained novice. It's to console you for the fact that you're not going to see my son again. And don't do the wide-eyed innocent and say, "What do you mean?" We both know you've got him mesmerised. Poor fool, he's just a child, and you've blinded him with sex. Cheap sex. Now, if you'll kindly get out of my way . . . and do close your mouth. You look like a landed cod.'

In the toilet Edie cried hot ears that burned her eyelids and caused her nose to run. She'd been treated like trash, cheap trash to be brought off with a ten-pound note. It was burning a hole in the pocket of her overall now, and she half-wished she'd torn it in two and thrown it in that smug bitch's face. It wasn't fair! Not that she cared about Tim. He was as weak as a drink of water, and so green that sex had been an ordeal. But he had seemed a step to better things.

After a while she dried her eyes, and splashed her face with cold water. It wouldn't do for anyone to see she was upset. She looked at herself in the mirror. Eyes bright, mouth smiling, that was it. Eventually she'd see her day with the Parker-Lanes of this world. 'I will get on,' she said aloud. 'I will. I will. I will.'

Chapter Thirty

Cathy

SHE WOKE EARLY, AND lay listening to sounds of life in the street outside. After a while she raised herself on her elbow and reached for the small medallion on the bedside table. Gold on one side, painted enamel on the other. She held it in her hand, enjoying its perfection. The scene was as Gunther had described it: swans on the Rhine at Badesheim. She closed her eyes, remembering his face. She had hoped he would return the next day, but he had not. Perhaps he had left Paris?

That thought made her so melancholy that she struggled up in the bed. Why did she feel like this? He had been good-looking, but not extra special. And they had spent so little time together – why did she feel as though she knew him through and through? He had been trying to tell her something, she had felt that from the beginning. What had he meant about his life being planned? She sat on the bed for a while trying to work it out, still half-imagining she had dreamed it all. But the bowl was still there, and the cloth she had used to bathe his wounds.

When she had put on a robe, she went downstairs to retrieve the post, hoping there would be something from home. She felt empty, as though something that should have come to fruition had instead melted away. There was one letter from Mags, and another in Stella's round hand, so that was something. She made tea and sat, her elbows on the table, to drink it and enjoy her letters.

She opened Maggie's letter first. The wedding had gone well. 'Joe's sister was a brick, Cath. On my side all the way, which is more than can be said for his mother. But I'll win her round in the end, because she loves her son, and I mean to make him happy. I wish you could have been there, Cath, but they took some snaps so you'll see it eventually, when they're developed. I thought of Mam and Dad in the church. Joe's side was full, and his Mam and Dad there behind him, once his Dad sat down. His sister and her man sat on my side, though, and her little girl gave me a horseshoe for luck. And they chucked pennies to the crowd outside the door, how about that? And a sweep for luck! I'm very happy, Cathy. Joe is the right man for me, and if it wasn't for you I would have lost him. One day there'll be someone for you. I hope that with all my heart. '

She folded the letter when she had read it and put it back in the envelope. Stella's letter was short. She wished Cathy and Maggie were back home. Mrs Schiffman was kind, but Edie was bossing everyone, especially her. 'Can I come out and live with you when I leave school? I can't stick our Edie for ever.'

A longing to go home overtook Cathy, but how could she go now, when there was always the possibility that Gunther might return?

Alec was waiting with coffee when she arrived at the Lido. 'Cheer up,' he said. 'They've decided to give you a little solo spot.'

She stared at him in consternation. 'Don't look like that,' he said sternly. 'You're good, you'll walk it. And it's only a minute long. Now get your gear on, and we'll have a run-through before the pack arrives.'

On an impulse Cathy leaned forward and kissed his cheek. 'You're a nice man, Alec. I'd hate it here without you.'

'Well, I'm not going anywhere, so let's get cracking. With a bit of luck and some sweat, Bluebell'll think you're a natural.'

A few minutes later she was going through the new routine. Only a few moves, but it was progress nevertheless, so that, for a little while, she forgot even the swans of Badesheim.

When they broke for a meal she went out into the fresh air, preferring walking to eating. Her coat was belted over her basic costume, and it reminded her of that day in the rehearsal room, the girls auditioning in their shiny leotards, all believing they were going to Paris. She had been one of the lucky ones, and it was certainly a new and wondrous world. All the same, what she would give to have Maggie there, a shoulder to cry on? 'He didn't come back to say goodbye, Mags.' If she told Maggie that, she would know how to comfort her. Inside her pocket she clutched the little medallion. Surely he would come back one day to reclaim it?

There were leaves on the pavement, and Cathy enjoyed the sensation of scuffling through them as she had done in childhood. In London . . .which was only a few hundred miles away, and yet felt like the other side of the moon.

It was time to turn round, then, and go back into the Lido to don her finery and show Miss Bluebell that her faith had not been misplaced. She noticed several scrawled signs on the wall as she retraced her footsteps. She couldn't understand them, but the name de Gaulle was in most of them. Alec had explained to her that General de Gaulle had been forced out of power the year before. A bit like Churchill, she had thought. Good enough to win the war, but not good enough for the peace. According to Alec, he might return one day. So might Churchill, which would be good even if just to annoy Mrs Essex. But thinking of home, even with Mrs Essex there, made her feel worse. She fingered the medallion one more time, and then went through the stage door, chin up, shoulders back, as she had been taught. She was a Bluebell Girl after all.

Gunther's letter came a week later. 'I am so grateful to you for rescuing this traveller in distress, and being brave enough to offer him shelter. You are very special, Catherine, and I will not forget you. The enclosed is simply to repay all you gave me. I would have come back to repay you in person, but I was needed at home. My fiancée joins me in sending thanks. We are to be married next month – you can imagine the hustle. Elizabette is my second cousin, so our wedding will be a big family occasion. That was why I wanted René at my side. Sadly, I have learned that he was killed during the liberation of Paris. Such a waste, but that is the nature of war. All wars. Still, my trip was not wasted as I made a friend in you. If you are ever in the Badesheim area, indeed in Germany, do let me know.

'I remain your grateful waif and stray, Gunther von Sachs.'

Chapter Thirty One

Maggie

T HE HOUSE WAS IN the centre of a long terrace that ran down to the line that carried coal away from the pit. It was No 33, Wainwright Street. It had two bedrooms upstairs and one big room and kitchen below. The stairs to the bedroom ran up from the living-room, there was a hallway the size of a cupboard, and a lavvy down the yard, which was called, she had now learned, a netty.

'What do you think?' Joe asked. She could hear the anxiety in his voice and she hugged her arms to her chest in an attempt to show pleasure.

'It's wonderful, Joe. Four rooms . . . and lovely paint. I like green. Apple green. Can we paper the little bedroom, nice and clean for the baby?'

'We'll paper everything, right through. Paint as well, if you like. Once we've got furniture and stuff.' His face had clouded then at the thought of the magnitude of their needs.

'Don't worry, we'll manage,' she said. 'Your Mavis showed me the second-hand shop, and your Mam says we can have the bedding.' They wandered from room to room, hand in hand, marvelling at their new possession. 'We'll have a deputy's house one day, Meg. Bigger than this, with a garden for the pram.' No. 33 had only a yard out the back, and a front door that opened directly on to the street. A deputy's house would be posh.

'Manager, one day,' she said. 'That's where you'll wind up.' Managers, so she had been told, lived in mansions with grounds and a gardener, and Joe was bright enough to make it to the top.

He was looking at her quizzically: 'Manager? You've married a hewer, Meg, not a bloody genius.'

She took him in her arms then, awkwardly because of the size of her belly. 'You, Joe Harrington, are the best man that ever walked, and if you hadn't got me in this state, I'd show you.'

They walked back together through a Belgate full of people who called out to Joe and nodded in her direction. 'Everybody knows you,' she said admiringly.

He looked at her in surprise. 'Of course they do, Meg. I'm a Belgate lad, aren't I? So are they. And so are you now, a proper Belgate lass.' In a strange way it reminded her of London – not her London, but the London of the Polaks and the Choats and the gyppos and the Jews, all of them knowing each and every member of the group. She belonged to Belgate now, and she had . . . she sought for Joe's favourite word – 'solidarity', that was it. She had solidarity, and all was well with the world.

A letter from Cath was waiting for her when she had waved Joe off to the pit and got back to her in-laws' house. It was full of chatter about the club, and the other dancers, and Churchill's visit to Paris where everyone had cheered him to the echo. 'There was a huge crowd to cheer him in the rue du Faubourg Saint-Honoré, and they chanted his name till he came out to them. I felt really proud, Mags, because he was ours, and we had done such a good job in the war. They wouldn't have a free country if it wasn't for him and us.'

Churchill had gone to Paris for a party at the British Embassy, given by the Duff Coopers, who Maggie knew were important, although she didn't know why. Fancy Churchill getting all that applause in a foreign country! At least they were grateful, even if his own country wasn't. Not that she could say that in front of Joe, who was not a Churchill fan.

On the face of it, everything seemed to be going well for Cathy. She was living well and able to send money home, and had a nice friend called Alec, who was a poof, so nothing to worry about there. But there was something wrong with the letter. Maggie read and re-read it, trying to put her finger on the flaw. Was Cathy fed up with the club? Had it not turned out as she had expected, and was she sticking it out for the sake of the family? The very thought of this made Maggie feel guilty. Was the dancing too hard, even impossible for someone who had had no training? Had she fallen out with this Alec, who had seemed to be her friend? No, towards the end there was mention of him taking her to a restaurant and showing her how to eat spaghetti with a fork and spoon.

'She's sad,' Maggie decided at last. 'No matter how much she tries to hide it, she's sad.'

She felt a sudden twinge in her belly. It must be indigestion. She didn't know much about giving birth, but she'd heard enough about it to know it wasn't twinges you got, it was pangs that made you yell out loud. Maybe Joe's mother would have some bicarb. She was tucking the letter back into the envelope when her mother-in-law entered the room. They got on well enough now, but Maggie still felt an outsider, an 'incomer' as they caller it in Belgate. Her arms were full of a billowing object which, when she flung it over a settee, turned out to be an eiderdown. 'I made this for you,' the other woman said. It was quilted and hand-stitched, one side blue satin and the other a paisley pattern in pink.

'It's beautiful,' Maggie said, her eyes filling with tears. The next moment her mother-in-law's arms were round her, and they were both crying. Another twinge came then, but she brushed it aside. Something important was happening here.

'I'm sorry, I'm so sorry. I thought . . . I thought . . .'

'I know,' Maggie said. 'You thought I'd caught Joe for a soft sitting-down. But I love him, I really love him.'

'I know, I know you do.'

But Maggie had pulled away, aware of a sudden wetness between her legs, and a small but widening pool on the floor between her feet.

'My God,' Mrs Harrington said, her hands flying to her face. 'My God, your waters have broken.'

The next few hours were a blur, faces looming above her, Joe black as the ace of spades straight from the pit, eyes white and wide with excitement, the doctor, the midwife, the doctor again. The smell of antiseptic, and waves of pain that came and went, and then, as suddenly, were over. The air was filled with a thin, needy cry, and someone was saying, 'It's a boy! A bouncing boy!' And someone else was laying a shawl-wrapped bundle on her breast, and a peace such as she had never known was stealing over her.

Chapter Thirty Two

Stella

STELLA TRIED TO CONCENTRATE on what the teacher was saying, but it wasn't easy. She had never liked history – who cared about what happened hundreds of years ago? It was hard enough dealing with now. She thought of Mrs Schiffman's face this morning. Her eyes had looked tired, a bit red as though she'd been crying, and when Edie had gone on about wanting an egg for breakfast the old lady's chin had trembled.

For a moment Stella imagined giving Edie a good hiding. The thought gave her satisfaction, but she knew she would never do it. Edie had the upper hand now, and no one could do anything about it. She hadn't paid heed to Maggie or Cath when they were at home, and she was worse now. In the beginning, Stella had hoped that Mrs Schiffman would get the better of her, but it had been foolish to hope for that. Not with Edie being the way she was.

Suddenly she realised the classroom had gone quiet. She looked up, hoping not to find every eye on her. But they were, and the teacher had stepped from behind her desk and was advancing towards her.

'Stella, tell us where you are, because you're certainly not here with us.'

'I don't know what you mean, Miss.'

'I mean you're day-dreaming, which is something you

ought to have a diploma in.'

'I wasn't, Miss. I was listening.'

'Then what was I talking about?'

Stella looked around, hoping for inspiration. Her fellow-pupils' eyes were on her, but no one was mouthing a tip. They were enjoying her discomfiture, and she swallowed an uncomfortable lump in her throat.

'Well? I'm waiting.'

'I don't know what you were talking about, Miss.'

'At last. A confession. You don't know what I was talking about because you weren't listening.'

The teacher gave a sigh. 'I've made allowances for you, Stella, because of your home circumstances, but there are limits. I want a hundred lines by tomorrow.' She turned to the board and wrote on it with chalk that squeaked like a living creature: '*I am here to listen.*'

When she added the full stop, she did it with such force that the chalk snapped in two.

At the end of the class, as the others were leaving, the teacher beckoned her over. 'You're a very pretty girl, Stella. Exceptionally pretty. But it's a harsh world, and you won't go far on a pretty face alone. I've made allowances, because I know your home life has been far from easy. But you'll be leaving soon, and what am I to say on your end-of-term report? That you're good at gazing out of windows? And it's no good turning on the waterworks: it doesn't work with me. Now, go away, and let's have more effort from you tomorrow.'

Hot tears were smarting behind Stella's eyes, but she struggled to contain them. It would only be worse for her if the other girls saw she'd been a cry-baby. 'Yes, Miss,' she said, and turned away.

There was some sympathy for her from the others on the walk home. 'I'd do some lines for you,' one girl offered, 'but she'd spot the writing.'

'It's OK,' Stella said. 'I'll manage somehow.'

The talk turned to *Oklahoma* then. 'My Nan's seen it, and she says it's wonderful. It's at Drury Lane. She says the cast got eleven curtain calls the night she went.'

There were murmurs of appreciation, but no real interest as none of them were likely to get to the Drury Lane Theatre. What did arouse enthusiasm was the royal wedding and everything connected with it. They discussed the dresses, the carriages, the congregation and, above all, the bridegroom.

'Do you think they did it before the wedding?' one girl asked.

'Did what?' Stella was curious.

'It, silly. Our Daisy says everyone does.'

'Not royalty!' Stella was horrified.

'Well, I would if I'd been her. He's like a film star, better than a film star.'

'So is she,' Stella said stoutly. 'She was a picture in that dress. And she's got lovely skin, everyone says so.'

'My Mam says it's a good marriage for him. He's penniless . . . well, he was. He's King of England now.'

'He's not!' This came as a scandalised chorus. 'He can't be king. He's only a duke.'

'Duke of Edinburgh, Earl of Merioneth, and Baron Greenwich of Greenwich in the County of London,' Stella said proudly.

'Ooh, who's swallowed the dictionary?'

'I read it in the paper,' Stella said. 'And I know all the bridesmaids' names as well. Two hundred million people around the world heard it on the radio.'

'They never!' This was said in awe rather than contradiction.

'They did,' Stella said proudly. 'And they got 2,500 wedding presents from around the world, and 10,000 telegrams of congratulation as well.'

'It's a pity we didn't do the wedding today, Stel,' someone else said. 'You'd've got full marks.'

They separated then, each to go their way. Stella thought ahead. She would need somewhere quiet to do the lines. Her jotter was in her satchel, and she'd counted the lines: she'd have to do three and a bit pages. Still, it was only a few weeks till the end of term, and her last day at school. 'Last day in prison,' Edie had called it, and she wasn't wrong. If she got a job . . . she was working out how she'd spend her wages when she came through the door of the flat. Mrs Schiffman was sitting in the chair by the fireplace, and this time there was no mistake, she had been crying.

'What's wrong?' Stella asked, panic making her voice catch in her throat. The older woman nodded towards the clothes-horse. Edie's best dress hung there, pink Moygashel with breast pockets, and a self-belt, and a big brown mark on the skirt where the iron had burned through.

There was nothing to be done, and no words to reassure. There would be hell to pay, Edie would see to that. Stella made a cup of tea, and urged Mrs Schiffman to drink it, but the same feeling of foreboding engulfed them both.

And then Edie was back, throwing her bag on to a chair and advancing on the table. 'Is that tea fresh? Get me a cup, Stella . . .' and then, as her eye alighted on the clothes-horse 'Oh, my God! It's ruined. It's bloody ruined, and I need it for tonight.'

She turned on Mrs Schiffman. 'How could you let that happen? Can't I trust anybody to do things properly when I go out and work to keep this house? It's all on me . . .'

There was a sound from the doorway. Cathy was there, putting down her case. 'I could hear the shouting down the street. I don't know what's going on, but it's not all on you, Edie. Not any more. I'm here now.'

BOOK 3
1952

Chapter Thirty Three

Cathy

SHE HAD BEEN LATE to bed last night. One of the dressers was leaving, and that had been her last night at the Windmill, so there had been tears and farewell speeches, and quite a lot to drink. Mrs Schiffman had had cocoa and biscuits waiting for her when she let herself into the flat. 'You shouldn't've stayed up,' she had chided, but Mrs Schiffman had shaken her head.

'You don't need sleep when you get to my age. Soon you will sleep for ever, so for now you keep awake.'

Cathy had smiled but a pang of panic had gone through her. If Mrs Schiffman died, how would they manage without that indomitable presence? Even though Stella was grown up, 'I still need her,' Cathy had thought. 'She is the lid on the family. Take her away, and I will feel exposed.'

Stella had already gone, picked up by Edie in her little car. 'Women driving cars, Catherine! Everything's changing.' Mrs Schiffman's tone had suggested the change was not for the better, and they entered into a reminiscence of what had been good which now was lost. 'Rag-and-bone men,' Mrs. S. offered. 'They were grateful for whatever you had. And the horses . . . you seldom see a horse now.'

Cathy licked her lips and mourned the passing of coconut ice. That had gone with rationing. And candy floss and liquorice bootlaces and sherbert dips. 'And kids don't skip in the street or play hitchy dabba, like we did.' She had taken off her court shoes and rubbed her feet, weary from a night of dancing at the Windmill, and she felt nostalgia well up in her for the days when the sight of her father coming home had seen all four girls throw down their chalk or skipping ropes, and go running down the street to cling to any part of him they could reach.

This morning she was going into town to do some shopping. She paused on Pinkney Street to look at the stalls there. There was a pretty chiffon blouse blowing gently in a July breeze. Turquoise was Stella's colour. She beat the stall-holder down to £2 10s, and bought it. She worried about Stella: she seemed to like working for Edie, but Edie was carried away with herself now. Mags was scathing when they spoke on the phone. 'How's Lady Muck of Vinegar Hill, then?' Not that Edie cared a jot for her sisters' opinion or anyone else's, for that matter. She had a flat in Daventry Street, which she said was in Notting Hill, but which was actually in Ladbroke Grove, and a little Morris Minor in sea-green. Men were in and out of her flat, but no one gave off any sense of permanence.

Cathy pulled herself up sharply, then. Who was she to criticise? There had been no shortage of men in her own life since she came back to London. Men clustered around the stage door, sent flowers and chocolates. Mostly she avoided them, but just occasionally she would allow one of them into her life for a while. But they were always looking for the glamour of the theatre – when they found an ordinary woman behind the costume, they lost interest. Or she did. Anyway, it never worked out.

She had walked into the job there. One mention of Miss Kelly and the Bluebell Girls, and she had been regarded as Terpsichorean royalty. She forbore to mention at the interview how brief her stay in Paris had been. That was her own business, Cathy thought.

She paused on the corner to look back down Jubilee Street. Whatever else in London was changing, the street wasn't. She lingered for a moment, and then moved on. She was almost at the end of the market when she saw it. A picture standing on an easel. A river scene with swans. She moved closer. Could it be Badesheim? Surely not.

She willed herself to walk on. She needed a picture like she needed a hole in the head. Besides, all that was years ago. She saw her bus ahead, and sprinted the few yards to the stop, but once she was seated on the upper deck, the damned picture kept intruding. 'In summer you can row on the river, and the swans will circle your boat, hoping for bread.' That's what he had said, and she had said, 'It sounds beautiful.' She had waited a whole week to hear from him, after he left. If she could not stop thinking about him, surely he must be thinking of her? And then the letter had come.

Cathy had tried to put it behind her, willed herself to get on with life, but it hadn't worked. Alec had done everything he could to help, although he believed she was suffering from homesickness and not from the collapse of a dream.

In the end, the longing to run for home and lick her wounds had been overwhelming. Miss Kelly had tried to persuade her to stay, but in the end she had packed and caught a train to Calais and the ferry, without even writing ahead to say she was coming home. A week later, a letter had arrived from Alec. 'We miss you, Catherine. A girl called Louisa has taken your place, but she is not a *mentsch* like you. I hope you are happy. No, that's a lie. I hope you are miserable and regretting running away. Your place is here, Cathy, when you're ready to come back.' He had signed off with love, and that had been precious to her. She would always remember him, but she would never return to Paris.

When she closed her eyes she did not remember Montmartre, or the chestnut trees, or the smell of crêpes cooking gently in the open air. The only memory that surfaced was the letter's arrival. She had opened it, and seen the money order, which was for more than anything she had done for him that night. She didn't want it, anyway. And then she had read on: 'We are to be married next month' . . . it meant the end of dreams. Paris had been a dream time, nightmarish in some ways, magical in others. But it was over, and so was holding on to a man who had stumbled into and out of her life in one night.

Now she put thoughts of swans and rivers and moonlight on cobblestones out of her mind, and got on with her shopping. But on the way home, all the same, she bought the painting. It had captured her imagination, and she could not let it go to a stranger.

There was a shock awaiting her when she got back to the flat. 'You have a visitor,' Mrs Schiffman told her in the hall. 'In the living-room. You'll be surprised.'

'Cathy!' He rose to his feet as she entered the room.

'Paul! Well, this is a surprise, but a nice one. Where've you been the last few years?' She held out her hand and he grasped it firmly.

'Getting on with things. I'm CID now. Detective-Sergeant.' He cleared his throat. 'Actually, nice as it is to see you again, I'm here on business. We think we've found the man who murdered your mother.'

Chapter Thirty Four

Edie

SHE HAD HIT THE alarm as soon as it sounded, and then turned over and gone back to sleep. Now she was rushing round, trying to find the things she needed to see her through the day while cramming toast and marmalade into her mouth. Someone had entered the apartment. Stella? She had heard the soft click of the door closing, but there was no sound of steps on the thick pile carpets. Wall-to-wall carpets. Ultimate luxury.

'It's me.' Stella was obviously bursting with news.

Edie drew the back of her hand across her mouth to dislodge crumbs, and gave up on being on time. 'What's up?'

'You'll never guess!'

'I don't want to guess, Stel. I want you to tell me now!'

'They've found him!' Stella's eyes were round as headlamps, but her words infuriated her sister.

'Who's found who, Stel? Honestly, I wonder why I pay you sometimes. Gravy for brains, that's your trouble.'

'The man who murdered Mam. Him. They've got him. Paul Steele . . . remember him, the policeman?. . . came round to tell Cathy last night.'

'Why didn't you ring me? What's the point of having a phone?' The ivory telephone stood on the side-table, and she gestured towards it.

'We didn't think, Edie. It was a shock.'

'Did you ring our Maggie ?' She saw at once that her words had gone home. 'You did! You rang the one that's three hundred miles away, but the one on the doorstep . . . oh no, no need to tell her. She's just the sister who doesn't count! That'll be our Cathy's idea.'

'She asked me to come and tell you, Edie.' Stella's blue eyes were threatening tears, but it wasn't going to wash. Not this time.

'You could've got off your arse and found a phone box. Or got on a bus. I've given you a job, and you can't even tell me my mother's murderer's caught.'

'I'm sorry. I . . . we . . . we thought you might be out. You usually are at night, Edie.'

'You could've bloody tried, Stel. Why am I always the odd one out? Anyway, I can't waste time now. Who is he, and what happens next?'

Stella outlined the few facts she knew. A man had been caught red-handed with a dead woman. Police had questioned him, and become suspicious. Eventually the man had confessed to other murders, and one of the victims was their mother.

'How can they be sure he isn't a nutter?' Edie was holding a can of hair-spray in one hand and tongs in the other. 'People confess to all sorts, sometimes. Trying to get attention.'

'No, it's true, Edie. Paul says he never gave up. It was him that reminded them of Mam's case when they got the man for the other murders.'

'I suppose he's after our Cathy again. Beats me why. Anyway, how was Maggie when you rang?'

'I didn't ring,' Stella said hastily. 'But Cathy says she's OK, and it's only three more weeks.'

'She shells kids like some women shell peas.'

Edie turned to look in the gilt-framed mirror, running her fingers through the neat curls until she got a just slightly dishevelled look. 'Three kids in seven years! It wouldn't do for me.' She turned to get a sideways reflection, holding in her tummy and jutting her breasts. 'You never get your figure back. Now, chop chop, Stella. Get my coat, it's on the bed, the one with the Hardy Amies label. And pick up those brochures. We should've been out of here ten minutes ago.'

Edie enjoyed arriving at the salon, seeing everyone snap to attention because the boss had arrived. It might be Mr Edward's name on the deeds, but no one was in any doubt about who was in charge of the business. Except that, today, no one seemed impressed by her entrance. 'The King's dead!' someone said. 'They've just announced it. Died in his sleep.'

She left them all mulling over the news: it was sad, but hardly the end of the world.

When she was in her office with the door shut, she sat down at her desk and pretended to shuffle papers. So they had found the pig who had killed Mam. Well, he should burn in hell, and hopefully he would. But how was she going to manage the revelation when it came to telling Leonard? She had no illusions – he wanted her, but he wanted advancement more. At the moment she was his ideal accessory: having her on his arm when he was meeting clients made him look good because she was a successful businesswoman, and squeaky clean into the bargain. She had never told him about her mother's murder. He had assumed both her parents had died in the war.

A pink-overalled assistant appeared with a tray of coffee. 'Ta,' Edie said, and lifted the ivory phone. After all, she thought as she dialled, half of Leonard's deals were dodgy, so, providing she steered clear of any publicity, what did an event from the past matter? When she put down the phone, she felt satisfied. She had told him the bare facts, and he hadn't flipped. So far, so good.

She drove Stella home at six p. m. They were meeting Leonard and a friend later on, but first she wanted to see if there was any more news.

Cathy was on the verge of leaving for the Windmill when they arrived, but she gave a brief outline of what she knew. 'He's fifty. A plasterer with his own business. And a wife and children. He's admitted it – says he gave her a lift, and she egged him on.'

'She wouldn't,' Edie said, but she avoided meeting her sister's eyes as she said it.

'I've got to go.' Cathy was already at the door. 'There's nothing more, really. He'll go to trial, and Paul says he'll get life.'

'He should hang,' Stella said vehemently. Her sisters looked at her, alarmed. She was defiant, though, and repeated: 'He should hang for what he did.'

'Well, maybe he will.' Cathy was gathering up her things. 'You'll look after her, Edie?'

'Yes, I'm taking her out tonight. Leave her to me. She says our Mags is OK?'

'Yes.' Cathy was halfway through the door. 'Happy as a pig in muck, our Mags.'

'You rang her straight away, which was more than you did for me! Why am I always the last to know anything?'

'Sorry, Edie, can't stop to argue now. And keep your voice down. Mrs S. is having a lie-down, so don't disturb her.' And with that, Cathy was gone.

As she waited for Stella to collect her things, Edie looked around her. How had she existed here? Cheap furniture, clutter, all Mrs S.'s icons and religious paraphernalia. 'It's a slum,' Edie said to herself. 'It's a slum, and I'm never coming back.'

In the car on the way to her flat she outlined the evening. 'We're going to Rules, a very smart restaurant. We'll have a nice dinner there, and then go back to Gordon's place. You'll like Leonard's friend, Gordon. He's posh, but he's OK. You must keep him sweet, Stella, I'm relying on you for that. Leonard needs him in a good mood, so do your stuff. You can borrow my red lamé if you like, but don't get it marked.'

She looked sideways to see if Stella was taking it all in, but she was day-dreaming as usual. 'If only they all had my gumption,' Edie thought as she brought the car to a halt. 'We could have moved mountains.' Still, better one than none.

As she opened the door to the flat, she wondered briefly if she should talk to Stella about contraception but . . . Gordon was a gentleman. Nothing would happen tonight. Tomorrow would be soon enough to talk. Besides, there was only enough time to get washed and dressed – she meant to look her best tonight – and you couldn't get through the birds and the bees in five minutes. Not with a greenhorn like Stel.

She thought ahead to the evening: hopefully they would have a good time, and not talk about the King dying all night, as they'd done at the salon . . . on and on about the poor Princess having to come back from Kenya. In a luxury plane, no doubt, with every convenience. 'I should be so lucky,' Edie thought. Still, it was bad losing a parent. For a moment her conscience pricked her, then she got down to her make-up and forgot all about affairs of state.

Chapter Thirty Five

Maggie

LITTLE JOE HAD GONE off proudly to school, his prized satchel, nearly as big as its owner, banging against his chubby legs. It was a relief to have one of them off her hands, especially with the new baby being a handful, but Maggie had still cried all the way home the first day she left him. Now Amy was safe in the garden, playing with her dolls, and the baby was asleep in his pram. Time to get the kettle on for Joe coming home from his shift.

He came stooping through the door, a giant of a man, bending to kiss her and then peeping in to make sure his children were safe. The wireless was full of news of General Eisenhower winning the Republican nomination for the American presidency. 'He's bound to win,' Maggie said. 'A war hero, and all that.'

Joe wiped his lips. 'He's a Republican, Meg – worse than a bloody Tory, and that's saying a lot. God help America if he gets in, you mark my words.'

She changed the subject, then. No sense in winding him up before he went to bed. Once he got on to politics he was like a man possessed. She loved her husband, and he was a brilliant father, but when it came to union matters he changed. She poured him more tea and regaled him with stories of the children's doings, until at last he mounted the stairs that led up from the living-room. 'I'll wake you at four o'clock,' she said, and kissed him between his shoulder blades as she propelled him towards bed and sleep.

When she heard the last footfall above her, she poured herself another cup of tea and took out Cathy's letter. Now that they had the phone in for Joe's council business, it was nice to feel she was in instant touch, like the other night, but she still loved receiving letters.

'He's been remanded, and he'll come to court when the case is all ready. Paul says . . .' The letter was filled with 'Paul says'. So he was back on the scene again! No harm in that. Cathy was a good catch for any man, but Paul Steele had been faithful to the family, so he deserved her. There was the usual moaning about Edie and her hoity-toity ways, but Edie had got on and no mistake. Own flat, own car, and to all intents and purposes her own business, because Mr Edward seemed to have no say at all. She'd been able to give Stella a job straight from school, and a canny wage for a kid, so thank God for that.

Maggie sat back in her chair and thought about the day Paul Steele had come to tell them about Mam. Everyone had turned and looked to her, as if she were now the head of the family, and she had felt like a child inside, robbed of its mother and scared to death. She sat on, remembering her mother. When she had had a husband, she had been a happy soul. They had had fun . . . many of her memories were of laughter. 'We didn't have much,' she thought, 'but by God, we were happy.' And then Dad had gone out one day and never come back – not even as a corpse, because his body had been so badly burned it could not be shown, even to grieving relatives. 'How do they know it's him?' her mother had said, and for ages after that they'd all expected him to come beaming through the door, saying it was all a big mistake. October 1940 Dad had died, and the Blitz had gone on until the following May. London was bombed by the Luftwaffe for eleven weeks on the trot, every single night until

Londoners' homes lay in ruins, and the dead numbered tens of thousands. A man in uniform had told them all 'to be proud of your Dad', but you didn't want to be proud, you wanted him home.

Eventually she carried the pots to the sink, and left them soaking. She didn't call Amy in until the baby was parked in his pram outside the front door. That was the good thing about Belgate: you could park your bairn on the front street, and know it would come to no harm. When she had Amy on reins she set off down the street towards the shops. All the streets in this part of Belgate were identical: narrow terraced houses, one window down, two up, doors painted a uniform green. As she walked, slowing her steps to accommodate Amy, she thought about the detached houses on the edge of the village, with gardens and wrought-iron railings, for the various managers, the aristocracy of the pit. Joe's ambitions lay elsewhere. 'Politics, Meg, that's the way for me. Union first . . . well, I've cracked that already. And the council, God willing, come the election, and after that the nomination.'

A Member of Parliament! If he got the nomination, he would win. Belgate was solid Labour: 'They don't count votes round here, Meg. They weigh them.' If he got into Parliament, they would move to London, for part of the week at least. Just for a moment the idea thrilled her, and then she remembered the hustle, the smog, the restless pace of life there. Besides, the kids couldn't be moved about, not when little Joe was settled at school. 'We're better off here,' she thought, and went into the fruit shop.

Back at home she unloaded her shopping, settled a sleepy Amy on the settee, and made herself a cup of tea. With a bit of luck Amy would sleep on for an hour or so – she'd certainly been up early enough. Maggie put her feet up on the chair opposite, and thought about the day ahead. Lately, she'd felt a bit low – for no real reason, she was a very lucky woman. She just felt a bit blue. Probably because the news about Mam's murderer had brought back all the misery of that time. VJ night: a date she certainly wouldn't forget.

The mood in the country in the past few weeks hadn't helped, either. People should have realised the King was dying when they saw that picture of him seeing Princess Elizabeth off to Kenya, but, somehow, you never thought royalty would die like ordinary mortals. The news that he had died in his sleep had taken everyone by surprise, and their grief had been genuine. The pictures of the three Queens, draped and veiled in black, had struck a chill in her. The old mother, losing a son and not allowed to weep and wail like anyone else. The Queen, who was losing not only a husband but a position. According to Maggie's neighbour, she would have to take a back seat now . . . 'and she won't take kindly to that.' And then the young Princess, Queen now, looking scared behind the veil, rushed back from a holiday to take on a country. 'Same age as me, give or take – and all that on her shoulders.'

The country had come to a halt, all cinemas and theatres closed, and BBC programmes cancelled except for news bulletins in which there was nothing cheerful. Flags in every town had flown at half-mast, and sports fixtures were cancelled, while the crowd outside the Palace grew and grew in spite of the cold and the rain. Edie had got it right when she phoned: 'It's as though they're hoping he'll come out on the balcony, and say it was all a mistake.' Londoners had queued for hours to file past the coffin in Westminster Hall. Cathy and Edie had gone, and Maggie had cried because she couldn't be there with them to pay her respects. Only Stella had stayed away. 'She feels it,' Cathy had said. 'But you know what she's like about death.'

The rest of the day passed like every other day. She collected Joe from school. Fed the children, Amy at the table like a good girl managing a fork but not yet a knife, the baby at the breast.

When little Joe came home she gave him bread and butter with sugar on, and an apple sliced into pieces, just the way he liked it. Eventually brother and sister went out into the garden to play and squabble and make-up and squabble again, while the baby slept, its mouth still pursed as though around the nipple, fingers curled like tiny crabs.

She sat for a few moments, just savouring the peace, then she brewed the pot of tea and carried it upstairs. It was dark in the bedroom until she drew back the curtains. Joe stirred in the bed and groaned, before pulling himself up on the pillows. 'It's never four o'clock already?'

She held out the tea. 'It's just past.'

He took the tea from her and set it on the bedside table. 'Come here, bonny lass.'

She went into his arms willingly. They had not made love for a long time, months before the birth. He was kissing her, but gently. She put down a hand, and felt his penis grow hard suddenly at her touch.

'We can't,' he said. 'Not yet?'

'We can. I know best. Move over and let me in.' They were together in a swirl of discarded clothes and blankets. 'Oh, Meg,' he said. 'Oh, Meg.'

He was trying to hold back for her sake, but she urged him on. Her satisfaction lay in feeling him collapse, spent. 'There now,' she said, 'that's better.'

She lay in his arms, both of them content, until, downstairs, the baby cried. Time to go. She got up, retrieving her clothes as she went. She was half-way out of the door when he spoke. 'I love you, Meg.'

Chapter Thirty Six

Stella

SHE LIKED IT WHEN she and Mrs Schiffman had breakfast alone. It was nice to be fussed over, to be made to feel special. Sometimes she remembered times when Dad had made her feel like that . . . safe, and sort of fuzzy inside. Her memories of her mother were a little less satisfying: Mam had been in a hurry most of the time, and after Dad died she had cried a lot. That didn't mean she wasn't missed. She was . . . but Mrs Schiffman had made all the difference.

Stella knew all about her life before the war. Cathy had told her. 'They had a really good life in Germany, a place called Cologne. Her daddy made violins, expensive ones, and she had ballet lessons and everything. And then Hitler made everyone be really bad to anyone who was Jewish. He wanted to drive them out.'

'Is that why London's full of Jews?' she had asked.

Cathy had nodded. 'Well, partly. They've always come here, for centuries, but a lot more came because of Hitler. Mrs S. was married, and her husband knew things were getting dangerous, so they packed up everything and left.'

'And her family didn't, and they all got killed in the camps?'

'That's right. In Dachau, I think. So she has no one.'

'She has us.' Stella's voice had been indignant, and Cathy had hugged her.

'Of course, she has, chicken. And thank God we've got her.'

She had plucked up her courage to ask Cath a question: 'She told me something once, Cath. She said people who she thought were her friends, the neighbours and shopkeepers, people like that, were all horrible to her. That wouldn't happen here, would it?'

'I hope not, Stel, but you can never tell with people.' Cathy had tried to explain about the Holocaust, but it had all seemed vague. Later on Stella had borrowed a book from the library and read about it, until it got too terrible and she took the book back. But what she had learned only made her more determined to be nice to Mrs Schiffman, because what had happened hadn't been fair. The Jews hadn't threatened anybody. According to the book, they had been less than one per cent of the German population, so how could they have constituted a threat? And yet in 1933 the SS had stood outside every Jewish-owned business to warn people away, and had painted the word *JUDE* on the walls. Nowhere in the book could she find a convincing explanation of why they'd done such a thing.

And then, two years later, at Nuremberg, they made Jews second-class citizens without rights. No wonder Mr Schiffman had thought it was time to go. She had been taught about Kristallnacht in school, the Night of Broken Glass, when storm-troopers smashed the windows of all Jewish homes and businesses, even synagogues; but in the book it was worse even than that. That was the beginning of Jews being taken to concentration camps, and the moment when she closed the book.

When she next saw Mrs Schiffman, Stella had given her the biggest hug. Mrs S. had looked pleased, but startled. 'What is that for?'

'Just things,' Stella had said, and changed the subject.

Yesterday Cathy had talked to her about Mam, and what might come out in court. 'There's always lies told in court, Stel.

That's how the criminals try to get off, so you mustn't believe anything they say about Mam.'

The trial was only a few weeks away. Cathy had said she was going to be there, and Edie was, too, but Stella had been afraid to say she would rather not go, until she talked to Mrs Schiffman. 'Just tell them, *liebling*, if you can't do it. They will understand.' So she had told them last night, and even Edie had understood.

Today, though, she was feeling guilty. Was it disloyal to Mam to stay away? Mrs Schiffman's eye was on her when she looked up. 'What is going on in that head of yours, *liebchen*?'

Stella smiled as brightly as she could. 'Nothing,' she said. 'Nothing, really.'

She concentrated on pouring a cup of tea, and carrying it through to Cathy in the bedroom they shared. 'Are you OK?'

Cathy was rubbing sleep from her eyes. 'Yes, thanks, chuck. Is that tea? Lovely!' They talked for a few moments, and then it was time for Stella to hurry downstairs to wait on the kerb for Edie's car.

'I want to talk to you tonight,' Edie said as they negotiated the crossroads. 'You can leave early to get ready, but before you go . . . well, lunch-time, really, we need to talk.'

It sounded important, but not as though Edie was annoyed with her, which was a relief. She changed into her pink overall and welcomed her first client. The woman was fat and panting in the summer heat. Stella helped her up on to the couch and averted her eyes while the woman removed her blouse and bra. She could do back massages now, after instruction from Edie. She poured oil into her palm as the woman heaved herself on to her front, then she lifted her hand and let the oil trickle on to the broad expanse of flesh. It was soothing, giving a massage, until your shoulders began to ache. You couldn't stop then: you had to carry on, even when your muscles were screaming out for you to stop. There were moments of relief when you sought out single vertebrae, and gave them a little thump, but you could only do that now and again. What the client wanted was stroking. 'They're all like cats,' Edie had told her. 'Stroke them, and they'll purr – then they'll tip you, and it's your turn to purr.'

Which would have been nice if Edie hadn't made her go shares with the tips. 'Only fair, Stella. I can't have clients now that I run things, so I'm entitled to something.' Stella was saving her half of the tips, though, towards a holiday. Somewhere warm and sandy. Or by a river, like the one in Cathy's picture. White swans floating on blue water. There was a gasp from the woman on the bed, and she realised she'd got carried away. 'Sorry,' she said, and reached for more oil.

She did two more massages after that, cut a woman's toe-nails and massaged her feet, and helped another assistant with a face-pack.

When lunch-time came, she slipped into the cubby-hole where they took their break. Edie followed her in, shutting the door behind her. 'We need to talk,' she said again. Which was odd, because Edie usually just threw whatever she wanted to say right at your face. Why was she beating around the bush?

'It's like this,' she began again. Stella felt her stomach lurch: she was going to be sacked. After six weeks!

'Look, Stel, I'll say it right out. You'll be having sex soon, if you haven't already. You need to make sure you don't fall wrong. We've had that in the family already, and we don't need it again. Keep those in your handbag, and shove one of these up as well, just in case.' Stella knew what the first packet was: French letters. A girl had brought one to school once and showed it round. But the other packet was a mystery.

'Volpar Gels,' Edie said. 'You shove them up, and they dissolve. But you need to make sure he uses something as well, so always have those with you.'

Stella felt a terrible impulse to laugh. As if you could tell a man something like that, much less hand him one.

'Don't look so glakey, Stella. Have you taken that in?'

Stella nodded. What else could she do?

'Cut off at four o'clock. I'll pick you up at six-thirty, and look your best. Tonight's important. Now, put those away before someone sees them – and not a word to Cathy. The less she knows, the better.'

Stella got ready in a mood somewhere between anticipation and apprehension. They were going to see *Limelight,* and she was looking forward to it. She hummed the theme tune to herself as she got ready. After the film there would be a nice meal somewhere posh, and if Mrs S. was up when she got back, she'd be able to tell her all about it. She looked at herself in the mirror. She looked all right. Edie would be pleased with her, and whoever this new bloke was might be nice. Nicer than Gordon, who had scared her a bit. 'I'll be loving you, eternally,' she hummed. It was a sad sort of tune for a Chaplin film, but everyone said it was good, so it must be.

She was almost ready to leave when she remembered the packets Edie had given her. She wouldn't need them tonight, but Edie made such a fuss if you didn't do exactly as she said. Better shove them in her bag.

Chapter Thirty Seven

Cathy

THEY WERE SEATED AT the breakfast table, all of them still in their night-clothes because it was Sunday and there was no need to rush. 'It was dark this morning because of the rain,' Stella said. 'I didn't want to get up.'

Cathy looked at her sister quizzically. 'Seems to me you're never keen on getting out of your pit, nowadays.'

Colour flooded Stella's cheeks, and her head went down.

'She's worn out,' Mrs S. said soothingly.

'Something's going on,' Cathy thought, but she couldn't debate it today. Instead she referred to something in the morning's paper. 'It says here that there were hundreds out last night to see London's last tram-car make its final journey from Woolwich to New Cross.'

Mrs Schiffman shook her head sadly. 'London without its tram-cars!'

Cathy stood up. If Mrs S. got on about London changing, they would be here all night, and she had things to do. Paul was taking her out of London for the day, 'before the winter closes in'. It was still high summer, but Paul tended to think ahead. It would be nice out in the countryside, but conscience was pricking her at leaving Stella behind. She was going somewhere with Edie at night, but Sundays could be a drag. 'We could go down the market before I go,' she suggested.

Stella brightened a little. 'If you've got time.'

The market was alive with noise. They brought onion pretzels, and ate them as they wandered between the stalls. '*Vehr kohft, vehr kohft?*' 'Who's buying, who's buying?' was the cry. Yiddish was the language of Whitechapel and Spitalfields. Every second face and voice were Jewish, with here and there a gypsy, handsome and somehow reserved, even when they were plying their wares.

They bought bagels for Mrs S. and two scarves, filmy things with fringed ends. 'One each,' Cathy said, but Stella shook her head. 'Edie'll only greed it off me. You keep them.'

'Well, you can borrow them, borrow anything of mine.' They walked on a little way before Cathy spoke again. 'You get on all right with Edie, don't you? I mean, she doesn't bully you, or anything?'

'She likes her own way,' Stella said ruefully.

'Stand up to her, Stel. She's all right, really. Always been a little prima donna, but she's our sister. Mam would want us to stick together.'

'I know.' Stella's voice was uncertain.

'You would tell me if there was anything wrong, wouldn't you?'

'There's nothing wrong. Everything's fine.'

Cathy was not convinced, but Stella had quickened her pace to show the conversation was at an end. When they got home, she just had time to get ready before Paul was at the door in his Wolseley, but she made a mental note to talk to Stella again.

An hour and a half later, they pulled up in the car-park of an inn. 'I've had good reports about this place,' Paul said, handing her out of the car. 'The roast comes recommended, and they have their own beer.'

'You can't drink and drive,' she teased him. 'You're a policeman.' He looked handsome today. He was handsome. And nice. Any woman would be glad to have him. Any woman but her. 'Is there something wrong with me?' she wondered. Perhaps she was just not cut out for love and marriage? Or perhaps she was crazy to remember a face, a voice, a smile. It was becoming harder to remember that voice, that smile. Perhaps the memory would go altogether with time, and she could just be happy with what she had.

Over lamb and Yorkshire pudding washed down with a good red wine, they talked about the trial. 'You don't need to worry. There'll be someone with you all the way.'

'Not you?'

'No, not me. I'll be giving evidence, but I'll make sure it's someone you'll like.' He put out a tentative hand and touched her wrist. 'You're looking like a little girl again . . . like you did that first time I saw you.'

Cathy withdrew her hand. 'Well, I'm not a little girl, I'm positively ancient, and don't you forget it.' But her eye had alighted upon a couple at a nearby table. There was a baby in a high-chair and the woman was leaning over it, her whole body arched in tenderness. Would she ever know that thrill of motherhood?

'Penny for them,' Paul said, and she threw back her head and laughed.

They talked about the new Queen then. 'I'm sorry for her,' Cathy said. 'Two lovely children, and she must hardly ever see them.'

'I'm sorrier for him. He's had to give up a good naval career, and walk two paces behind her for the rest of time. And they say . . . someone in the Royal Protection Squad told me . . . that he was livid about the name change.'

'Name change?'

'Well, he thought his children would be called Mountbatten. It's what any man would think. They say Churchill got at the Queen, and stressed the importance of being British, with no suggestion of a German connection. So she announced that they'd be called Windsor. Way back in April, I think it was. He couldn't take it, felt it impugned his manhood, and all that kind of thing. Caused a real rift.'

'You don't mean a split?' Cathy sounded scandalised.

'Oh, they won't split, but he feels it just the same, and that gentleman doesn't take anything lightly. He'll make his displeasure felt.'

They walked in the woods when the meal was over, and then sat in chairs on a pub terrace in the evening sunshine, glasses in hand. 'This is lovely,' she said, only to regret her words when she saw the pleasure they invoked.

'We could do it more often, if you left that job. I work long hours, but at least I get some nights off.'

'So do I.' Cathy felt defensive. Any minute he would say, 'Marry me and give up working.'

'Do you? Christmas day, and a week or so a year. It might be all right for kids, Cathy . . .'

'Oh thank you! Now you're telling me I'm ancient.'

'I'm not. Anything but. You know what I'm saying. Shall we have one for the road?'

He was quiet on the drive back into London, but as they swung off the ring road he pulled into a lay-by, switched off the engine, and turned to face her. 'Cathy,' he began, but she put a finger to his lips to silence him.

'It's been lovely, Paul. A lovely day. But that's all it can be. I like you too much to ever hurt you.' On an impulse she leaned forward and kissed his cheek.

He smiled ruefully. 'I get the message: a peck on the cheek. OK, if that's all there is, that's all there is. But I won't stop trying, Cathy. I never do.'

He switched on the engine and drove back on to the carriageway, but she didn't feel relief. She felt sad because she knew she had hurt him. But how could she explain how one night could change a life? Stella's words came into her mind:

'Germans are wicked. They tried to kill us.' But Gunther had been gentle, and she had felt safe with him.

She felt her eyes prick and started to stare at the signs speeding by. Time to go home.

Chapter Thirty Eight

Edie

OUTSIDE HER OFFICE DOOR, she could hear chatter and laughter. Good, that meant the salon was full. 'More pennies for little Edie,' she thought and reached into the drawer for another marron glacé. It would have to be the last for the day, because the one thing she couldn't afford to lose was her figure. It irked her that you needed to use face and figure to get somewhere, but when you started out with nothing, as she had, you had to make use of whatever came to hand. Men were useful: give them what they wanted, and you could get anything out of them. She'd already managed to double her savings with tips from Leonard, and when the time came that she could really go big, Leonard, or some other mug, would guarantee a loan for her. If Stella would only wise up and make use of her assets she could achieve almost anything.

Edie turned and inspected herself in the mirror. Her looks were OK, and she made the best of them, but her secret weapon was personality. Stella was a little lacking in that department, but with a face and figure like hers perhaps personality was too much to expect. She was a good little companion, though, someone to take the strain off her. You could only keep one man happy at a time, and the bastards liked to hunt in pairs. She would watch out for Stella, though. That was the least she could do.

She allowed herself one more marron glacé, and then got back to work. Mr Edward left all the figures to her now, which came in very handy. He was without a boyfriend at the moment, which was a bit of a relief because the last one had been too nosey by far. Edie was running her eyes down the monthly figures when she saw a larger than usual debit: £642 to Avis Toiletries. Six hundred and forty-two pounds! That would pay the wages of twelve more assistants.

She swung round in her chair and took some Avis products from the shelf behind her. What was in the bloody stuff? Frankincense and myrrh? The packaging was good: white and silver, and with almost femine curves to the glass. The feel of the jar in her hand was comforting, which was why they flogged gallons of the stuff to clients. As she had told the girls again and again, any client leaving the salon without buying a product was a failure. She unscrewed and sniffed: nice but not nice enough to cost that much. It was only lanolin, after all. She looked at the list of ingredients: glycerine, petrolatum, zinc oxide, white vinegar, cetyl alcohol, perfume oil . . . nothing extra-special there. Certainly not six hundred and forty-two pounds' worth. She sat for a moment, thinking, then she got to her feet and fetched her coat and keys.

'I'm going out for a bit,' she told the receptionist. 'Don't let anything go wrong while I'm away.'

It was nearly twelve-thirty, the time when executives went out to lunch. She settled down in a side street from where she could see the front door of Avis Toiletries. People came out in ones and twos, some of them laughing, others intent on some unknown destination. At last she spotted a bespectacled man in a well-cut suit. Spectacles usually went with intelligence. With a bit of luck, he might be one of the chemists. If not he'd know one. She got out of the car, locked it, and began to follow him.

She was beginning to wish she'd worn a lower heel when he turned in at the door of a restaurant, Le Manoir. So it was

French, or what passed for French in London: ten to one the chef was a Liverpudlian. The bespectacled man was seated in a corner booth when she entered, and she allowed the waiter to lead her to a nearby table. No sign of a wedding ring: another bonus. She ordered a salad Niçoise and a glass of very dry white wine, and then sipped and stirred the food around on her plate. She never ate at lunch-time, but she had to look authentic.

She let him get through his avocado mousse and chicken omelette, and then she caught his eye. 'Hello,' she mouthed, and he smiled back, obviously embarrassed. Another good sign: not a man of the world. She finished her salad by pushing it to one side, and aligning her knife and fork alongside it. Wiping her mouth with a napkin, she signalled for the bill, flashing him another smile as she did so. He was just beginning what looked suspiciously like bread-and-butter pudding, but was sure to have a fancy name. It was disgraceful what they got away with in restaurants, nowadays. She might well think about diversifying into food one day: it was money for old rope.

When she had paid her bill she gathered up her bag and got up to leave, taking a route past his table. She leaned towards him to make sure he got a whiff of her Je Reviens. 'Forgive me for saying hello just now, but I'm sure we've met. Do you, by any chance, work at Avis?'

After that it was easy. She identified herself as one of Avis's best customers, and swore she'd seen him on one of her many visits there. He offered her a glass of his wine, and she accepted gratefully, sliding into a seat beside him. 'Although I shouldn't. I'm due back at the office, but you have such an interesting face. I thought that the first time I saw you.'

He was quite good-looking when he blushed and got a bit of colour into his cheeks. She put her elbows on the table and cupped her chin in her hands. 'Tell me all about Avis,' she said. 'It seems a fascinating business.'

By the time she got up to leave, he was putty in her hands.

She knew he was twenty-nine, had a degree in accountancy, was unmarried and living with his mother, and had been at Avis for five and a half years. His name was Henry Maxwell. They were to meet the following evening, and when she held out her hand to shake farewell, his was trembling.

On the way back to the salon she envisaged their advertising: 'Edwina Jackson Products.' Except that Jackson was such a common name. 'Edwina Creams'? Too downmarket. 'EdMax'? Definitely not. She was parking the car when it came to her – 'Edwina et Cie'. Perfect! She tried to remember where she had got that from. She hadn't the foggiest idea what it meant. All the same, it sounded French, and that always went down well. It would have to wait until she had Mr Edward out of the picture, but that could be tolerated. You couldn't conceive a global enterprise just like that!

Chapter Thirty Nine

Cathy

CATHY SHOOK OUT THE paper. 'It says here Charlie Chaplin's coming to London. We're going to see his new film tonight. *Limelight* . . . you've seen it, haven't you, Stel? You know, the one with that lovely song.' She hummed a few bars.

That was enough to spur Mrs S. into full flow. 'I read all about it. It's about the London where he was born. He was born to a terrible life, poor little boy. And now he's a famous actor.'

Cathy read on. 'It says they won't let him back into America. They say he's a Communist.'

Mrs S. was tut-tutting. 'No, surely not! But naughty with women, I think.' She went on to details some of the details of Chaplin's crowded love life, and they chuckled about his exploits. She turned to look at her sister, then. 'What about you, Stel? Naughty boy or what?'

'What d'you mean?'

'You weren't listening. Still, it doesn't matter.'

Across the table, her eyes met those of Mrs Schiffman. Stella was normally quiet, but this was different: she seemed cut off, somehow. Perhaps it was the trial. In half an hour, Edie would arrive to accompany her to the Old Bailey, and Stella would go off to hold the fort at the salon.

'Cheer up, Stel,' she said. 'It'll soon be over.' All she got in return was a watery smile.

'What's up with our Stella?' Cathy asked, as Edie threaded the car through the London streets.

'Search me. She's all right. She always was a moody little cow, Cath.'

'Well, it takes one to know one, Edie – except that Stella hasn't got a moody bone in her body. Something's up, and I mean to find out what. You haven't been pushing her too hard, have you?'

'Oh, I knew it would all come down to me. If the Queen's assassinated, it'll be my fault. No, I haven't been pushing her. She only does half of what the other girls do. And now, can you let me concentrate on finding us a parking spot?'

Cathy had expected the Old Bailey to be intimidating, and it was. The judge, perched far above them, looked like a great eagle on a crag. 'I wouldn't like to be up in front of him,' Edie whispered, and Cath could see that even irrepressible Edie was over-awed. They sat through what seemed like useless protocol, and then the defendant appeared. 'My God,' Edie breathed. 'He's just a pathetic little wimp.'

The man was short and skinny, dressed in a suit and shirt that stood away from his neck and looked several sizes too big for him. The hands that clutched the dock rail looked weak, almost childlike, and she could see that his hair was thinning on top. He was Alfred Hindmarch, of no fixed address. Paul had already explained that the man's wife and family had disowned him and thrown him out of the marital home. 'I'm sorry for the family,' Paul had said last night. 'None of them deserve the publicity they're going to get.'

That publicity would indeed be massive, Cathy realised as the list of charges was read out. '. . . that on the night of May 15 1944 you did wilfully murder Mary Syme . . . on the night of August 14 1945 you did wilfully murder Estelle Jackson . . .' There were three more but Cathy hardly heard them. She was too busy fishing in her bag for a hanky for Edie, who was sobbing quietly beside her.

'He's not like I thought he would be,' Edie said, when they were safe in a cubby-hole in a nearby pub.

'How d'you mean?'

'I was expecting something . . . well, scary. Big. Evil. But he's just a pathetic, weedy little man.'

'He's a murderer, Edie.'

'Edwina. You've got to get into the habit, Cath. It's Edwina. Edie is . . . well . . .'

'Not posh enough. Anyway, Edwina, something more important. What's up with our Stella? You fobbed me off in the car, but now I want answers.'

'How should I know?'

'You see her every day.'

'So do you.'

'For five minutes, if I'm lucky. You work with her.'

'Well, as far as I'm concerned she's fine. Bright as a button at work. If she's not like that at home, it must be down to you. Anyway, didn't Paul look impressive in the witness box. He'll be Commissioner one day, you mark my words. You want to nab him, Cathy, while the going's good.'

She was obviously not going to get anything more out of Edie, but the way she had changed the subject made Cathy certain something was up.

They went back in after the lunch break, but a lot of the afternoon was taken up with what Paul had told them would be counsel's special pleading. And all the time the little man in the dock sat quietly, as though he couldn't say boo to a goose. At first Cathy tried to take an intelligent interest, but it was stifling in the court-room, and once or twice her eyelids drooped. Edie stayed awake, but she fiddled with her handbag all the time and once would have used a file on a nail if Cathy hadn't stopped her. 'Not in court, Edie, for God's sake!'

All in all it was a relief when the judge rose and the court emptied. 'God, they use a lot of words,' Edie said as they descended the steps. 'And all the bowing and scraping. "Yes, Your Honour. No, Your Honour. Three bags full, Your Honour." Why don't they just take the man out and hang him? Everyone knows he did it all, so why the palaver?'

'It's justice,' Cathy said.

'It's more like Old Tyme Music Hall to me.'

Paul caught up with them as they walked back to the car. 'What did you think?' he asked.

'It was a bit slow,' Edie replied, 'but you were good.'

They were passing a glassware shop, its window sparkling in the sun, when Cathy saw him. It was unmistakably Gunther von Sachs, shepherding a woman in a yellow suede coat into a black limousine. She could see the sunlight glinting off rimless spectacles as he turned his head. So he wore glasses now! 'We're getting older,' she thought. He folded the woman into the seat, and closed the door, then he moved round to where the chauffeur was holding the door for him. Cathy felt her heart leap into her throat, and her lips move, as though she was about to call out.

'Look at that!' Edie said. 'Parking there, when we have to walk two blocks. Arrest the driver, Paul!'

He was laughing. 'I'd like to oblige, Edie, but look at those plates. CD, Corps Diplomatique. He's a diplomat . . . or she is. It'd be more than my job's worth.'

Cathy stayed silent, intent on not betraying the fact that her heart had leaped into her mouth. And that it had also broken, for the woman with Gunther had been just as she had imagined her – beautiful beyond belief.

They parted company on the corner, and Paul gave them a mock salute as they drove off. 'You're a fool, our Cath. Still, you always were a bit slow. Get a move on!'

She simply smiled at Edie's exhortation. What else was

there to say? Mercifully, there was just time to give Stella and Mrs S. a potted version of the day's events, and then she was out of the house and heading for the theatre. If she could throw herself into a dance routine, the pain would pass . . . but as the hustle of the dressing-room enveloped her, she felt a sudden revulsion.

'I've been here too long,' she thought, but there was no escape at the moment. Nothing to do but twitch the top of her costume into place, and go out to the footlights with a smile on her face.

Chapter Forty

Stella

FOR A SECOND MORNING she awoke feeling sickly, and gripped by fear. Her period was late – two days or three, she couldn't be sure. She got washed and dressed, trying to look cool and unhurried, but she could feel tears threatening to fall. Edie would go mad. So would Cathy and Mags, but, worst of all, Mrs S. would be disappointed in her. She buried her face in her hands, trying to block out the memory.

'You're a pretty girl, Stella,' he had said, taking her chin in his hand. She had tried to turn her head away, then, to avoid the big, fleshy lips. But his grip on her chin had tightened until his fingers were digging into her face. 'Please,' she had said, although it was hard to speak. 'Please . . .'

'A little tease, are you? Well, we know what to do with them.' He pushed her down, holding her in place with a knee while he loosened his clothes. She closed her eyes at the sight of his hairy flesh, and then he was tearing at her clothes and she felt herself invaded. The pain came, then, so that she would have screamed if she could have drawn breath. At last it was over.

'You should have told me it was your first time.' He was looking disconcerted. 'I didn't know. I thought . . . but there's no harm done. No harm at all. You should have said . . . they should have told me.' And then, as he tried to protect himself:

'Don't get any ideas. I know how it goes – put a man in a bad position. You knew what you were doing – or, anyway, she did. Been here before, that one.

'Now, don't be a silly girl, there's nothing to cry over. It'll all seem the same in the morning. And let's be grown-up about things, Stella. We're going to go back in there and pretend this never happened, aren't we? Because we all know what will happen if we don't.'

He had left her, then, and she had lain for a while, until, afraid that Edie would come and find her, she struggled to her feet and repaired her clothing. It was only then that she remembered the boxes Edie had given her, still in her bag.

At the breakfast table, she tried to look composed and happy, but Mrs Schiffman wasn't fooled. 'You look peaky, chicken. Why don't you go back to bed?'

She couldn't do that. That would bring Edie round, and she would have it out of her in seconds. 'I'm afraid of her,' she admitted to herself. 'I'm afraid of her tongue.' She wasn't afraid of losing her job – she had come to loathe the salon. And besides, she was useful to Edie, she knew that. No, Edie would keep her on, but would go on and on about the packages. 'She'll make me do away with it,' she thought, and then felt faint at the fact that she had acknowledged that a baby might be a possibility.

Mrs S. was not about to give up. 'Is it the trial? Is that what's upsetting you? It's all taken care of, you know, as Paul will tell you. They have all the evidence. That man will go to prison for a very long time, for the rest of his life.'

Edie had tried to smile, and say nothing was bothering her, especially not the trial. 'I'm glad they've caught him, because that means he can't hurt anyone else. And I know it'll come out all right in the end. There's nothing bothering me, honestly . . . except I'll be late for work if I don't rush.'

'Then what is it, *liebling*?'

'It's nothing, Mrs Schiffman, honestly. I'd tell you if there was.' It was a relief to escape into the open air, and watch for Edie's car coming up the road.

Her first client was a woman she disliked. Spoilt and imperious. 'But a good tipper,' Edie had said, when Stella complained. 'Just keep your mind on what you'll pocket. I used to do that. It makes it all seem simple.'

Stella tried to keep her mind on profit as she kneaded and stroked, but the impulse to slap the peachy body on the couch was almost overwhelming. 'I'm hurting,' she wanted to say. 'Someone be nice to me!' She pocketed the ten-shilling note at the end of the session, and smiled as sweetly as she could; but the next client was another, a matron but just as spoiled, complaining about the heat of the room and the softness of the pillow beneath her head. Stella muttered soothing words, but her own frustration was growing. She remembered the first time . . . the wine on his breath and the wetness of his lips; the pain when he entered her, and his almost pathetic astonishment when he knew it was her first time. 'They should have told me. Now, don't be a silly girl. There's nothing to cry over. It'll all seem the same in the morning.'

Except that it hadn't. There had been two others since then. Businessmen, Edie called them, business friends of Leonard's. Tonight they were going out again. 'To L'Ecu de France,' Edie had said gloatingly. 'I love L'Ecu, it's got character.' Never mind that the food stuck in your throat at the thought of what lay ahead . . . L'Ecu de France was posh, and that was all Edie cared about

At coffee-time, Stella tried to avoid catching Edie's eye. 'She'll know,' Stella thought. 'She'll be able to tell.' Half-way down her cup, she felt a sudden wetness between her legs. She felt faint suddenly, and then afraid again. Was it a false alarm? It must be. She couldn't escape this easily. But when she shut herself in the lavatory, the blood was there, reassuringly red and plentiful. She kneeled down on the cold floor, and laid her head against the wooden seat. 'Thank you, God. Thank you.'

But the respite, she knew, was temporary: it would all start again. There would be other times – there had been other times already. She was useless with the French letters and the other things. There was never an opportunity, and she was too embarrassed to mention them, even if there had been.

At last she got to her feet and let herself out into the washing area. Cold water splashed on her face was not only cooling, it hardened her resolve. She went back into the salon, trying to move at a leisurely pace, and went to the cupboard where coats were kept. No time to take off her overall: Edie might emerge from her office at any time. She moved towards the front door, her coat over her arm. With every step she expected to hear her sister's voice, but there was only the hum of chatter from the curtained cubicles. The next moment she was out in the street, the door closed behind her, and she was running for dear life.

She had not intended to tell the truth, simply to say she was fed up with the salon and wanted out. But seated across the table from the woman who had mothered her for the past seven years, more of the story came tumbling out. She expected Mrs S. to be shocked, disgusted even, but she stayed calm. 'You've done the right thing, Stella. That life is not for you. Now you must start again. You are a good girl, *liebchen*; your sister is different.

'She . . . well, nothing will hurt her, she will see to that. But you are a little chicken. One day there will be a good kind man to take care of you. For now, you have your sisters and me. Are you going to tell Catherine?'

Stella hadn't thought about telling anyone, but there would need to be some sort of explanation as to why she had left the salon. Another, more fearful, thought occurred.

'What will I do about Edie? She'll go down my neck.

I had clients, you see . . .'

Mrs S. held up an imperious hand. 'You can leave Edwina, as she likes to be called, to me!'

Chapter Forty One

Maggie

' SHE SAYS NOTHING'S HAPPENED yet, just them trying to kiss her and stuff, so thank God for that. But you know our Stella, it doesn't take much to upset her. What was Edie doing, letting her near bastards like that?'

'Do you want me to come down?'

Maggie leaned her elbow on the table and transferred the phone to her other ear. Cathy was saying that everything was now under control, but a fury was growing in Maggie. Damn Edie! She'd always been a selfish little bitch. 'We should never have let Stel go there, Cath. I feel ashamed. It was the easy way out. We never sat her down and said, "What do you want to do?" We just left her to Edie's tender mercies, and now look what's happened.'

Through the window she could see her daughter playing in the garden. One day Amy would be Stella's age, and the thought of anyone laying a finger on her . . . 'I'll kill Edie when I see her. What does she have to say for herself?'

Cathy was trying to reassure. 'I think she's sorry, Mags. Shocked, even. Her story is that she thought Stella could take care of herself. And anyway, no harm's done. I gave her "No harm", I can tell you. I'm not in any doubt that she was using her. A pretty face, someone to keep tired businessmen happy . . . you know what she's like.'

'What happens now?'

'Stella's going to stop at home for a bit, while she thinks things over. I've told her she can go to college if she wants to.'

'How will you manage without her wage? I reckon we could help a bit.'

'With three kids to support? I don't think so. We'll be fine. Anyway, Edie's giving Stella a month's wages . . .'

'Conscience money!'

'I don't care if it's blood money, Mags, as long as it spends.'

They chatted about other things, then, before parting with promises of meeting up soon. When she had put down the phone, Maggie tried to go about her household tasks but she couldn't settle. At last she went back to the phone and dialled directory enquiries. 'I want Maison Edwina, Charlotte Street, London please.'

At last she got through, mindful of the telephone bill. 'Is that you, our Edie? I'll keep this brief. You can go to hell in a handcart if you like, but try taking our Stella with you, and you'll have me to reckon with.'

There was squawking from the other end before she put down the phone with a satisfying plop.

She listened to the wireless as she prepared the meal, a nice rich pannacalty, made with corned beef this time. Layer upon layer of onion, corned beef, and potato, Joe's second favourite. As she made the gravy, they were on about people flooding out of East Germany. Joe had always said dividing Germany wouldn't work, and it looked like he was right. 'You can't split a nation, Meg. Just draw a line with one brother on this side, another on the other? Stands to reason it'll fail.' Now the announcer was saying that 16,000 people had fled East Germany in the last month. At that rate, there would soon be no one left on the Russian side. She must remember to tell Joe about it tonight. He was on day-shift so he would be at home for his tea.

When he arrived she could see he was nursing news, but she

knew better than to ask outright. He liked to impart news at his own pace, and from the spring in his step it was good news. She had decided not to tell him about Stella – partly out of a desire to put it behind her, and partly out of pride. You wouldn't catch anyone in his family getting up to Edie's tricks.

'Well,' he said, when his plate was scraped clean.

'Well,' she repeated. 'I knew there was something the moment you came through the door.'

He leaned over to wipe the baby's mouth with the corner of its bib, and she bit her lip in frustration.

'Well,' he said again. It was too much.

'Well, well, well. Is that all I'm going to get? The Gestapo should have had you, Joe. The Resistance would have cracked without a finger laid on them.'

'I'm telling you, give us a chance. I've got the nomination.'

'You haven't!'

He had long coveted the nomination for their ward on the council. If he had it, he was as good as elected. They'd both known he would get it, but having it actually in the bag was a relief. They talked politics as they cleared the table and washed up, one washing, one drying. He shook his head about East Germany. 'Zones, Meg! American zone, British zone, Russian zone, and now a blooming French zone . . . as if they did anything useful in the war! It'll end in tears.'

After that it was time to put the children to bed, bathing the baby in front of the fire, and topping and tailing the other two. He carried them up to bed, one on each shoulder, she following behind, beseeching him not to wind them up before sleeping. In truth, she loved the rough and tumble of bedtime when he was at home. Loved him being home any time. When he was down the pit, there was always a knot of fear, the fear that every pit wife had . . . of pit boots being thrown in at the door, and a voice saying the rest of him was in the infirmary or, worse still, already in the mortuary.

They sat by the fire when the children were at last asleep. The wireless burbled softly in the background as he shared his plans. 'Five or six years on the council, Meg. Maybe a little bit more. And then a seat in Parliament . . . the Easington one'll be up around then. Jim Coulby's clocking on.'

Maggie pretended to be sceptical. 'You think you'll walk it, don't you? Pride comes before a fall, think on that.'

'I will walk it, Meg. If you stand for Labour hereabouts, it's a doddle. But I won't take it for granted. I want to make a difference. I saw things in the war . . . I don't want that for our lad. They're still making weapons, Meg. I had it from a lad at Labour headquarters, who got it from a journalist. They're making a bomb in America that could blast us all to hell and back. A hydrogen bomb, a thousand times more powerful than the one they dropped at Hiroshima. Imagine that! They don't know what they're dealing with, Meg. Even if they did, imagine what would happen if it got into the wrong hands. I'm not having that for our Joe.'

'He wants to be a fireman. I was telling him about his granddad . . . I didn't say how he died, just that he was a fireman and brave.'

'Firemen are all right. I was thinking he might be a barrister, or a doctor . . .'

'Why stop there? Put him in the House of Lords!'

Joe suddenly looked sheepish, and she launched herself into his lap. 'That's where you'd like to wind up. I suddenly see it . . . delusions of grandeur. I thought you didn't believe in lords and ladies.'

His hand moved to cup her breast. 'I don't want them lording it, Meg, but if it was the likes of you and me . . . Lady Harrington. I can just see you having tea with the Queen.'

She slapped his head gently. 'You're daft as a brush, Joe Harrington.' In her heart, though, she knew he was the best man alive, and she the luckiest woman born.

Chapter Forty Two

Edie

SHE HAD GIVEN UP on the trial now. In the beginning she had
had a deep-seated urge to see the man who had murdered
her mother, to spit in his face or, if that was impossible, to see
him manhandled by burly policeman as he was taken,
shrieking, from the dock to be hanged. But, like most things in
life, it hadn't turned out like that.

She had expected him to be the dominating figure, the man
who had murdered multiple women with his bare hands. In
fact, he was so insignificant that the dock almost swallowed
him. The figure that drew all eyes was the judge, massive in his
robes, eyes hooded under the wig. Paul had told them he was a
good judge, fair but firm. 'They're pleading diminished
responsibility, but I don't think he'll let them get away with it.
It'll be life, at least, more probably a death sentence.'

How the jury ever came to a conclusion, Edie did not know.
On the three days she had attended, it had all droned on and
on, the barristers leaping up and down to make points about
issues she could barely understand. Why there was so much
need for nit-picking, when the facts were there for everyone to
see, was beyond her; but as long as they hanged him, she would
have to accept it. It wasn't as if her being there was going to
make a difference. If it had been necessary to secure his
hanging, she would have sat there till her bottom froze to the

seat. But the plain fact was that she was wasting her time there, and doing no good for anyone. And the less that was said in front of Stella the better. She tried to be tactful when she told Cath she wasn't going any more, but, to her relief, Cath had simply nodded and said 'Me neither.'

Besides, she had loads on her plate at the moment. All the fuss about Stella – although hopefully that was over, and she'd been more than fair about the wages. More importantly, her contrived meeting with Henry Maxwell was paying off. They'd met up twice since then, and getting him to talk about Avis had been pathetically easy, because work was his only topic of conversation . . . that, and his widowed mother, who lived in Barnes, which was definitely an upmarket area.

She had hoped there would be a genius behind Avis creations, but it all sounded horribly humdrum . . . earnest young chemists testing things to make sure they wouldn't bring the women who bought them out in hives. That was a point, though – she would have to be careful about safety, and skins were tricky things because no two reacted alike. Her first idea had been to get Henry to defect, bringing with him the Avis formulae, but she had dismissed that notion at their first proper meeting. He would never do anything so potentially dangerous, however much money was dangled before him. Patiently, she teased from him details of the five chemists, writing their names on a pad inside her handbag while she distracted him by holding his gaze with apparently rapt attention.

The next step was to put Henry on the back burner by pleading family pressures. She couldn't afford to dump him altogether, not yet. Until she found a better one, he was her only link to Avis.

She took Leonard's advice about finding a reliable private detective, using the same excuse of family pressures. 'It's not little Stella, is it?' he had asked, alarmed, but she had reassured him. 'It's Cathy,' she said, 'the dancer. She's always been a handful. Now some of it's catching up with her.'

The man he recommended was a shifty-looking individual, but he asked few questions when she said she wanted a dossier on five people: their marital status, family background, financial position, and any weaknesses. Especially any weaknesses. 'What exactly are we looking for?' he asked.

She didn't want to give too much away. 'I might be in a position to employ one of them,' she said. 'But their character is of the utmost importance, so if they have any weaknesses . . .' He charged abominably, but he had the results in under a week. She pondered for a long time, torn between two: Elizabeth Mayhew, aged twenty-eight, living with a widowed mother in Clapham, and known to be deeply in debt. And Oliver Pocock, the senior technician, still unattached at thirty-three, but with an eye for the ladies and a liking for fast cars. Against his name the detective had written 'Flaky'.

It was 'flaky' that settled it. Elizabeth was probably too devoted to her mother to risk her job, no matter what financial inducements were offered. Flaky Oliver was the better bet.

Edie wasted no time, driven on by the thought of paying out another £642 to Avis for every month she wasted. The detective had supplied her with snapshots of all five, so it was easy to pick out Oliver as he left at five-thirty. He got into a low-slung car of obviously foreign make, and was off with a gunning of the engine that must have been heard in Southend. She almost lost him several times, but traffic lights were kind, and ten minutes later she was parking next to his car in the car-park of a Holborn pub.

Picking him up was easy. She perched on a stool, ordered a drink, and kept looking at her watch. As soon as he had noticed, she let their eyes meet once or twice, and then looked hastily away. After fifteen minutes he came over to her. 'If he stood you up, he's a fool,' he said. 'Can I buy you a drink?'

She had to stifle a smile. Men were such babies. You didn't

even need to bait your hook, all you had to do was reel them in.

She was careful at first. The detective could have got it wrong, could even have been deceiving her. But, no, cheating a client would mean no more recommendations: she had the right data, all right. She sat through interminable meetings, plying him with drink and kind words, waiting for the right moment. It came on the fourth meeting, when he confided that his one aim in life was to own a new Triumph Roadster. 'Lovely lines, Edwina. Sleek. Four speed gearbox with synchromesh on the top three ratios, transverse leaf sprung independent suspension at the front, and a live axle with half elliptic springs at the rear.'

'Speak English,' she said, 'that's double Dutch to me. But if it's your heart's desire, what are you prepared to do to get it?'

A week later he had a Triumph Roadster, and the promise of a job in the firm that she would found. She had the formulae for all Avis products, and a debt to Leonard that made her eyes water. 'Business is business, mind, Edie. I don't do favours with money.'

'You'll get it back, Leonard. And in the mean time you're making me pay interest, so it's certainly not a favour.'

'You'll have to change the formulae in some way,' Oliver had warned her. 'If you use identical ingredients in those same proportions, they'll have you bang to rights'. He had gone slightly pale as he spoke, and she knew he was thinking, 'And me, too.'

She had patted his hand and told him not to worry. 'Of course I'll change them . . . I only wanted a starting-point. No one will ever know. Now, enjoy your new car.' She forbore to say, 'Because it's all you'll be getting.' If he thought she would actually give a job to someone who would steal from his employer, he had another think coming. The Triumph had dented her savings, so she'd have to bide her time a little – but she was on her way!

For a second or two, the magnitude of what she was

contemplating made her mouth dry, but only for a moment. She had conquered bigger hurdles than finding someone to whip up some face cream. Once she got down to it, it would be a doddle.

Chapter Forty Three

Cathy

'WHAT ARE YOU GOING to do today, Stella?' Cathy asked, trying to keep her voice casual. 'The nights are drawing in now. You ought to be getting out while there's still some sunshine.'

Mrs S. put a protective hand on Stella's arm. 'Never mind the shorter days. Tea rationing's over. No need to swap our sugar and jam any more. What a relief.'

'You can't believe we still have rationing,' Cathy mused. 'Not seven years after the war ended. That only leaves butter and sugar, now.'

'And sweets,' Stella said desperately. 'Don't forget sweets.'

They fell to reminiscing then, remembering the sound of sirens, the scream of police vehicles rushing to where a bomb had landed, or, even worse, a V2.

'They scared me,' Stella said. 'You'd hear them up above, and then the noise would stop and you knew they were going to just drop on someone. On you, maybe.'

'It was bad,' Mrs Schiffman said. 'Night after night bombing the East End. Flying in from the east, first dropping incendiaries to light up their targets, and then the bomb . . . the high explosives. They would fly over, then turn at Tower Bridge, and do it again. Night after night. They were after the docks, that's why Limehouse got it.'

'And the delayed-action bombs,' Cathy said. 'Timed to go off as people were leaving the shelters. That was diabolical.'

'Good job we had the church crypt,' Mrs S. fingered her lips. 'Babies were born there, poor little babbas.'

'Germans were wicked – they still are,' Stella said vehemently. 'Trying to kill us.'

'Well, they didn't and . . .' Cathy was about to say, 'we all survived' – but they hadn't all survived. They had lost a father to the flames and a mother to a murderer. 'And it's all over,' she said instead. 'Now I've got to get a move on.'

She had squirmed inwardly when Stella had said that about Germans – they weren't all like that. Seeing Gunther in the street had awakened all the feelings she had cherished over the years; but it had also made her see the futility of allowing him to occupy her heart. The woman with him, obviously his wife, had been beautiful and utterly, utterly fashionable. He was a diplomat, and she was a fitting wife for him. 'While I', Cathy told herself sternly, 'parade around in a skimpy costume with feathers on my head. I'm a hoofer, nothing more.'

That was what the girls at the Windmill called themselves . . . 'dancers' in public, and 'hoofers' when they were together in the dressing-room. But there was a hierarchy even there. The dancers who kept their clothes on preferred to be called soubrettes. Those who posed nude, the legendary Windmill Girls, were considered to be a lesser breed, although the fortitude they displayed in standing stock-still for long periods made them heroines in Cathy's eyes. It was nudity that filled the Windmill seats every day, in rolling shows that continued until 10.30 at night. The Lord Chamberlain had ruled that: 'If you move, it's rude,' so stock-still they must stay in what Mr Van Damm called *tableaux vivants*. There were tricks, though, such as a nude girl holding on to a spinning rope. It was the rope that moved, rather than her, so they could get away with it.

Cathy had never stripped off, but it was the girls who did

who filled the seats, and therefore paid her wages. The thought of going in tonight filled her with distaste. She had never liked the 'Windmill Steeplechase', the moment when one show ended and patrons stood up to leave as other patrons from the back rows made a dash over the top of the seats to grab the front rows. She hated seeing a girl clutching a wisp of chiffon or a fan, anything to hide her pubic hair, loathed the stage-door Johnnies bringing presents of chocolates, or pressing banknotes into a girl's hand, in what was little more than an invitation to sex. She always relied on one of the male dancers, known as 'ginger beers' because so many of them were homosexual, to escort her into the street, and beyond the men pressing round. At least at Madame Bluebell's she had had some dignity. Here, if she was honest, there was precious little.

It was time she got out. The average age of a Windmill girl was nineteen. 'I'm twenty-five now,' she thought, 'and what have I got to show for it?' Her mood was so sombre that she almost took down the picture. What did she want with swans sailing on some mythical river? She wasn't even sure it was the Rhine. In the end she left it for another day and tried to get on with real life.

Paul took her out for a meal that evening. They found a booth in the nearby pub and ordered casseroled chops. 'The trial's nearly over. I'd like to have taken you somewhere posh to celebrate,' he said as they clinked wine glasses. 'Maybe I will when we get the actual verdict.'

'I'd like that, but I'm a working girl, remember?'

'I do remember. Constantly. And wish you would retire.'

'You don't mind what I do?'

He was smiling. 'No. I'm proud of you. But you can't go out there night after night for ever.'

'What else can I do?' It was a flippant answer, and the wrong one.

'You could marry me. We need to do something. I can't

make love in the back seat of cars when I'm an inspector.'

He was joking, but only half-joking. Last week she had let him make love to her. She had held him close, and tried to make him feel wanted, when all the while her mind had been elsewhere. There had been other men since she came back to London. She had lost her virginity to a stage-door Johnny – had done it quite determinedly, because it was time. Now, when she tried to remember it, it was strangely insubstantial, rather as though it had never happened. She could remember some of the others . . . no, all three of them, but they were insubstantial too, like ships that had passed in the night. Paul was different: she liked him, even loved him, in a way. But she had not wanted him to make love to her: it was something she had done for him, not for herself.

Now she changed the subject by telling him about Stella's exit from the salon.

'I'm not surprised, Cath. Stella is . . . well, a stunner, you know that. She's also an innocent, if I'm any judge. Vulnerable. And your sister Edie moves with a racy crowd.'

'Racy? What d'you mean?'

He went on about links between business and crime in London. 'I'm not saying they're villains, but Edie should watch her step.'

His tone was serious enough to worry Cathy, but a bigger worry as she went home was the memory of his mock proposal. One day he would say it for real, and expect an answer. 'I do love him,' she thought. 'I just don't love him enough.'

Mrs S. and Stella were sitting at the table when she got home. 'We've got something to tell you,' Mrs S. said. She was smiling, so it wasn't bad news. Cath sat down.

'I've made up my mind,' Stella said proudly. 'I know what I want to do. I want to be a nurse.'

Cath looked at Mrs S. and received an emphatic nod of the head. 'She means it.'

'Well . . .' Cath began to unbutton her coat. 'I can think of worse things. And where do you intend to do this?'

Stella was off, then, rattling off dates and times and details, even down to the length of uniform dress she would wear.

'You're certainly keen,' Cathy said, but she said it vaguely. Her eye, and her attention, were on the newspaper lying on the table. A headline said: 'German diplomat and wife injured in crash' and the name of the diplomat was Gunther von Sachs.

Chapter Forty Four

Cathy

YESTERDAY HAD BEEN THE last day of the trial. The tension in the court had been almost measurable until the judge entered, took an age to settle his robes, and then nodded to the Clerk, who turned to face the jury as they filed in. None of them had looked in the direction of the dock. 'They never look at the defendant if they've found him or her guilty,' Paul had told her. 'It's almost as though they feel bad about their verdict.' So did that mean Alfred Hindmarch was going down? And did it really matter, when Gunther was lying somewhere, alive, or perhaps dead? It was two days now, and she had not been able to find out a thing. The court had fallen completely silent, and she forced herself to concentrate.

'Have you reached a verdict on which you all agree?' There must have been some kind of signal, or a murmured response, but she didn't see or hear it. 'Will the foreman of the jury please rise.'

The foreman was a forewoman, tall and erect, and looking like a lady doctor. 'On count one, the murder of Mary Syme, do you find the defendant guilty or not guilty?'

The reply was loud and clear. 'Guilty.' There was a buzz in the court that turned into applause, and was quickly quelled. It was over. One by one the verdicts were all 'guilty'. She had come home to break the news to Stella and Mrs Schiffman, all the while wondering whether Gunther were alive or dead. She had phoned the hospital named in the newspaper report, but they would tell her nothing, so she had had to go to work and dance as though everything in the garden were rosy.

In the morning paper next day there was a small paragraph about the verdict, but mostly it was full of the new Queen opening her first Parliament.

'Poor young woman,' Mrs S. said. 'Pitched in head first, just when she was enjoying being a wife with her babies.'

Cathy was less sympathetic. 'She'll ride in a gilded coach, Mrs S. Rain won't fall on her, she'll never have to worry about the gas bill. I'd swap with her.'

Talk at the breakfast table turned then to Stella's plans, and the need to implement them as soon as possible. Cathy tried to keep her mind on Stella but, in reality, she could think of only two things. Was Gunther still alive, and how could she find out?

'So it's the London Hospital you're going to?' Mrs S. enquired.

'Well, not exactly.' There was a new and welcome excitement in Stella's voice. 'I'll go to the Preliminary Training School first for a nine-week period. There are two tutors and a Home Sister, so I'll be well looked after. We'll start the day with morning prayers, and then begin the training. A lot of basic things at first, like cleaning and stuff. That'll be followed by the real stuff, anatomy and physiology, personal and communal health, theory and practical nursing and bandaging. And they have doctors, too, to give lectures. We do First Aid as well, so I'll be able to take care of you two. Oh, and I'll have a cap, and mauve overalls – purple passions they call them – until I get my student's personal uniform made. And we wear Daniel Neal brown lace-up shoes.'

Cathy tried to look interested. 'Sounds marvellous. Do you need any cash for the shoes and things?'

'No.' Stella was looking faintly embarrassed. 'Our Edie said she would pay for them.'

As soon as she could, Cathy made an excuse about needing to shop, and left the flat. In a coin-box she fed in her money and dialled the hospital again. She was hoping for a different telephonist from yesterday, but it was the same one and she was still adamant. No, she could not confirm there was a Mr and Mrs von Sachs receiving treatment. No, there was no point in putting anyone through to the ward. If there was a ward, which she was not at liberty to say. She sounded so self-important that Cathy was convinced Gunther actually was there, and she had been told to stonewall any callers.

Edie was in the flat when she got back. She was less than enthusiastic about Stella's plans. 'It's a waste. You could really have done well yourself with a face and figure like that. You got the looks in the family, and you're going to bury them in a blue sack and put a bandage on your head. Still, if you're determined. It wouldn't do for me.'

'I bet the patients will be glad about that,' Cathy said, but she said it half-heartedly. Her thoughts were still on Gunther. She had scoured the morning paper from front to back, but there had been no further mention of him.

Talk turned to the trial then. 'What did he look like when the judge put on the black cap?' Edie asked.

'The same as he's looked all through . . . like an inoffensive little man who's wandered into the court by mistake, and wonders when someone will show him out.'

Mrs S. was nodding. 'They are like that, the real murderers. Remember Nuremberg? They looked like harmless old men.'

'Did he look upset, though?' Edie persisted. 'I mean, you can't hear someone say you're going to hang and not show some emotion.'

'Paul says he won't actually hang. They'll appeal on the grounds of diminished responsibility, and he'll get life.'

'But he'll never come out, will he?' Stella's voice was cracking.

'No, Stel, he'll never come out.'

'Good,' said Edie. 'Serves him right. I thought about being there – I wanted to see his face when they told him he would hang. But then I thought, as long as it happens, that's what counts. And I had things to do. Well . . .' She was getting to her feet and reaching for her bag. 'Can't sit here as though I had corn growing.' She examined her nails for a moment. 'I might as well tell you . . . it's not definite yet, but it will happen. Mr Edward is retiring.'

'What does that mean?' Cath asked.

'It means your little sister will be owner of three salons, darling. Up to her neck in debt, but the boss nevertheless. And I'm launching a line of toiletries. Not right now, but soon. So, you see, I've got my work cut out.'

'Congratulations.' Cath tried to sound approving, but it wasn't easy. 'I've got to stop resenting her,' she thought to herself. 'She wants to get on. That's not a crime.'

But it was a relief when Edie left and she could plead the need to lie down for a while, and retire to the bedroom. 'Are you sure we can't get something for you? Tea . . . anything?' Stella was looking anxious. Cathy waved aside all offers of help. The only help she needed was information, and no one could get that for her.

She had tossed and turned for half an hour when it came to her. There was one person who could find out anything and everything about anybody: a metropolitan policeman. Her heart was beating as she dialled the Scotland Yard number. Would they be able to locate Paul in that huge organisation?

When at last he came on the line, she almost sagged with relief.

'Cathy? There's nothing wrong, is there?'

'No . . . well, yes, but nothing to worry you. It's a friend of mine, a German I knew when I was in Paris. She is a Mrs von Sachs, and I've been told she was in a road accident two days ago. Her husband as well, but I don't know him. He's a diplomat.' She felt her face redden as she told that particular lie. 'I've rung the hospital, but they won't give out any information. Could you find out?'

'I expect so.' His words were reassuring, and she felt tears prick her eyes. She had lied to him, but how could she have told him the truth? 'I want you to find out if the man I love is alive or dead. He's the reason I can't marry you, marry anyone. I love him, Paul. I barely know him, but I love him. If anything has happened to him I won't be able to bear it.' She couldn't say that to him . . . to anyone.

'Give me your number,' he said. 'I'll ring you back as soon as I can.'

She gave him the number and put down the phone. Outside the phone-box, London swirled around her, pedestrians scurrying past on pavements, cars and buses competing on the road. She had had to replace the receiver so that he could ring her back, but she huddled over it, pretending to be still on the phone, in case anyone else came along to use the phone-box.

His return call came ten minutes later, ten minutes in which she had alternately sworn and prayed – that Paul would be quick, that no one would oust her from the box, but most of all that Gunther was still alive.

'I've found out, Cath, but it's not good news.'

She felt a tremor low down in her abdomen and pressed her legs together, afraid she was going to wet herself. 'What is it?'

'Your friend is dead. Dead before the ambulance got there. The husband is alive, though. Seriously injured, but hanging on. I think they're shipping him back to a German hospital later today. I'm sorry. I wish it had been the other way around.'

She could let out a sob now, knowing he would think it was grief when, actually, it was a cry of joy and relief.

BOOK 4
1958

Chapter Forty Five

Maggie

IT WAS ALWAYS NICE to get a letter from home. She had picked it up from the mat when she took in the milk, and tucked it in her pinny pocket to enjoy later, when she had the house to herself.

Joe had been gone for hours, on day shift. Now she waved young Joe and Amy off to school, and stood at the gate to watch little Alan until he teamed up with his mate and his mother, whose turn it was to see both children safe to the Infants' School gate. The two women waved at one another, and Maggie went back into the house. The kettle was on the hob and she swung it back on to the fire. When it boiled she would make the tea, and then put the irons on the glowing coals. There was a right pile of ironing waiting for her as soon as she'd had her tea.

The letter was packed with news. Edie was opening her fourth salon, this time in up-market Notting Hill, and occasionally there were adverts for her face-cream on the new television channel. The world must be full of women with more money than sense, Maggie thought. Stella was now working on a children's ward, and seeing a young doctor. 'At least I think she is, Mags, but getting anything out of her is like drawing blood,' Cath wrote. 'Still, she's mentioned him once or twice, so we can but hope.'

Paul had moved into his flat near Euston Station, and was expecting a promotion soon. That would be to inspector. She read on, hoping for some news of him and Cathy really getting together. A wedding would be nice, now she'd got her figure back. You'd think with three sisters you'd get at least one. She poured another cup of tea, and indulged in a nice vision of her daughter as a bridesmaid . . . or flower-girl if Edie and Stella wanted the role. The thought that Amy might be too old, and wed herself, by the time any of them got around to it drove her back to the letter.

The last paragraph was less cheerful than what had gone before. Mrs S. had a nasty cough, and was losing weight. 'She's adamant she won't see a doctor, but Stel will persuade her. I told her, "She'll do anything for you, Stel. You've got to make her go."'

When the letter was back in the envelope, she set about preparing Joe's meal. Mutton stew with dumplings. If she put the meat in now it'd be ready for the dumplings about three, which was just right for his homecoming at four. And the bairns could have some, too. She chopped and peeled and set the stew away. With potatoes and greens, it would be a grand spread. Cooking done and cleared away, she set up the ironing board and fetched the first iron from the fire, spitting on it to make sure it was hot enough. It gave a satisfying hiss, and she began on one of Joe's work shirts. She liked the way the iron cleared a smooth path through the wrinkled cotton. Ironing was one of the household tasks she didn't mind. Dusting didn't appeal, though – she could stand and watch the motes of dust shimmer in the sunlight and then settle back on the surface she'd just wiped.

A couple of nights ago she had broached the subject of getting a job now that Alan went to school, but Joe had vetoed the idea straight away. No woman of his was going to work, not while he had breath in his body. A woman's place was in the home. He had gone on and on until she had sealed his lips with a kiss, and promised never to mention it again, not even set foot across the door. It wasn't as though they needed extra cash: he made good money, and, by large, they had everything they needed. Even a TV set. On an impulse she crossed to the set and switched it on. There was nothing to see but the test card, but she quite liked the little girl, composed and demure in the middle of the screen. Joe said they had colour TV in America, but black-and-white was good enough. All the same, if Edie's adverts were coming on, they would have to think about colour when the time came. She didn't want to miss out.

She would have listened to the radio while she ironed, but she was tired of hearing them go on about the Munich air crash. All those Man. United players dead, young men in the prime of life. Joe had likened it to an accident in the pit: 'dying beside your marrers, well . . . in a way, you couldn't ask for more. But it's a waste, Cath, a tragic waste.' He was right, of course. The plane had crashed trying to take off from a slush-covered runway at Munich airport. The 'Busby Babes', handpicked by Matt Busby, and the cream of footballers, were on board along with a number of supporters and journalists, and twenty-three of them had died. Belgate took its football seriously, and the news had gone round the village like a drum-roll. There had been heroism involved, especially the Manchester United goalkeeper, Harry Gregg, who had stayed behind to pull survivors from the wreckage.

As the pile of newly ironed clothes grew, Maggie reflected on the amazing times she was living in. People flying everywhere, even football players. And everyone talking about self-service shops where you could just walk in and help yourself. The shops themselves were claiming to save shoppers money, but she couldn't see that working. Some women were daft enough to go mad if they were surrounded by reachable groceries. 'Give me the counter every time,' she thought.

The mutton was smelling now, rich and flavoursome. Joe would sniff the air when he came in and say, 'Something burning?' That was his little joke. The kids would go mad and mimic him, and Alan would fetch his fire engine from under the stairs and push it round shouting, 'Fire, fire!' Bedlam, it would be bedlam! Afterwards, when the kids were in bed, they would sit and watch the TV. Except Joe would go off on one of his hobby-horses: civil rights in America, or the evils of the Tory party were his pet subjects at the moment. She knew the story of Rosa Parks by heart, so often had he repeated it. All the same, she was a brave woman, sitting down on a whites-only seat in a bus, though she was black, and refusing to budge. Joe's latest topic was nuclear disarmament. He was threatening to go on a march somewhere in a few weeks' time. And news that no more debutantes were to be presented at court had brought on such orgies of pleasure she had thought he risked a stroke. She would get it all tonight before he'd washed his food down.

When he was all talked out and the picture on the screen had dwindled to a dot, they would go up to bed and make love. 'Do you never get tired?' she had asked him once, and he had chuckled and loved her again. She was happy in Belgate now. She understood pit life: back-shift and fore-shift, tub-loading and the bliss of day-shift, pit clays as opposed to best clothes, superstitions, and tricks on cavilling day . . . she knew it all.

Chapter Forty Six

Stella

S HE SMOOTHED HER APRON over the new pink dress. She was a staff nurse! The wonder of it swept over her – no longer a lowly probationer. Next step, a navy-blue Sister's uniform. She checked her cap was at the regulation angle . . . woe betide her if she passed Matron in the corridor with it a centimetre out of place. Behind her she heard laughter. 'What's up?' she asked, turning to her colleagues.

'We're laughing at you admiring that uniform. You'll still have to wipe bums, Stel!'

'I know,' she said. 'Haven't you got anything more interesting to talk about than scoffing at me?'

'Well, Elvis has been called up.'

She feigned incomprehension. 'Elvis? Who's he?' For a moment she had them fooled, but only for a moment. Everyone knew Elvis Presley, bought his records, worshipped him as the King of Rock and Roll. He was all right, but nothing special, as far as she was concerned.

The others were still drooling over a newspaper picture of Elvis in uniform. 'Come on,' she said, remembering her new status. 'Let's get back to work.'

She was working on the orthopaedic ward. Children on that ward were usually in for long stays, so you got to know them well. The downside to that was that it was an awful wrench when at last they went home, and you felt as though you were parting with one of your own. Still, it was nice to see them better, so she was really enjoying her time there.

The one cloud on her horizon was Mrs Schiffman. She had somehow lost her sparkle, and now seemed like an old lady: she appeared to have aged overnight, and was often lost in a brown study. 'I love her,' Stella thought, 'she's been like a mother to me.' She winced, remembering the night Mrs S. had stood up to Edie and freed her from that nightmare. 'You leave Edwina to me,' she had said. Stella could stick up for herself now, if she had to. Not that she had much to do with Edie these days. She was always off somewhere, setting up some new scheme, or grumbling if an old one wasn't paying off. 'Why was I such a fool?' she thought, remembering how she had trailed in Edie's wake, smiling to order, letting herself be pawed.

She was aroused from that unpleasant memory by a call of 'Staff!' Nurse Gibbons was standing in the doorway, cap awry, face red as beetroot. 'He's at it again, causing chaos. Everyone's crying. I was only trying to do his dressings . . . I can't stand it!'

Stella knew exactly what she was talking about: young Alexander Brown. He had been in and out of the ward for most of his short life, and he hated hospitals and everyone who worked in them. 'Right, Nurse,' she said. 'Leave him to me.'

He was there in his bed, mutinous, trying hard to hold back tears, glaring in a way he hoped would repel retaliation. She sat down on the edge of his bed. 'Get off,' he said.

She stood up and he looked surprised. 'If I ask nicely can I sit down?'

He looked at her and she saw he was trying to work out what she was up to. 'No,' he said.

She nodded. 'All right, I won't. It's your bed.' She was trying to give him back his dignity, some sense that he was in control of his own space. 'Can I talk to you if I stand here?'

A grudging 'Yes' was the answer.

'OK. I know how much you want to go home, Alex. And as soon as we're sure you're really better you can. That's why we need to see what's going on under those dressings. If you let me do them, we're one step nearer you going home.'

He thought for a moment. 'Would you be doing them?'

'If that's what you want.'

'Well, only a little bit.'

'Then only a little bit it is. I'll just wash my hands, and I'll be right back.'

She was walking towards the hand-basin when Dr Slater caught up with her. 'Nicely handled, Staff Nurse,' he said. She smiled her appreciation, and hoped that was the end of it. He was becoming a bit of a constant presence on the ward, and it made her uneasy. 'I was wondering,' he said, as she turned on the tap and began to lather, 'I was wondering if you were free tomorrow night?'

'Sorry.' The word came out in a rush. 'I'm afraid not.'

'I see,' he said. 'It's an Amami night. Well, never mind, I can always try again. And I will.'

'I'm usually busy,' she said apologetically. 'I'm not being awkward, it's just that I have a lot on.'

'I know,' he said solemnly.

'What do you mean you know?'

'I have ways and means. I pick up things. As a matter of fact, I have a dossier on you this thick.' He held up thumb and forefinger an inch apart.

'Very funny. And now I have to get on.'

He walked with her to Alexander's bed. 'You're lucky,' he told the little patient. Alexander scowled, his usual reaction when he wasn't sure what was going on. 'Well,' Dr Slater continued, 'she'll do anything for you. She won't do a thing for me.'

'Could you go away, doctor? I do need to get on.'

'See, Alex, that's how she treats me. "Go away, doctor."

Could you put in a word for me, old chap? Any time. No rush, I'm a patient man.'

Alexander's scowl deepened. 'If you go away,' Stella said desperately, 'I might, just might, think about a coffee some time. But not tomorrow night.'

Dr Slater was turning on his heel. 'See,' he called to the little boy in the bed, 'you got her to say yes. Thank you.'

Alexander watched the doctor walk away. 'He's crackers,' he said, defiantly.

'How right you are!' Stella sighed with relief. 'Now, let me just lift a corner of that dressing and see how we're doing.'

Chapter Forty Seven

Cathy

S HE HAD THREE DAYS of her week off left. On Monday and Tuesday she and Paul had gone on expeditions. Today they had pottered around his new flat, which was spacious and airy; she had made a Spanish omelette for an early dinner; and now they were settling into good seats to watch the film everyone was talking about: *A Certain Smile*. She had loved Rossano Brazzi ever since she had seen him in *South Pacific*, and was looking forward to this film. Paul had bought her chocolates.

As the lights dimmed, she slipped her hand into the crook of his arm, and gave herself up to the lush music of the theme song. It was sung by a young black man, a café pianist in the film, and the words kept repeating in her brain long after his song was finished. '*A certain smile, a certain face, can send an unsuspecting heart on a merry chase.*' The story of the film was bleak: Dominique, a young student, was in love with Luc, older and married. As the film ended, she was facing up to the fact that Luc didn't really love her. She had been a whim, no more. He was with his wife, and he always would be. It was stupid, she thought, as they stood to attention for 'God Save the Queen', and then filed slowly out into the evening air . . . it was stupid to let one moment in time colour the rest of your life. '*A certain smile, a certain face . . .*'

'You like that tune,' Paul said, and she realised she was humming it.

'Yes, well, it's catchy.'

He was smiling down at her, and she felt a surge of affection for him. He had always been there for her, right from that awful night when he had brought news of her mother's death – thirteen years ago, and yet, at times, it seemed like yesterday.

'Do you want to go for a drink?'

She shook her head. 'Let's go back to your place.' It could be her place, too, at the drop of a hat, she knew that. 'I'll stay tonight, if you want me to?'

'Silly question!'

She curled up on the settee while he went into the kitchen in search of drinks. '*A certain smile, a certain face . . . a fleeting glance can mean so many different things. All at once you know why your heart sings.*'

Paul didn't make her heart sing, kind and loving though he was Without him her life would be much bleaker, and he was a thoughtful lover. But Gunther had set it singing without doing as much as kiss her cheek. 'I was young, then,' she reasoned. 'Daft and impressionable. It was Paris and night-time. I had an unsuspecting heart. But this is now, this is real.' Even as she reassured herself, the song intruded again: '. . . *in the still of night, exactly like a bitter-sweet refrain, comes that certain smile to haunt your heart again.*' Gunther would be back in his castle in Badesheim now. Probably remarried, or with some other beautiful woman in his life. Paul had kept tabs on him while he was in hospital, and told her when he was shipped back to Germany. Six years ago, six long years. Anything could have happened in that time – 'and my life hasn't moved on at all,' she thought.

Paul was back, a bottle of champagne in one hand, two glasses in the other. 'What's the special occasion?' He didn't answer. Instead he prized off the cork and there was a satisfactory foaming.

'Careful!' She was laughing but her heart had begun to thump.

'You', he said, 'are looking at Inspector Steele. And now, for the fourteenth time, Inspector Steele is asking you . . . will you marry me, Catherine Jackson? You can't refuse an inspector. I could have you arrested. '

She was laughing, and clinking glasses, and offering congratulations, but she could not bring herself to say the one word he wanted to hear.

They made love later. He was a tender lover, anxious to please, holding back to pleasure her until his own need overcame him and he was thrusting inside her. Even afterwards his concern was for her pleasure. 'I love you, Cathy,' he murmured, his lips against her skin.

She lay without sleep for a long time after he slept. When she was sure she wouldn't wake him she slid from the bed and went to the window. Outside, London was still awake. Cars crossed and criss-crossed at the corner. Lone pedestrians trudged homewards. She leaned her forehead against the glass, and let her breath form a cloud on the glass. '*A certain smile, a certain face, can lead an unsuspecting heart on a merry chase.*' Was it time to end the merry chase? She could be happy with Paul; they could have children, build a home. She was tired of dancing, and the hectic and tawdry life of the Windmill. This week of freedom had shown her that. She imagined his face if she said 'yes', but even as she imagined his smile the song intruded. It was not any smile she craved, it was a certain smile . . . '*exactly like a bitter-sweet refrain, comes that certain smile to haunt your heart again*'. And suddenly she was back in Paris, in the narrow, scented streets. The faint sound of accordion music in the air, and magic in the surroundings.

She had been walking home that night, the wine and brioche Alec had given her in her bag. She intended to have a little feast, then write a letter to Mags before rolling into bed for a sound sleep. And then she had heard the shouting: 'Bloody Boche!' A pool of light spilling from a window and a body lying there. She had thought of her mother alone in a deserted street – that's why she had helped him, and given herself a wound that would not heal.

'Italy,' he had said, 'Monte Cassino.' He had been a German soldier, and she should have hated him – he had said as much: 'You're English. Don't you hate all Germans?' And he had chided her when she insisted he stayed the night. 'You are very kind. And very brave. And also, perhaps, very foolish.'

He had thrown back his head to laugh at her cheeky reply, and she had felt a sudden thrill. He was handsome. But it was something else, something that afflicted her still. He had talked of his home and the swans that would circle your boat, hoping for bread, until she could see he was tiring. 'Get some sleep,' she had said. 'You can tell me more in the morning.'

Now she let the curtain fall into place, and went back to Paul's bed, only to relive again the rest of that magic night.

Chapter Forty Eight

Edie

S HE HAD DEALT WITH everything on her desk by eleven o'clock, and the rest of the morning yawned before her. She was lunching with someone from a public-relations company, but that wasn't until one o'clock. Two whole hours. Edie drummed her fingers on the desk, and then, afraid of breaking a nail, folded her hands in her lap. For a moment she wondered what would happen if she got up, marched into the reception area, donned a white top and trousers and dealt with the next client herself. Edwina et Cie hands on! Where had she got the name from? She tried to remember the day she had come up with it. It was French, but she hadn't had the foggiest idea what it meant back then. Now she knew exactly: Edwina and Company. Big time!

If the market got really big, she might do away with the salons eventually. She had never really enjoyed pandering to rich women's needs, nor did she relish receiving treatments herself . . . although she always required new staff to perform on her first. If they didn't make the grade, they didn't get a job. For two pins she would junk the salons, now that the beauty products were doing so well. She picked up a copy of *Woman and Home,* and turned to the back page. There it was: a beautiful girl draped in chiffon, lying on a chaise-longue holding aloft one of the distinctive pink and grey pots. Edwina et Cie – she rolled it round in her mind. Edwina Jackson with a French touch. Had it been worth it – the tears, the tension, the ruthlessness needed to get the product she wanted, the product that would sell? Twice she had almost given up, but something inside had forced her on. 'I had to win,' she thought, 'I had to win, or I would have wound up like the rest of them. Amounting to nothing.'

She moved to the window to look down on the bustle of Charlotte Street, people window-gazing or walking purposefully, people with something to do. She looked at her nails again, perfect red ovals. She could have a re-polish, or a hand massage, to fill in time. Except that she liked to stay aloof from clients nowadays, and she didn't want staff making themselves at home in her room. She went back to the desk and picked up the newspaper lying on it. There was a rebellion in Algeria, and de Gaulle was involved somehow because his name jumped out of the print. She leafed through the pages, finding nothing of interest until she came to the theatre page. *My Fair Lady* was opening at Drury Lane. Rex Harrison and Julie Andrews . . . she'd hated that little brat, always jumping up to sing – squeak, really – in the war. And now she was a star. Well, she wasn't the only one.

Edie threw the paper aside and looked at her watch. Five past eleven. She shook it and held it to her ear. It was ticking, but surely it must be later than that? She walked to the door, quite why she wasn't sure, and asked for coffee. It came in the pink cups with the grey cipher that were served to clients. After that she settled down to study the plans for the new salon in Notting Hill, but that was a jumble of figures and projections, and she wasn't in the mood. If only she could phone someone. It couldn't be poor Leonard, he was a guest of Her Majesty and would be for a while. Anyway, men were nothing but trouble. If only Cathy would get the phone in. Edie had even offered to pay for it, on the grounds that she needed to know they were all right, but Cathy was a stubborn bitch. Nor could she bring herself to ring Maggie now – another lecture on the evils of capitalism was the last thing she needed. As if making money was a crime! They'd probably never heard of profit in the coalfield. Prissy little Stella would have a blue fit if she rang the hospital. Edie sighed, and started to run through the hundreds of people she met, but didn't really know well enough to telephone without a reason. At least Maggie was bringing the kids to London soon. That would be something to look forward to, as long as she didn't go on and on about the rights of the workers.

They never mentioned boredom in the life stories of the cosmetic queens. Edie had studied them all in the hope of picking up tips. In fact, it was the way they'd managed to make something out of nothing that had inspired her, but the books didn't get down to fine detail, such as what you did when everything was going swimmingly and crises hardly ever happened. Still, they were giants, those women, and she aspired to be like them: Helena Rubenstein, daughter of a Polish corner-shop owner; Estée Lauder, who was really Mentzer, daughter of immigrants who kept a hardware store and started selling creams concocted by her uncle. And Elizabeth Arden, the one Edie most admired, who had been born in Cornwall as Florence Nightingale Graham, and started out as a "treatment girl" just like she had. Graham was as ordinary a name as Jackson, so no wonder she had changed it for a name she got from a poem. 'Arden' had class, which was the quality Edie most wanted for her own products. And it was Arden who had pioneered the 'makeover' in her salons. There was money in make-overs.

Edie pulled out the file to see how far they were getting with her own plans to transform the generally dowdy into women of style. Compared with the giants of the industry, she was still small . . . 'but I'm young,' she thought, 'I've got plenty of time.'

She must get around to creating a signature scent, like Arden's Blue Grass. That was the next step.

Her coffee had gone cold, but she didn't fancy another cup. She didn't fancy anything today. 'I'm bored,' she thought. 'It shouldn't be like this, but it is.' Five minutes later she was in the car and speeding towards the East End.

The old place hadn't improved. Most of the bomb sites had been cleared up, and bloomed now with rosebay willowherb or nettles, and occasionally an ugly warehouse or small factory. But the tenements were just as dreary, the flats even worse. At least Jubilee Street had been kept clean while she was growing up there. She passed a back lane, and had to slow for a ragman's horse and cart emerging. When she glanced down it, she saw lines of washing, and two women standing, baskets at their feet, pegs in their mouths. She wrinkled her nose at the thought of what the inside of their homes would be like: smelling of dust and wee and boiled cabbage, cigarette smoke and paraffin heaters; shoddy furniture with nothing matching. For a moment she felt a sliver of contentment, as she thought about her own apartment with everything co-ordinated. But it was only a sliver, and content soon disappeared.

The traffic was moving on and she changed gear. Only then could she put up a kid-gloved hand to wipe her eyes.

Chapter Forty Nine

Cathy

S HE HAD SET HER clock to wake early. She wanted to be up when Mags and the family arrived. Mrs S. was already in the kitchen, shuffling around more slowly but still busy. As Cathy made toast, she thought about the old lady. If she herself moved out to be with Paul, could Mrs S. afford the rent, even with Stella paying her share? Still, today was not a day for problems. Joe was in London for a trade-union meeting of some sort, and Maggie and the kids, all three of them, were coming with him. Two whole days of her big sister. Stella would be around later, and even Edie had promised to look in, 'if I have time'. Cath forbore saying 'Time is money,' but it had been a temptation.

The family would be staying in a B & B in the Gray's Inn Road, 'but we'll be with you all day. Or as much of it as you can spare.' She had managed to wangle a precious night off, but it hadn't been easy. 'I'm thirty,' she thought. 'I'm thirty, and there are only two others in the line-up who are older than me.' The Windmill was no place for an ageing dancer who wanted nights off.

'What are you going to do today?' The old lady was smiling with her mouth, but her eyes looked wary. 'She's tired,' Cathy thought. 'She wonders if she's up to a house full of kids.'

She leaned forward and put a hand on the blue-veined one opposite. 'You can have a nice lie-down later on. I'm taking

Mags and the kids on a river trip, to Hampton Court. We'll be gone all day.'

'It's nice that you will all be together. Four sisters.'

'You had brothers, didn't you? And a sister.'

'Two lovely boys. One older, one younger. And my sister Miriam. He was a funny boy, David, he was the younger one.' She looked up and held Cathy's eye. 'Yes, they died in Dachau. They sent me papers: mother, father, two brothers, one sister, one sister-in-law, one niece, one nephew, all nicely documented. The Nazis were good record-keepers.'

There was silence and then, suddenly, the room was full of children, sleepy from a night on the bus, but eyes bright with curiosity just the same. They perked up after orange juice and biscuits. 'I suggested them having a sleep when they got here,' Mags said, 'but they weren't having it.' Joe had already gone off to a meeting, and Mags had brought the children on her own. 'In a taxi,' young Joe told Cathy, eyes round.

'It cost a lot,' Amy said reprovingly. 'A lot of pennies.'

Cath ruffled her niece's hair. 'Never mind, you don't get taxis often, do you?'

She got them all out of the house as soon as Maggie and Mrs S. had had a joyful reunion. 'Such children!' the old lady said wonderingly. 'I saw the photographs. Wonderful, I thought. But here, in the flesh – film stars, every one of them!' Maggie glowed with pride and Cathy felt a degree of satisfaction too. She liked being an aunt. She would like being a mother even more if it ever happened but she was beginning to think it never would.

She felt better when they were out on the river, embarking at Westminster Pier and sailing off, the children drinking in every word of the commentary as they followed the route of the Royal Barge belonging to King Henry VIII, and the monarchs who followed him. The children were fascinated by the locks as the river twisted and wound towards Hampton Court; there was a breeze off the river; and gin and tonic in paper cups tasted like nectar.

'So,' Maggie said eventually, when they were settled in a seat out of the wind. 'I can see something's on your mind. Just tell me it isn't our Stella in trouble.'

'It's not Stella.' They were passing Kew Gardens now, and the commentator was talking about botanics.

'Well, spit it out. I'm not here for a month. We've only got two days, and any minute now the kids'll get fed up and want attention.'

And Cathy finally told her sister about Gunther, and Paul, and the damning effect of a smile on an unsuspecting heart.

'Oh, Cathy, you should've told me before. You were just a kid then, and he must've seemed so glamorous . . . you always were a sucker for stray dogs. But that was years ago. He'll be old and fat, now, and have a wife who looks like Bessie Braddock.'

'His wife's dead, Mags. In a road accident. It happened here in London, and I read about it in the paper. He was injured, too, but he survived, and was taken back to Germany.'

'So he could be married again. Sure to have, if he's as good-looking as you seem to think. You have to move on, Cath. Paul's a good catch . . .'

'You don't have to tell me that. He's lovely, everything about him is right. I know it. I just can't stop thinking about Gunther. And he didn't forget it either. He wrote to me after.'

'He wrote to tell you he was getting married, Cath. If he'd been as knocked out as you were, he wouldn't have done that.'

'He was engaged, she was already his fiancée. He had to do the honourable thing. They're like that, nobility – especially German nobility. Sticklers for protocol. He was engaged. End of story.'

'And he couldn't break it off? Be honest, Cath . . . did he do anything to suggest he'd fallen for you? No. He was just grateful, that's all.'

Maggie was right, Cathy knew it. Gunther's wife had been beautiful, stunning even . . . 'and I am ordinary.' She fingered the medallion in her pocket. Swans on a river. A keepsake, and probably all she would ever have of him. She turned her attention to the river then, and let the drama of London's riverbanks take over.

That night they gathered in the flat, and ate cod and chips hot from newspaper stained with vinegar and crystallised with salt. Paul was there, hefting the kids around, being at hand to offer help, installing Mrs Schiffman in her chair and propping her up with cushions until she sat proudly like a queen.

'Do you remember . . .?' Edie said, and then they were away, talking of bombs and nights in the shelter, whelk stalls, hot chestnuts, street parties and the old magic of the East End.

'And then it was all over,' Stella said suddenly, and they knew she was referring to the night her mother had died. Funny how the light could go out of a lifestyle with the passing of just one person.

'Time to put this lot to bed.' Maggie was scooping up her youngest, and they trooped out to the waiting taxi. 'Will we all get in?' Joe asked anxiously, but the taxi swallowed them up as though by magic.

'See you tomorrow,' Maggie called.

'Yes, early,' Cath replied.

Back in the flat Edie was pouring herself another drink. 'That was nice,' she said, but she didn't sound joyful. Her eyes were on the old lady, who had fallen asleep in her chair.

'I don't like the look of her, Stella,' she said. 'Do something.'

Stella was stroking the wispy hair from the old lady's forehead. 'She's tired, that's all. I'll get her to bed shortly.'

In the kitchen, Edie helped Cathy wash the glasses. 'The old lady's fading, Cath. And God help our Stella when she does go. She's like a little puppy with her.'

When Edie had gone, Cathy looked around the flat to see if

anything needed tidying up. That was when she noticed the post on the sideboard. She sifted through the envelopes . . . bills, circulars, and one with a foreign postmark. It was from Alec, and the address was Haifa. So he had made it to the Promised Land! Her eyes filled with tears, but she wiped them away so she could read what he had written.

'Do you remember, when we drank wine in those smoky bistros, my toast was always: "Next year in Jerusalem." And now I am here in this land of desert and waterfall, blossom and rocky ground. We aim to make the desert bloom, Cathy. Quite how we will do it I do not know, but we talk a lot, this melting pot of doctors and lawyers, artists and professors, scientists and planners and the odd *schlemil* like your friend. We have to make friends with our neighbours, that is certain. They were here before us, so it is their land, too. If we learned anything from the Holocaust, it is that nation must make friends with nation. There has been enough killing.'

He ended with an invitation to visit him one day. 'You would be surprised how often I have thought of you: Cathy, who was a good dancer but a better friend. *L'chaim*. Alec.'

L'chaim – to life. He had taught her that toast also. She folded the letter. Dreams did come true for some people – that was good to know.

Chapter Fifty

Stella

S HE COULD HEAR A child crying at the end of the ward. It was the red-headed boy with the tubercular leg. He was strapped to a frame which was torture for an active child, but essential if he was to emerge with a healthy limb.

She moved to his bedside and reached for a tissue to dry his tears. 'What is it, David? Tell me, and I'll try to make it right.' His lip was still quivering but his howls abated. 'Go on, tell me. Perhaps I can fix it.'

He let out a big shuddering sigh. 'I want to go home. I want my dog. I want to go outside . . .'

She put a finger to her lips. 'Wait. How about I ask your mummy to bring your dog outside the window, so you can see him.'

His mouth was still dubious but his eyes had brightened. 'Bet she won't.'

'Bet she will if I ask her. She'll probably bring it this afternoon. I'll telephone her, and you can blow kisses.' It would be weeks, even months, before he went home to his beloved dog.

'Bet you don't,' he said.

'Cross my heart I will. That dog will likely be in the grounds this afternoon.'

'And you'll be in hot water with Sister.'

The voice came from behind her, and she knew who it was who had spoken. Dr Slater. She felt her cheeks grow suddenly hot, and tried to compose herself before she turned to face him.

'Probably, Doctor. But that's nothing new.'

He was leaning over the bed and speaking to his patient in conspiratorial tones. 'She will get the dog there, David, because everybody's frightened of her. Even Sister. Especially me.'

'You'll frighten him, Doctor. Did you want something special?'

'Tea. Tea, please, milk, two sugars, and the pleasure of your company. Come on, you can't refuse a desperate man. It would be a denial of your oath.'

She was tucking in David's sheets. 'I haven't sworn an oath, as well you know. I'll make you a cup of tea, but then I have to get on.'

They walked up the ward towards the kitchen. A probationer was sitting in a chair, rocking a baby to sleep. 'Keep an eye out, Nurse,' Dr Slater said. 'If Sister comes back, just scream.'

'You'll get us all shot,' Stella said. 'She's only gone to Matron's office. She won't be long, and then we'll all be in trouble, you included.'

When the kettle boiled, she scalded the tea and poured him a cup.

'Thank you. Now, about that little proposition . . .' He was always asking her out, and she was always saying no. Why, she wasn't quite sure. She liked him, liked his way with the children, his humour, the clean cut of everything about him. But she couldn't stand complications. Besides, there were other things.

'Come on, say yes. My sister's here, just for the weekend. We could go out together if you can't bear the thought of me on my own.'

'It's not that . . .'

He was laughing at her. 'You might as well say yes, because you know I won't give in. I'll go on and on and on, until you come down with repetition disease . . .'

'There's no such thing!' She was trying not to laugh.

'I just discovered it. I'm writing it up for the *BMJ*. It'll make my name, and then you'll be dying to go out with me, but I'll be too famous.'

Before she could answer, the probationer's head came round the door. 'She's in the corridor.' Within seconds the cups were drained and cleared away, he was out of the door, and she was smoothing her hair back under her cap and just praying that guilt didn't show in her face.

'Nurse?' Sister stood in the doorway, eyebrows raised.

'Everything's fine, Sister. I've done the pre-med on the talipes, and I think everything else is as you left it.'

'Good. Cut along then, and find something to do.'

Stella knew what she had to do: use the phone in the consultant's room to phone David's mother. If Sister made herself a cup of tea, that should give her time. Her shift finished at three, but she stayed on long enough to make sure the dog appeared, and left a small boy ecstatic at the sight. She had had to shift his bed a little to get him a better view, but the SEN had promised to shift it back before Matron's round.

Dr Slater was waiting at the gates as she left. 'Alms!' he cried piteously, 'alms for the love of Allah. Take pity on a starving man.'

'If you don't stop showing me up, I'll do more than pity you.'

'Ooh, that sounds exciting. Come on, Jackson – a couple of hours of your company, it's not much to ask.'

He looked younger in his tweed jacket, a college scarf slung round his neck. She wanted to say yes, but if she did . . . it wouldn't end there. With men it never did.

'I've got to go,' she said. 'Honestly, I can't be late.'

On the bus she felt like crying, she wasn't sure why. She just did. It felt better to get inside the flat and see Mrs S. smile a welcome. 'I've had a visitor,' she said. 'Your sister's been round with a tonic. Look!'

The bottle of Wincarnis stood on the table.

'Cathy brought that?' Stella said, astonished. 'She didn't mention it last night.'

'It wasn't Cathy, it was Edie . . . Edwina. Now there's a surprise.'

The ignoble thought that Edie must be after something came and went. She was home and safe, and that was the best feeling in the world. She made tea and they sat in companionable silence for a while, the old lady relaxed in her chair and Stella, waist-band loosened, sturdy shoes off, unwinding from the bustle of a busy ward.

'How was your day?' Mrs Schiffman was eyeing her closely.

'Good. Yes, a good day. The Colles fracture went home . . . I told you about him, the little boy with mended spectacles. And I managed to get David's dog into the grounds so he could see it from the window. That cheered him up.'

'He's the little one who must stay for a long time?'

'That's right.'

'And your friend, the doctor?'

'Oh, he was there, making a nuisance of himself as usual.'

'I see,' Mrs Schiffman said, and stirred her tea.

Chapter Fifty One

Maggie

SHE WAS MAKING TOAD-IN-THE-HOLE with chips and peas – that would bring a smile to Joe's face. The bairns, too, they'd do anything for a batter pudding. In the background the radio was burbling away, but suddenly a name sprang out at her: 'Imre Nagy.' She knew that name because Joe had gone on and on about it. He was the politician who had been in charge of Hungary when the Russians invaded in 1956. She could remember his voice on the radio, appealing for help as the Russian tanks rolled in. Joe had had tears rolling down his cheeks, and she had struggled to understand why one Communist army was fighting another when they were supposed to be part of a brotherhood.

And now it seemed Nagy was dead . . . hanged. There would be hell to pay when Joe found out. She would try to keep it from him till he'd had his meal. He had a hearty appetite after a shift, but he could be turned off his food if something put him out.

She had cleared away the peelings, and was washing down the bench when she heard the knock at the door.

'Come in!' she called. No one stood on ceremony in Belgate, or if they did they knocked at the seldom-opened front door.

The knock came again, and she was moving to open the door when the latch lifted and it opened itself.

'Mrs Harrington?'

The moment she saw the man's face, she knew it was trouble. The sight of the pit boots in his hand confirmed it. 'What's happened?' she said.

'He's not dead.' The man was as anxious as she was. 'Sit down, lass. There's been a fall of stone, and they've taken him to the Infirmary. You can go there directly. Have you got someone to see to the bairns?' He was putting down the boots, placing them carefully side by side.

'Yes,' she said, 'my sister-in-law. She'll see to them.' She got to her feet. 'I've got to go. Where is he? Which ward?'

'He'll be in Casualty, pet. And then likely they'll operate. But they'll sort it once you get there.'

'How will I get there? I need a taxi.' She seized her purse from the dresser. Was there money enough? There had to be.

The man was getting more agitated. 'Don't worry about that. We can sort all that. Look, give me your sister-in-law's address and I'll fetch her. I'd run you to the hospital, but I've got to get back. There's others, not just Joe.'

'It's all right. You've been kind. She lives in Bethune, 39 Bethune Avenue. Her name's Mavis Cowley.'

'I know her man. I'll fetch her now.'

Within minutes, the house was full. The mechanism that had existed down the ages when there was injury in the pit was swinging into action. 'Leave your lot to us.' The speaker was a chubby woman from a few doors down whom she hardly knew, but her eyes were kind and the plump fingers that helped her button her coat were comforting. It was like being a little girl again and having your things done up for you.

A car appeared at the door. 'Get in,' Mavis said. 'I'm coming with you.'

'The bairns?'

'Meg, there's four women in there, all with bairns of their own. I dare say they'll manage.'

When they got to the hospital, Maggie left it to Mavis to do the talking. Someone took her arm and led her along a corridor, and then she was in a waiting-room. 'Why are we here?' she asked. Mavis patted her hand. 'Someone's coming to speak to you, and then you can see Joe. Try to keep calm, Meg . . . I know it isn't easy, but he needs you to stay calm.'

The walls were cream, and she could see a line where they'd stopped washing them, the height of a woman's arm. She would tell him about Imre Nagy, but not straight away. She would have to make sure no one else mentioned it, in case he got himself worked up. When she got him home, he would be all right. She could sort him once she got him home. . .

The doctor was young, Asian – dark-skinned, anyway. He wore a white coat, and had a stethoscope round his neck. His eyes were full of compassion, and that frightened her. 'I'm afraid your husband is badly injured, Mrs Harrington.' He was going to detail the injuries but she hadn't time for that.

'But you can fix him, Doctor? You can sort it out?'

He was looking to Mavis, appealing for help, which was a disgrace because doctors were there to sort things, not ask someone else to help them out.

'Come on,' Mavis said gently. 'Let's go in and see our Joe.'

He was a strange and remote figure on the bed, with a mask over his face and a great metal and plastic collar around his neck.

'Joe?' His hands lay on the coverlet. His big scarred hands with the blue flecks that marked him as a collier, and could be so gentle when they touched her body. She lifted one to her lips. It was warm. He was alive.

'I'm going to find out what's happening, Meg. Shout out if you need anything.'

His eyes were closed, but what looked like a tear had escaped a closed lid. She put out a finger and it transferred itself to her skin. She put it to her mouth, and it was cold and salty on her tongue.

'I'm here, Joe. Here's a fine thing you've done! I hope you'll be more careful in future. Still, you never listen. Do you know how much I love you, Joe? Me and the bairns? You mean the world to us. You've got to get well. You promised I could be an MP's wife, remember? I fancy that. You'll be a good one, Joe, because you're a good man. But I love you anyway. I love you, Joe.' She lifted the hand and put it to her mouth.

Mavis had come back into the room, a doctor and nurse behind her. Maggie knew from their faces that it was almost over. The doctor crossed to the bedside and put his fingers to Joe's neck.

'I'm sorry,' he said.

She put the hand to her lips again. It was still warm. 'There must be something you can do.'

The doctor shook his head. 'His injuries were too extreme. His chest was crushed. There were multiple fractures of the limbs, and his spleen was ruptured. If it's any consolation, I don't think he knew much about it.'

When Joe had left that morning, he had teased her. 'I want my dinner on the table when I get back, and you in your best nightie ready for action.'

She had slapped him and said he would be lucky to get fried bread, never mind any carry-on, but she had known she was making toad-in-the-hole for him all along. Why hadn't she told him? He could have looked forward to it all day, and now he would never know . . . she could hear someone wailing, a high, thin sound that echoed off the walls. 'Hush,' Mavis said gently, and she realised the wailing was her own.

She sat on for a long while, not thinking, just holding Joe's hand until it began to grow cold.

'Would you like to lie down for a while?' a nurse asked sympathetically.

'No, thank you,' Maggie said. 'I have to go home and see to his bairns.'

Chapter Fifty Two

Cathy

They set out at eleven o'clock. Paul was there to load up the luggage, and help them get Mrs S. into the back seat.

'Are you sure you're up to it?' they had asked a thousand times, but the old lady was adamant.

'Maggie needs her family,' she had said firmly, and defied them with a glare to suggest that she was anything but a family member. Stella sat in the back with her, almost monitoring her every breath, while Cathy sat alongside the driver. 'Right,' Edie said, letting out the clutch. 'We're off.'

Cathy mouthed, 'Thank you,' at Paul through the window, and settled back for the journey. As they negotiated their way out of London, she was impressed by Edie's driving. The small, manicured hands were firm on the wheel, the neat suede shoes on the pedals. But that was Edie all over: when she set herself to something, she didn't look back. 'She's different from the rest of us,' Cathy thought. For a moment she wondered if Edie had been sired by the milkman – but it was a ridiculous idea, really.

'What are you smiling at?' Edie asked, glancing sideways.

'Nothing. I wasn't smiling. There's not much to smile about, is there? The more I think about our Mags, the worse it seems. Alone in a strange place, and God knows what she'll have to live on.'

'There'll be pensions and things,' Edie said firmly. 'And

compensation. We'll get a lawyer if we have to. She'll come back to London, where we can keep an eye on her. It'll work out, you'll see.'

Cathy didn't argue. It didn't pay to argue with Edie, but it was far from as simple as Edie made out. Maggie could come back, but where would she go? The only one of them who had a spare room was Edie, and Edie with three little kids running round didn't bear thinking about.

The last few days had passed in a blur. She had heard the news from Edie, who had appeared in the flat, for once not coming in as though she owned the place. 'Have you been crying?' Cathy had asked, and had known in that moment that something was very wrong.

'Sit down,' Edie had said, and then, 'Where's Mrs S.?'

'Lying down. Do you want her?'

'No, leave her where she is. It's our Mags, Cathy. Her sister-in-law just phoned, and I came straight over.'

'She's not . . . just tell me, she's . . .'

'No, it's not Maggie. It's Joe. He's dead. Killed in the pit.'

They had drunk Mrs Schiffman's sweet sherry, uncaring that it was borrowed without permission. Tomorrow it could be replaced.

'What are we going to do?' Cathy had asked, but Edie was already outlining plans.

'She'll have to come home, of course. Back to London. We'll help her get set up. It'll be nice having her back here – the family back together. And we can see to the kids, give them advantages. You'll see, it'll all work out. She was never meant for a mining town, not our Maggie.'

'She's been happy there, Edie. You can't deny that.'

'I daresay, but that was because of Joe, and now he's gone. No, all things considered, she'll be better off here.'

Since then they had spoken to Maggie many times, trying desperately to console her at a distance until they could get there to console her in person. The funeral was tomorrow, and now they were on their way.

Mile after mile, England rolled past. They stopped at Leicester, and then at Doncaster, and eventually Durham was on the road signs.

'You turn off here,' Cathy said, looking at Maggie's written instructions. The roads grew narrower, and less built up – and then Belgate was before them.

'Good God!' Edie said. 'Our poor Maggie.'

The pit seemed to loom above the village, its headstock outlined against the sky. The streets radiated off the one main street, and all seemed identical. Terraced and narrow. And then they were there: 33 Wainwright Street was small and narrow, and exactly like its neighbours.

The door was opened by a rosy-cheeked woman in a flowered pinny. 'Come in,' she said. 'She's expecting you.'

They trooped through the narrow hallway, past a door, and then they were in the room where Maggie sat, with two older women on either side of her. 'Maggie!' She was rising to kiss them, and hug Mrs Schiffman until Cathy feared her bones would be crushed. The other women melted away as if by magic, but one of them returned with a tray full of cups and milk and sugar. Behind her came another with cake and scones, and the third with a teapot. 'We'll be off now you've got company,' one of the women said. 'Just shout if we're needed.'

'Where are the children?' Stella asked. They were, she was told, at someone's house, being cared for. 'They come back here to sleep,' Maggie said. She was pale, but dry-eyed, the black jumper and skirt she wore making her look gaunt, and older than her years.

'I can't believe you've all come all this way,' she said and put out her hands to her sisters.

They stayed with her for an hour or two, hearing the painful details of Joe's death. 'Everyone's rallied round,' she said. 'Day and night, they've been there to help me.' For some reason that she couldn't fathom, the words 'acquainted with grief' came into Cathy's mind. It sounded like something from the Bible, but as she pondered them she understood why they had occurred to her. This was not the first death in the pit that Belgate had encountered. It would not be the last. And everyone rallied round, because they were glad it wasn't them, when it might have been – or because long ago it had been them, and they still felt the pain.

The sisters left when the children came back, wide-eyed and unusually silent. 'You've grown,' Cathy told young Joe, and saw him square his shoulders as befitted the new man of the house.

They found the B & B in Seaham Harbour, a few miles from Belgate. 'I heard about your sister's loss,' the owner said. 'Word gets round up here.'

They had two bedrooms, each with double beds and a view of the sea. 'I'll go in with Mrs S.,' Stella said firmly, and shepherded the old lady away.

'I guess it's you and me, then,' Cathy said, as brightly as she could. Sharing a double bed with Edie would be no treat. But this was a strangely subdued Edie. To be sure, she carried out her routine when she returned from the communal bathroom, laying out an array of creams that would not have disgraced a shop window.

'The place is clean,' she said. 'I'll give them that.' She was slapping cream on to face and neck as she spoke. She had changed into a satin dressing-gown, which came with a matching toilet bag. She peered anxiously at her face in the dressing-table mirror, and then lavished cream upon her hands as she talked about Maggie.

'She was amazing, wasn't she? I mean, no grumbling, no "why me?" I'd have been screaming from the rooftops if I'd lost my man.'

'She's numb, that's all. It'll hit her after the funeral.'

Edie was silent for a moment, considering her reflection. Eventually she spoke again. 'All the same, I envy her a bit. She's got kids, and she's got memories. You've got Paul. Stella . . . well, our Stella's a saint. She'll devote herself to Mrs S., and then she'll find another lame duck to mother, and she'll be perfectly happy.'

Cathy wasn't sure what to say. This wasn't Edie in her usual mode.

'What about you?' she said at last. 'You've got a thriving business, plenty of money – everything you've always wanted.'

'But that's just it, Cath. I'm not sure it is what I want. You've all got someone to love, someone who loves you. I'm on my own. I can buy what I want, but you can't buy things like that. I have thought about getting a dog, something small and handy. A Shi Tzu, or whatever they call them – ornamental little things.'

Cathy repressed a smile. 'You're only twenty-nine, Edie. Plenty of time to find someone. You can leave the pedigrees till later. Put the light out and come to bed, and stop making a drama out of it.'

But as they lay side by side in the dark, she wondered what Edie would say if she knew the truth – that she had Paul, but not that thing her heart desired. 'Perhaps we're not meant to be happy,' she thought, and turned on her side for sleep.

Chapter Fifty Three

Edie

SHE HAD SET HER clock deliberately early, guessing that the one bathroom would be in demand. When she was ready she looked at herself in the navy suit with touches of white at neck and wrists. Smart, but not too smart. No point in making people feel uncomfortable with a show of *haute couture*. They were decent people up here, but a bit simple. Not a lot of style.

She took over from Stella, then, making sure Mrs S. had a decent breakfast, and helping her into her heavy black. 'There,' she said, when she had pinned the jet-and-pearl brooch at the neck. 'That's a lovely piece. Was it family?' The old lady fingered it. 'It was my mother's. Yes, a family piece.' Edie cleared her throat, wishing she had kept her mouth shut. Mrs S.'s family had gone to the gas chambers: she wouldn't need reminding of it today.

The house in Belgate was full to bursting when they got there. Men in best suits that smelled of moth balls, and women flitting about with cloth-covered trays of food. Edie had spoken to Maggie on the phone, and offered to pay for a proper wake in an hotel, but it was all taken care of, Maggie had told her. Low though her opinion of miners was, Edie had to admit it was impressive: without any fuss they were providing support, men and women alike. Still, the sooner Maggie was out of here the better. The children were nowhere to be seen – Maggie had decreed them to be too young for a funeral, so somewhere, someone must be caring for them. More solidarity!

Eventually the undertaker took over: the coffin appeared from behind the closed doors of the front room, and was carried on broad shoulders out to the waiting car. 'Those are your flowers,' Maggie said, pointing to a wreath of white roses and chrysanthemums. Cathy had arranged that, and whoever had done them had done them proud.

'I want to cry,' Edie thought as she entered the church. 'I want to cry, but I have no right.' Her sister, who did have the right, was magnificent and dry-eyed in widowhood.

'I'm not in control of this,' Edie thought. 'Nobody's in control of death. You can do nothing about it. She rolled that thought around in her mind and was suddenly afraid. They sang 'Eternal father', and 'O Love that wilt not let me go', and suddenly and sharply she remembered her mother's funeral. They had sung that then. 'I give Thee back the life I owe . . .'

'I can't control everything.' Edie looked round, afraid she had spoken aloud. But everyone's eyes were on the altar, their mouths open in song. She sat as the vicar talked of the price paid for coal, looking often at her sister in the pew in front. 'She's proud,' Edie thought. 'I thought she was a fool for coming up here to marry a pitman. But she's proud of what she is, and what she has.'

Someone, a man, was reading something. His voice was shaky at first, and then became magnificent as he found confidence.

'Surely there is a mine for silver, and a place for gold that they refine. Iron is taken out of the earth, and copper is smelted from the ore. Man puts an end to darkness, and searches out to the farthest limit the ore in gloom and deep darkness. He opens shafts in a valley away from where anyone lives; they are forgotten by travellers; they hang in the air, far away from mankind; they swing to and fro. As for the earth, out of it comes bread, but underneath it is turned up as by fire. Its stones are the place of sapphires, and it has dust of gold. Man puts his hand to the flinty rock and overturns mountains by the roots. He cuts out channels in the rocks, and his eye sees every precious thing. He dams up the streams so that they do not trickle, and the thing that is hidden he brings out to light.

'But where shall wisdom be found? And where is the place of understanding? Man does not know its worth, and it is not found in the land of the living. The deep says, "It is not in me," and the sea says, "It is not with me." It cannot be bought for gold, and silver cannot be weighed as its price. It cannot be valued in the gold of Ophir, in precious onyx or sapphire. Gold and glass cannot equal it, nor can it be exchanged for jewels of fine gold. No mention shall be made of coral or of crystal; the price of wisdom is above pearls. The topaz of Ethiopia cannot equal it, nor can it be valued in pure gold.'

'That's on the miners' memorial in Durham Cathedral,' someone whispered. 'At least, a bit of it is.'

When it was over, they filed out into sunlight which suddenly smote the eyes. 'A lovely service,' Edie murmured as she shook the vicar's hand. 'I want to go home,' she thought as they stood at the graveside, 'I don't feel safe here any more.'

The coffin was lowered into the grave, neatly disguised with swathes of artificial grass. All around her she could hear subdued sobbing, and she wanted to cry but it would not come. As they filed past the vicar to shake his hand in farewell, she moistened her lips. 'That reading, vicar, the one about opening a shaft?'

'Job 28,' he said. 'In the Good Book,'

Back at Maggie's house there was sherry in the wrong glasses, but it was warm and sweet on the tongue. She would have appreciated a dry sherry, but this was all right – even comforting. There were pies and sausage rolls, and big slabs of cake, and an army of people with teapots the size of buckets and huge jugs of milk. 'Look at her,' Cathy whispered at one stage. Maggie was clasping her newly returned children to her, and smiling gratefully at the man and woman who had brought them home.

'Yes, the neighbours are good to her, but the sooner she's back with us the better.'

Cathy was shaking her head. 'I'm not so sure, Edie. I think she belongs here.'

'She's got a good sister-in-law, I'll give you that. Mavis has put herself out no end.'

When at last the mourners began to ebb away, it was time to make their own farewells. Mrs S. was beginning to flag, now. The sooner she was in the car the better. It would be midnight before they got to London. Late for an old lady.

'Thank you for coming, Edie,' Maggie said. 'They couldn't have got here without you, and I know you've got a lot of responsibility. It was good of you to make the time.'

'Did you really think I wouldn't come, Mags? We're sisters, remember.' Edie was about to say, 'I've got staff to take care of things for me,' but the words refused to come. They would have sounded out of place here. 'You must come back to London, Maggie. So we can help you.'

'We'll see, Edie. We'll see. But I'll bring the bairns quite soon. Joe always promised them they'd see Big Ben again one day, when . . . well, he always promised them.'

They were all in the car, and it was time to put it into gear and move off, but somehow Edie was reluctant to go. 'Come on,' Cath urged softly. 'Don't prolong the agony.' She put down the clutch, and moved off down the narrow street, sensing her passengers waving to the women and children they were leaving behind. The pit loomed up on the left, and Edie suddenly remembered what the vicar had said about the cost of coal. There was a price for everything, she thought. Even for getting on.

Chapter Fifty Four

Stella

D R SLATER WAS THERE at the gate as she crossed the compound. 'Don't make a scene,' she said desperately. Lately he had become more and more vociferous, especially if there were other nurses in the vicinity.

'Me?' His eyes bulged and then rolled, and she tried hard not to laugh. 'If you don't come for a coffee, I'm going to chain myself to the railings.' He fished in his jacket and brought out a set of handcuffs.

'They're plastic,' she said.

'So?' He clamped one around his wrist, and waved the other towards the gate.

'One cup of coffee,' she said. 'One coffee, and then I've got to go.'

'You', he said, when they were safe in a booth, cups in front of them, 'are hard work, Stella Jackson. In fact, I would say you have had a seriously deleterious effect on my welfare.'

'What's deleterious?'

'You know full well, and you a staff nurse. I've a good mind to bring my mother to you.'

'That doesn't scare me.'

'You haven't seen my mother. Seriously, though, why are you so determined not to . . . well . . . I don't bite.'

'I know.' She was suddenly contrite. 'It's just – family

things. I have responsibilities.'

'I understand that. But you must have some free time. Cookie says your parents are dead, and you live with one of your sisters?'

'Nurse Cook should mind her own business. I do live with my sister, but there's also an old lady, she's German . . . she was a refugee, and she's Jewish. Anyway, she sort of looked after us when my mother . . .' She hesitated, and then came to a decision. 'My mother was murdered. A random killing. The man who did it is now in jail.'

He was leaning forward to cover her hand with his own. 'I'm sorry. Go on.'

'My Dad had died in the Blitz, in the fire service. There were four of us, all girls.' She went on to tell him about Maggie, and Cat, and Edie who had gone up in the world and liked to be called Edwina. It was suddenly easy to talk to him, but Stella didn't mention the time when she had worked for Edie. The time that had marked her for ever.

'I heard about your sister's husband – when you had time off. I'm really sorry. Still, it was good that you were all there with her. How is she managing?'

'All right, I think. We're letting things settle before we ask her what she wants to do.'

'That's wise. We tend to rush things a bit after bereavement. Big mistake.' There was silence for a while and then he leaned forward. 'You've certainly had your share of trouble. I've been pretty lucky. My dad is a doctor, too – a GP. My mum was a nurse, a Sister Tutor, so you can imagine. I've got a sister and a brother. He's at Cambridge, and she is married to a market gardener and talks about nothing but plants.'

'I see.'

'As I've told you before, my name's Michael, if you think you could bear to let it pass your lips. Then I can call you Stella, which is a very pretty name, by the way.'

They had a second coffee, and then she stood up and tightened the belt of her raincoat. 'Got to go.'

'Got to go, Michael. Go on, say it, I dare you.'

'Got to go, Doctor.'

'God, you're a hard woman. Can we do this again?'

'If you stop showing me up, we might.'

'It worked!' He held up a thumb to indicate victory. 'Never knock something that works. First rule of medicine.'

They were outside in the street, and she suddenly wished they were still back in the booth. Until she remembered the things she hadn't told him. At the bus stop he leaned to kiss her cheek, and she let him; and then she was on the platform, the clippie was ringing the bell, and he was standing, waving, until the bus was out into the stream of traffic and he was lost to view.

She would have to stop this somehow, before he got closer. Before the moment when she would have to puncture his idea of her as someone nice and unsullied. She squeezed her lids together to stop her eyes smarting, and tried to switch her thoughts to the evening ahead.

To her surprise, Cathy was still in her dressing-gown when she got home. Stella looked at the clock. 'You'll be late.'

'I'm not going in. I called in sick. It's OK – there's nothing the matter with me. I've just lost interest in being in the chorus line, Stel.'

'How will they manage without you?' Over Cathy's shoulder she could see Mrs Schiffman shaking her head to dictate silence.

'Easily.' Cathy sounded resigned. 'There's a dozen girls thirsting to take my place, Stel – twenty years old, and with stars in their eyes, like I had. When you want to do it, you don't notice the aches and pains, the blisters, the nights you have to will yourself to smile. I watch them, thinking that it's romantic and they'll be stars one day and make their fortune. But you learn. You learn the hard way.'

Behind them the old lady stirred. 'I think we need a cheer-up.' She was rising from her chair, crossing to the bureau that held her treasures. The bottle was round and dark and mysterious-looking. 'What is it?' Cathy asked as it glugged into three glasses.

'Just drink it,' Mrs S. said. 'But slowly.'

It was liquid fire, and it had the desired effect. 'Schnapps,' Mrs S. said.

After a while Cathy helped her make the evening meal, and they ate it together round the fire.

'How was your day?' Mrs S. asked Stella when the plates were cleared.

'OK. No crises. A nice new patient. Perthes disease.'

'She's showing off again,' Cathy said wryly, and the old lady nodded.

'She's a good nurse, all the big words. But you were late tonight, Stella. What kept you?'

For a second she was going to lie, but it would be futile. 'I had a coffee with Dr Slater. Just a coffee. There . . . it's . . . we were talking about work.'

'Don't perjure yourself, Stel. You had a date. That's OK.'

'It wasn't a date. He's nice, but . . . well, you should talk, Cath. Poor Paul's been kept at arm's length for years.' She was suddenly contrite. 'I'm sorry, that was cheek. It's your business.'

'It's all right, Stel, it's the truth. Paul is too nice to be messed about. I don't know why I do it.'

Mrs S. was getting to her feet. 'This old lady is going to bed, and you two should talk. I say only one thing: life doesn't come in bunches. One life each is all we get. Don't let it slip through your fingers, either of you.'

After Stella had helped her to bed, and put out the light, she came back to sit beside her sister. 'I'm sorry, Cath. That was out of order earlier. It is your business, as I said.'

'It's OK, Stella. I do love Paul – I think I do. But there are things . . . things in the past . . . complications.'

This was the moment to confide, to tell it all, Stella thought. She could tell Cathy about the men . . . that it had been more than them just making passes. And Cathy would console her, and try to make it right. Except that it couldn't be made right. 'I am damaged goods,' she thought, 'and no one must ever know.'

Chapter Fifty Five

Maggie

EDIE HAD MET THEM off the bus at Victoria. The children had slept for most of the journey, but Maggie had stayed awake, wondering if she was mad to make such a journey with three children. And how would she manage with washing and everything while they stayed in Edie's posh apartment? Still, Cath would help out once she was no longer working. Only that was another worry – if Cath did marry Paul, how would Stella live? As far as she could make out, Mrs S. had little or nothing, and a nurse's wage wouldn't keep two people and run a home.

It was a relief to have Edie take over. She was good with the kids, considering she had none of her own, folding them into the car and chatting to them all the time. Maggie had a wistful moment when she looked at Edie's trim figure, and unlined face: she felt suddenly fat and tired and shabby. And then she remembered that she had been loved, and ceased to envy Edie at all. 'New car?' she asked, as she settled in the roomy front seat. Edie let out the clutch and the car glided forward.

'Only got it last week. I needed something bigger. The firm bought it, not me . . . well, the firm is me, but you know what I mean. Now sit back and relax, you must be shattered after that trip. Everyone's coming over tonight, so it's going to be a long day.'

Before long they were installed in the apartment, the kids

excited at the prospect of a bed with a padded headboard, and the little one asleep on something called a chaise-longue. 'You've done well, Edie,' Maggie said, hoping she didn't sound grudging.

'It's all right, isn't it?' Edie said, but she didn't sound thrilled.

That evening the apartment was full, as Cathy and Stella arrived with Mrs S. Paul brought them, but he didn't stay. 'Family only,' he said firmly as he took his leave. Maggie wanted to say, 'You're family.' He'd been in their lives long enough, that was for sure – but something in his face held her back. 'Cathy's going to lose him if she's not careful,' she thought.

Edie had catered carefully, delicious food obviously brought in at no expense, wine in a bucket for later when the children were tucked up in bed.

'They're tired out, poor *lieblings*,' Mrs S., said as the children were shepherded away.

Cathy nodded. 'This is nice. Just like the old days.'

'Except Mam's not here,' Edie said quietly.

'You were always her favourite.' Maggie's tone was not aggressive. 'She loved us all, but you were most like her. We take after Dad, I suppose.'

'What she means is you were the gobby one, Edie. We three are quiet.' But Cathy said it kindly, and Edie smiled.

They reminisced then until the needs of the present day intruded.

'So what comes next?' Edie said, looking round.

'Well, I'm staying in Belgate.' Maggie's voice was quiet but firm. 'I've thought it through. I'm happy there, and I've got friends, but I want to stay for the children. It's their heritage.'

'Are you sure?' Edie sounded anxious.

'Very sure. What's going to happen to the rest of you?'

It was Mrs S. who spoke. 'You are right to choose, Maggie.

And choice is good. We were not so lucky, Afrom and I. The choice was made for us. London has been kind to me, but I would have liked to choose,'

'Do you miss Cologne?' Edie was leaning forward as she spoke.

The old lady's lips trembled for a moment, and then firmed. 'I miss it sometimes . . . not the bad times that came, but the good ones before them, when I had a family. But you, your family, has filled the hole in my life. For that I thank you.'

'It's us who should thank you.' Cath and Stella spoke as one, but Edie's voice rose above them.

'I think you should go back, Mrs S., while there's time. Go and see all your old haunts, and then realise that this is where you belong now. Cath, you'll soon be at a loose end. You could go to Cologne with her.'

Mrs S. was smiling. 'A nice thought, Edie, but not possible.'

'If it's money you mean, leave that to me. I'm not saying you'll go first class, but you'll go, and Cath will go with you – Stella, too, if she can get time off. I was a right little cow to you after Mam died, and you took it all. I want to say sorry.'

Afterwards, when Mrs S. and the girls had gone home, and the children were asleep, Edie and Maggie sat on in the cream armchairs and drank wine and talked.

'What brought that on?' Maggie asked.

'What?'

'The generosity . . . you offering to pay for a coachload tour of Germany?'

'It won't cost that much. Anyway, I can afford it.'

'Maybe, but you've got to admit that you being kind to everyone isn't exactly what we've been used to.'

'I wasn't that bad, was I? Well, I suppose I was. But I've grown up, and I've done a lot of thinking lately. About what I want out of life.'

'You're not getting religion, are you? Shall I send for a doctor?'

'Yes, scoff, Mags. I'm not getting religion but, in a funny way, religion comes into it.'

Maggie leaned forward to refill her glass. 'Go on,' she said. 'You can't stop there.'

'Remember the funeral? No, that's a silly question . . . at the funeral there was a reading. About mining.' Maggie was nodding. 'Well, I wasn't really listening until I heard him say something about finding wisdom. I don't know why, but that struck a chord. I mean, that's what you need, isn't it? So I asked the vicar what it was. . .'

'You never did! Good girl.'

'Well, anyway, I went out and bought a Bible. Don't laugh. I haven't converted, I'm still an unbeliever, but I wanted to read it again, especially the bit about wisdom. It was lovely really, all of it. About how they find silver and gold and precious stones, but what it's really saying is that the most precious thing is wisdom – that you can't dig it out of the ground, and that man does not realise how precious it is. So I'm trying to be a bit wiser, Maggie. That's all.'

Maggie let out her breath. 'Well, there's never a dull moment in this family, and that's a fact.'

Chapter Fifty Six

Cathy

IT WAS QUIET WHEN Stella had departed in a flurry of missing keys and lost shoulder-bag. Cathy sat down at the table and pulled the paper towards her. Her first morning out of work for fourteen years. She might have hung on for a couple of years, but she hadn't. She had handed in her notice, and taken some holiday coming to her in lieu. There was no going back now: no one, especially not Vivien Van Damm, would rehire a thirty-two-year-old dancer. So, what lay ahead?

She put thoughts of the future out of her mind and thought about last night. 'You're looking at an ex-dancer,' she had told Paul, and then winced when she saw the way he was taking it.

'Do you mean . . .?'

She had lifted a hand to stay his words. 'It doesn't mean anything, Paul, except that I've packed it in. I'll have to find something else to do, but I can take a couple of weeks off to fit in a trip to Germany, and I'm going to. After that, I'll start looking around. '

He had been quiet after that, and it had been a relief when he delivered her to the door and they said goodnight, not with the usual kiss, but just a peck on the cheek. All in all, it hadn't been her finest moment.

She shook out the newspaper and stared at the headline: 'Scandal of Notting Hill Riots'. Paul had been talking about it for the past couple of weeks, but reading a two-page article about it was still a shock. According to this piece, the riot had begun on 29 August when a gang of white youths attacked a Swedish woman they had seen the previous night arguing with her Jamaican husband. They had shouted racial insults at him, and were furious when she turned on them to defend him. Seeing her again the next night, they pelted her with bottles, stones, and wood, and struck her in the back with an iron bar, until the police intervened. The writer said there had been a marked increase in Caribbean migrants to Britain since the end of the war, and now white working-class 'Teddy Boys' were beginning to display hostility towards the black families in the area, egged on by groups such as Sir Oswald Mosley's Union Movement, and other far-right groups such as the White Defence League, who wanted to 'Keep Britain White'.

Cathy sat back, puzzled. London, her London, had always been a melting-pot. She had grown up amongst it, Poles, Jews, blacks, gyppos . . . by and large, they had all got on. Why were things going wrong now, when everyone had had the lesson of the gas chambers to remind them of what happened when race was set against race? She read on. There had been an increase in violent attacks on black people through summer. Paul had told her of an incident in which a group of ten white youths had repeatedly assaulted six West Indian men. They had been tracked down by the police in a manner that had caused Paul to glow with pride: 'They arrested nine of the gang after working non-stop for 20 hours.' But after the assault on the Swedish woman, a mob of three or four hundred white people, many of them Teddy Boys, attacked the houses of West Indian residents, night after night, and it was still going on. The police had arrested more than a hundred people already, mostly white youths, but also black people carrying weapons. Which was easy to understand, given the circumstances.

She put the paper aside, troubled. The whole thing had an

eerie echo of the stories Mrs Schiffman had told her of how things had begun in Cologne – assaults on Jewish homes, and attacks in the street. Surely such things could not happen again, not in Britain in the 1950s? She hid the paper under a seat cushion, hoping Mrs Schiffman would not find it and be afraid.

When she had cleared the breakfast table she looked in on the old lady. Still asleep. In a little while she'd take tea in, but letting her rest now made sense. The journey to Cologne would be an ordeal for a seventy-year-old. It would be the first time in an aeroplane for all three of them, but according to Edie it was a piece of cake. 'They look after you every inch of the way,' she had said last night. 'Take everything they offer you, and if you can't eat and drink it, then put it in your bag.'

Cathy's eyes had met Stella's, and she could see they were thinking alike . . . if Edie was paying, she wanted value for money. All the same, she was being generous. For a moment she thought back to how hard it had been to get her to hand over her tips – what had Maggie said about them? 'We'll never hear the last of our Edie's tips. They're like the loaves and the fishes, paying for everything.' All those years had passed since they had struggled to pay the undertaker, and meals had been conjured up from nowhere. She had gone to Paris thinking she would make a fortune and save the family. She had sent money home – but had it been worth it? She took out paper and sat down to write to Maggie, but words wouldn't come. She would have to do it tomorrow.

Mrs S. was sitting up in bed when eventually Cathy carried the tea in. 'Who's a lazy lie-abed then?' She put a cup into the thin blue-veined hands. 'You'll have to be up early on Friday. Crack of dawn.'

'I can't believe it. To see that city again after all these years!'

'It won't upset you, will it? It'll be very changed. Places always change, but Paul says Cologne was heavily bombed.'

'I know,' Mrs Schiffman said. 'I have read about it. No, it

won't upset me. It was necessary.'

Cathy sat down on the side of the bed. 'Are you sure you want to go? I know you remember a happy life before the war but . . . I'm not sure, but I shouldn't imagine there's a Jewish community there now.'

Mrs S. was nodding. 'All dead, Cathy. Or run away, like me. Perhaps that's what I need to see – that it is gone. Over. No more ghosts, just a new city rebuilt with no traces of the past.'

Cathy stood up. 'If that's what you want, Mrs S. And it'll be a bit of fun, you and me and Stel. I'm looking forward to it.'

Paul was picking her up at five-thirty, and they were getting out of London. She left Mrs S. with a tray at the ready. 'And Stella will be in later. She's doing an omelette tonight.'

'She's a good girl. But I worry about her, Catherine – she is too serious for a young woman, a child. She shouldn't be home cooking for an old woman, she should be enjoying herself, finding a handsome young man.'

'There's that doctor at the hospital . . . she's mentioned him once or twice. You've heard her on about him teasing her.'

'Mentioned? What's with mentioned? Mentions don't make wedding rings or babies.'

'Give her a chance. She's not twenty-five yet!'

'Exactly. Twenty-four. I was married at nineteen.'

'Where does that leave me then? I'm thirty-two?'

'You are a silly girl.' The old lady's tone was suddenly sombre. 'You think you can keep something on a string. One day you will pull in that string, and find there is nothing on the end of it. I know there is something, someone else, Catherine . . . but in all the years he doesn't come, he doesn't write, he doesn't phone. Paul is here, Catherine, a live, breathing man. What more do you want?'

'It isn't that simple.' Cathy turned away to end the conversation, but the old lady continued. 'No, it isn't simple. It's tommy-rot and you are *meshugene*. Paul is a *mentsch*, but you will go your own way.'

'It's *meshugener*,' Cathy said absently. 'With an R on the end.'

'No,' Mrs S. said firmly. 'That is a crazy man. You are a crazy woman: *meshugene*! Are you trying to teach your grandmother to . . . what is it you say?'

'Suck eggs,' Cathy said. 'Fat chance of you letting me do that.'

It was a relief when Stella let herself into the flat. 'Paul's downstairs.'

'Ta,' Catherine said, and made for the door. She managed the quick exit she had wanted, but not before she noticed that her sister's eyes were red.

They drove out to Windsor and ate beside the river. There were swans on the water, and she watched them glide. 'Like your picture,' Paul said, and she nodded. 'Yes. I've always loved that picture, I don't know why.'

They ate and drank well, and afterwards sat on in companionable silence. 'Are you coming back with me tonight?' he said at last.

'Not tonight. I'm a bit worried about Stella. She looked upset when she came in.'

'I thought she looked a bit subdued.'

'Do you mind?' She put out a hand to his.

'Of course I mind. I mind that you're not beside me every night. That you're always holding back. That I've spent a large part of my adult life hanging round like a lovesick swan. I understand you want to see to Stella, but that's not really it, Cathy, is it? Last night, when you said you had left the Windmill, I thought . . . for one foolish minute, I thought this is it! Well, more fool me. Now, for both our sakes, I think the present situation has to end. When you come back from Germany, I want an answer. A simple "Yes, I'll marry you." Or "No, I won't."'

Chapter Fifty Seven

Maggie

Shewaved to her neighbour before she shut the door. The three children had gone off full of tales of their London trip to relate to their schoolmates, even her baby . . . she would have to stop calling Alan that.

'Did we meet the Queen?' Amy had asked at the breakfast table.

'No,' Maggie had answered solemnly. 'But I expect she knew we were there.'

She was smiling as she sat down. The teapot was still hot, and she poured a cup as she opened Cathy's letter. She seemed to be coping well with having left the dance troupe – certainly there was no kind of regret to be read between the lines. She was horrified at the riots in Notting Hill, and well she might be after what had been shown on the television. She thought of her children, and was glad they were not growing up in London – such goings on could never happen in Belgate. Most of all she thought of her husband, who had hated prejudice of any kind. 'We're all born equal, Meg,' he would say. 'Jew, Gentile, black, white, man or woman . . . let one of them be done down, and it'll come to you sooner or later.' He had had such belief, such hopes for the future, for his own kids and everyone else's. Surely all that conviction couldn't just die?

'It's up to me,' she thought. He had never wanted her to

work while he was there to provide for her. But he was gone now, and she would have to find a job of some sort. She'd still have spare time, time to find out about politics and who was best placed to make sure everyone got their rights. She would do something about it before the month was out.

She read on. Cathy was anxious about Mrs S., and whether or not she would withstand the flight. Edie was being a brick, and tipping up for everything.

The real purpose of the letter came in the second paragraph. 'I knew there was something up with Stella, so I buttonholed her. "Out with it!" I said. She wasn't going to tell me at first, but I made her. It was awful, Mags. When she was just a kid, working for Edie, and knocking about with her, she told us she wanted out from Edie's job, but not exactly why. She made out it was men trying it on, nothing more. But it went further than that, Mags, much further. She was held down and raped by a man old enough to be her father. And by one or two more. Why she didn't tell us the truth at the time, I don't know. Or why I didn't ask questions till I got the truth out of her. I can't forgive myself for that. What Edie was thinking of I don't know. I think they were both out of their depth. Thank God Stella didn't get pregnant, but she's now got the idea in her head that she's damaged goods. She had herself checked out for VD when she started nursing, and that was OK, which is a mercy. But I feel guilty. We should've protected her, Mags. Well, I should. And Edie should've known better. Now I don't know what we can do.'

Maggie sat for a long time when she had finished the letter. It was true: they should have looked after Stella better. Shipping her off to Edie had been the easy way out. And when she had come clean about part of it, they'd been only too ready to sweep that under the carpet, too. If only she herself had been there, in the home, things might have been different. Still, it was all water under the bridge now. She put the letter back in the envelope, and got ready to go to the shops.

When she came back, she put her shopping on one side and picked up the phone. 'Cath? It's me, Maggie. About the terrible thing that happened to Stella – do you mean what you said? She was actually raped?'

'I'm afraid so. She said the man was sorry after, when she cried, because he probably thought she had been up for it.'

'What was our Edie thinking of?'

'She didn't think back then, Mags. Except about how to get an advantage for herself. If it's any consolation, I think she's sorry now.'

'Yes,' Maggie said slowly, remembering the conversation about the Bible reading. 'Yes, I think she probably is.'

They talked of Mrs S. then. 'Better she dies happy, Cath, than sits there pining. The journey is a lot for an old lady, but your roots are your roots. You never know – seeing Cologne again might pick her up no end. But I've been thinking: if Stella sorts herself out and there's really something with this doctor, Mrs S. could come and live here. I mean, it's me or Edie, and I know which I'd choose. I'll talk to Stella some time about the other . . . you know.' She couldn't bring herself to actually spell it out. They were both avoiding the real purpose of the call.

At the other end of the line, Cathy was protesting that she would be there for the old lady, who could stay in her own home. 'Cathy, I hope to God you're not going to spend the rest of your life in that flat, on your own. With a cat, like Miss Ennis at No. 10.'

'Remember how we used to scoff at her? God, we were wicked kids!'

'I'm serious about Mrs S.,' Maggie ended. 'If she needs a home, she can come to me. What she'll make of Belgate, I don't know but there's a lot of kindness here.'

When she put down the phone, she felt suddenly mournful. Joe would have known what to do and say. He would have made it seem less shameful about Stella. 'She's young,' he would have said. 'She'll get over it.'

Maggie switched on the television. It was a bad mistake. There was a documentary on about costermongers, and the life of the East End. It brought back memories of a time when she had had a mother and a father, and felt safe in the womb of her family. Now she was the head of the family, and it was a frightening place.

Chapter Fifty Eight

Stella

THERE HAD BEEN QUITE a crowd of them at Heathrow: two cars, one driven by Paul and the other by Dr Michael, who had insisted on seeing Stella off. 'You can let me come, and I'll behave, or you can forbid me to come, and I'll turn up anyway and show you up. You choose.'

Stella had said he could come, because she wanted him there, even though, at the same time, she could hardly bear it. Encouraged by Cath, and knowing that this foolish charade had to end, she had taken the plunge in a quiet corner of the coffee bar a day or two earlier. He had listened as she poured it out: the rape, her own foolishness, the guilt she had felt ever since. He had looked at her sternly for a moment before he spoke. 'Do you mean to tell me that the past few terrible months, during which I have jeopardised my entire career by spending almost every waking moment on one ward, facing a stone wall of indifference, is all because of one admittedly regrettable incident over which you had no control?'

'Are you ever serious?' she had said.

'I'm very serious about you, Stella Jackson. Now, do I come to Heathrow with your blessing, or don't I?'

She looked at him now, hefting cases, and supporting Mrs Schiffman, who was positively glowing with approval whenever she looked up at him. 'Thank you,' she said, when it was time to go through the gates.

'Hurry back to me, Stella,' Michael said, and this time he wasn't fooling.

'Thank God for that,' They had settled Mrs Schiffman in a bulkhead seat with plenty of leg room. Now the two sisters were taking their own places, and buckling seatbelts. Cathy leaned back and let out a deep sigh. 'I thought we'd never get away, what with all the goodbyes, and Edie clucking like a mother hen. She's taking your doctor for a drink, in case you didn't know. I think she wants to make sure he's worthy of you.'

'He is, Cathy, so she can quiz as much as she likes.'

'Good girl,' Cathy said, and they both knew why.

Mrs Schiffman slept most of the way, or appeared to. 'What is she thinking?' Stella wondered, seeing the old eyelids twitch occasionally. What must it be like to be going back to a place where you had been supremely happy until you had had to flee for your life?

It was a relief to get her safely off the plane and into the hotel. On the drive from the airport to the centre of Cologne, the old lady had perked up, peering from the window, trying to identify landmarks that were either no longer there, or that she could not find. '*Oy vey!*' she muttered occasionally.

'It's bound to have changed,' Stella said gently. 'I've been reading up on it. On one raid alone, they used a thousand bombers. Think of that: a thousand planes raining bombs! Hundreds upon hundreds of high-explosives, and even more incendiaries. Hospitals and churches just disappeared – that's why you can't identify anywhere.' She looked at the old lady, expecting signs of compassion. There were none.

'Thirteen thousand homes went, and more than twice that were damaged,' Stella continued. Her voice dropped. 'Just under five hundred people died, and five thousand were injured . . .and that's just because a lot of people had already fled the city.' Surely now there would be some expression of sympathy?

Mrs Schiffman's eyes gleamed. 'They drove us out. It was their turn.'

After that there was silence until they reached the hotel.

The following day, they made three forays into the city, each time in search of some place that Mrs Schiffman remembered. Each one was a wild-goose chase. The place where her father's factory had been was now a wasteland tangled with weeds. The synagogue where she had been married was gone, too, and so was the place where she had gone to school. But then they found the house where she had gone for her dancing-classes: it was still there, the basement now a *ratskeller*, according to Mrs S. In spite of the off-putting name, it sold excellent salads, and at least it was a place to rest their legs. Each time they went back to the hotel, they implored the old lady to take a nap, but she seemed to be gaining in strength, rather than getting exhausted. Often, on their journeys, they espied the spires of the cathedral standing proud amid lesser buildings.

Now they were sitting in the hotel lounge, and Stella was flourishing a handbook. 'It's called the Kölner Dom, officially the High Cathedral of Saints Peter and Mary. It's Roman Catholic, and is the seat of the Archbishop of Cologne.' She read on: 'The cathedral is the largest Gothic church in Northern Europe, and has the second-tallest spires and largest façade of any church in the world. The cathedral suffered seventy hits by aerial bombs during World War II. It did not collapse, but stood tall in an otherwise flattened city.' She looked up. 'That's like St Paul's, isn't it?'

She went back to the book: 'The great twin spires are said to have been used as an easily recognisable navigational landmark by Allied aircraft raiding deeper into Germany in the later years of the war, which may be a reason that the cathedral was not destroyed. It is a renowned monument of German Catholicism and Gothic architecture, and is a World Heritage

Denise Robertson

Site. It's also Germany's most visited landmark, attracting an average of 20,000 people a day – so if we're going, we'd better go early, before the crowds get there.'

She read on silently for a second, and then looked up, frowning. 'It says the cathedral is "a powerful testimony to the strength and persistence of Christian belief in medieval and modern Europe" · That's what's always puzzled me: Germany had Christianity for centuries, and yet it still had gas chambers. How can that be?'

Mrs Schiffman simply shrugged her shoulders. She had long given up seeking answers. Cathy tried to formulate a response. 'I don't know, Stella, I don't think anyone knows. Germans say they were led astray by Hitler . . . ordinary men and women who wouldn't have harmed a fly, they just got swept away. They weren't all bad.'

'Why are you sticking up for them, Cathy? You know what they did – they killed our Dad.'

'But look what we did to them, Stel. Look at this city. If Mrs S. had still been here, we'd have rained bombs on her, just like they did to us.'

'I hate Germans,' Stella said. 'They're all nice to us now, but I can't forget. And you shouldn't either, Cath.'

But Cath had turned on her heel and was walking towards the lifts.

'What's the matter with her?' Stella turned to the old lady. 'She knows it's right, what I'm saying. They are awful people, as you know.'

Mrs Schiffman eyes had narrowed, and she was watching Cathy's retreating figure. 'I don't know, *liebchen*, but I think you should be careful what you say to your sister. She has a lot on her mind.'

Chapter Fifty Nine

Cathy

THIS WAS THEIR FOURTH day, and Stella had decreed it should be a day of rest. 'If you take it easy today, you'll be able to go sight-seeing again tomorrow. There's a lot we haven't seen. The Museum Ludwig has Picassos, and loads of other famous pictures. I've never seen a real Picasso. And there's the Old Town, which they say is very picturesque, and the Zoo. There's heaps more to see before we leave, so put your feet up today, just to please me.'

When the old lady retired for a late-morning map, the two sisters drank coffee in the hotel garden. 'She's really perked up since we got here,' Cathy said.

Stella nodded. 'Yes, but it's all adrenalin. She's very frail. Still, it was the right thing to do. I think she's laid a lot of ghosts to rest.'

Cathy nodded. 'We all need to do that sometimes.'

'I think I have laid mine,' Stella said quietly.

'Really?'

'Yes. When you look at this city, you realise you have to let go of the past. I'm sorry about that outburst the other night: I was fighting myself, really. Wanting to cling to old prejudices, and yet knowing I had to let them go. I didn't like Germans, I blamed them for Dad . . . well, fair enough, but I blamed them for Mam, too, in a way, which wasn't fair. When you meet them, though, Cath, they're just like us, some nice, some less nice. So goodbye prejudice.'

'What about other things?'

'Such as? No, that's silly. I know very well what you mean. Yes, I've laid that to rest too. I should've been braver . . .'

'You were a kid!'

'I know. Anyway, why are we wasting today? Or, more important, why are you wasting the day? No need for you to stay put, Cath. One of us here is enough.'

'If you're sure,' Cath said.

Yesterday she had made enquiries. The cost of a hire car and driver had made her eyes water, but she had drawn out 'emergency' money before she left London. Should she spend it on a trip to Badesheim?

Stella had one more question. 'Do you like Michael?'

'I think he's lovely, Stel. And very nearly good enough for you.'

An hour later she was on her way. As the car sped through the countryside, she asked herself why she was going. To find Gunther? He probably didn't live there any more . . . and yet he had spoken of his family home so warmly she couldn't imagine him leaving it. She had Stella's tourist guide in her lap, and she turned to the relevant page.

Badesheim had a famous main street, the Brudesgasse, and two castles, as well as a number of historic mansions, many of which were open to the public. There was also a wine museum, because Badesheim was surrounded by vineyards. Cathy smiled to herself. If she found him ensconced with a beautiful second wife, at least she could drown her sorrows.

When she put the book back into her bag, she took out the medallion. The swans still sailed serenely on their blue enamel river. The branches on the bank still trailed in the water. She held it in her hand for a moment. If she saw him, she could give it back. Reason returned as they drove through the outskirts of the city: it was six years since his wife's death, and he had probably remarried. Might have children from either marriage. Would certainly have taken up life again. She had been part of his life for one night – a few hours. He might not even remember her.

And yet, in her heart, she hoped . . . she knew . . . that he would. She leaned her head back against the seat and gave herself up to remembering.

At last the car was drawing up in the central square of Badesheim. She thanked the driver and asked him to wait. Gunther had spoken of the road to his home being steep. She got out of the car, and began to walk around. There were roads left and right, both leading uphill. Which one should she take?

In the end she went into a coffee shop, and ordered a coffee and strudel. The woman who served her knew the von Sachs name at once. More than that, she pointed to a poster pinned up near the door and translated: 'It is a *Volksfest* . . . how do you say it, a carnival. For the orphanage. Good things to buy there. Very nice. By kind permission of Herr von Sachs.'

It seemed like a gift from heaven. A village fair! Crowds of people. She could go, and be almost unseen. She took directions from the woman, and went back to the car.

The town had seemed to be unscathed by warfare, but on closer inspection Cathy could see masonry pitted by bullet holes, and here and there a new building erected between the older buildings on either side. So Badesheim, however idyllic, had not escaped the carnage.

The driver followed her instructions, and they came out of the town on a rising road that twisted and turned among trees. And then she saw it, just as Gunther had described it. It was indeed a castle above the Rhine. 'It has many windows,' he'd said. 'When I was a boy I tried to count them. I gave up at one hundred and twelve.' And there the windows were, glinting in the sunshine.

She asked the driver to wait, and got out of the car. A man and woman were seated at the gate, selling tickets. Cathy held out a handful of coins, and they selected the appropriate amount. She was in. Balloons were tied to the gatepost, and she could hear the excited chatter of children playing around a hurdy-gurdy. She moved among stalls piled with cakes and sweetmeats, bric-à-brac and old books. China and glass gleamed, and on another stall were teddy bears in all shapes and sizes. The house loomed over the proceedings, looking strangely vacant. Perhaps he was away. Perhaps he didn't live here any more, except that the woman in the coffee shop had said he had given permission for the fête. Though that didn't mean he would necessarily be there: landowners often fled charity occasions. Perhaps coming here had been a mistake? Perhaps the wisest thing she could do was run to the car, head back to the hotel, and put all this behind her?

And then she saw him, seated on a low veranda, gazing out over the jollifications.

He was just as she remembered, except for a little greying at the temples. His hands were resting on the arms of the chair, and he looked relaxed, even benign. For a moment she panicked: how would she address him? Gunther? Herr von Sachs? Should she simply say, 'Do you remember me?'

In the end she went up to him held out the medallion. 'I think,' she said, 'this belongs to you?'

He turned his head and smiled at her, holding out his hand. There was no hint of recognition in the blue eyes.

She put the medallion in his outstretched palm, and his fingers closed around it.

'Thank you,' he said. 'You are English?'

This was the moment to speak but his tone was one of polite disinterest. 'He doesn't remember me,' she thought, and almost turned on her heel. Instead she said, 'You seem to have attracted a fine crowd.'

He was smiling now. 'Yes. It is always a popular day, for the children.'

He was still looking at her, but she could see that, for him, the interview was at an end. She waited for rejection to strike home as she moved away, but, as her step quickened, she realised that all she felt was a growing satisfaction. She had closure. '*A certain smile, a certain face*' . . . the words sang themselves in her head, but they had lost their sting. 'I'm free,' she thought. 'He doesn't remember, and that sets me free.'

The slope was descending and she began to run towards the gate. She needed to get back to the hotel so she could ring Paul, and tell him she was coming home. And so much more, so much, much more. 'All these years I have held on to a dream,' she thought as the gates came in sight. 'I measured everything against that dream, and found everything wanting.' The eyes gazing up at her – blue, just as she remembered – had not lit up at the sight of her. They had been utterly disinterested.

In time she might regret the wasted years, but today there was no time to spare for regretting. 'Let's go,' she said to the driver when she reached the car. 'I have something very important to do.'

Epilogue

HE FINGERED THE OBJECT the woman had given him. Too big for a coin. Smooth on one side, chased on the other. Unable to see with his sightless eyes, he kept it in his hand until a servant came to check on his needs. 'What is this?' he asked. 'Someone gave it to me . . . an Englishwoman, I think. Is it a coin?'

'It's a medallion, sir. Swans enamelled on a lake, something like that. It's very pretty.'

By the time Gunther heard the man's words, Cathy's car was already leaving the Brudesgasse and taking the Cologne road. She was too far away to hear him breathe her name as he realised what it was he had been given, and by whom . . . the medallion his grandmother had given him as a child, his good-luck charm, the one thing of value his assailants had missed that night in Paris. He had given it to a young girl who had appeared like an angel out of the dark. A girl he had never forgotten.

She did not see him rise to his feet, reaching for the white stick at his side so he could go in search of her. She did not see the servant hovering behind in case of disaster. She would never know that he, too, had remembered down all the years.

Perhaps that was just as well.

If you've enjoyed this book and would like to find out more about Denise and her novels, why not join the **Denise Robertson Book Club.** Members will receive special offers, early notification of new titles, information on author events and lots more. Membership is free and there is no commitment to buy.

To join, simply send your name and address to **info@deniserobertsonbooks.co.uk** or post your details to The Denise Robertson Book Club, PO Box 58514, Barnes, London SW13 3AE

Other novels by Denise Robertson

All Denise's novels are available from good bookshops price £7.99

Alternatively you can order direct from the publisher with FREE postage and packing by calling the credit card hotline 01903 828503 and quoting DR10TP1.